The Traitor of Belltroll

BALANCE KEEPERS

The Traitor of Belltroll

Lindsay Cummings

KATHERINE TEGEN BOOKS
An Imprint of HarperCollins Publishers

Katherine Tegen Books is an imprint of HarperCollins Publishers.

Balance Keepers, Book 3: The Traitor of Belltroll
Copyright © 2016 by PC Studio, Inc.

 PC STUDIO

ISBN 978-0-06-227524-0

16 17 18 19 20   CG/RRDH   10 9 8 7 6 5 4 3 2 1

First Edition

To my dad, Don Cummings, for always being my Plot Doctor. And to my editor, Katie Bignell, who deserves all the dedications in the world. And, while we're at it, a raise.

Table of Contents

The Core

The Tower

Belltroll

Observatorium

Lake Hall

Professor Asante's Quarters

Professor Bigglesby's Quarters

Treefare

Main Chamber

The Pit

Library

Cedarfell

Waterfall of Fate

Canteen

Heart of the Core

Professor Flynn's Quarters

Watchers' Cavern

Ponderay

Cave of Fire

Cave of Whispers

Calderon

The Path Hider

The Way Inside

The Realm of
Belltroll

Bells of Belltroll

Troll Mountain

Ring of Emerald

Tunnel to the Core

Troll Mountain Range

Ring of Entry

The Realm always provides the Means

Prologue

The Main Chamber was as silent as a perfectly Balanced Realm.

There was a flicker, a shimmer and twist of the air, and then two figures appeared, seemingly out of nowhere.

The two stolen Master Tiles hung from the first figure's neck, glittering even in the darkness of a large black cloak.

The second figure was shorter, walking a few paces behind in a show of insignificance. The Apprentice.

"The boy," the Master said. "Do we have plans to bring him back to us soon?"

The Apprentice sped up, trailing the Master like a loyal dog. "I have set things in motion. But you, of course, have to push it all over the edge."

The Master liked the Main Chamber empty and silent. None of those awful, jittering Balance Keepers milling about, their heads held higher than they deserved to be held. Their foolish, insignificant, regular Tiles hanging from their necks.

"Tonight," the Master said, stopping near the door to the Realm of Belltroll. "Tonight, we will draw him in."

"We'll need to be careful," the Apprentice said.

The Master spun around, cloak billowing like a dark cloud. The two black Tiles clinked on the chain around the Master's neck, and the Apprentice took a step backward, cowering.

Pathetic, the Master thought. *So much weakness in one body.*

"I know exactly what we need," the Master hissed. "We need chaos. We need destruction. We need an Imbalance, and Belltroll is the key."

The Apprentice stooped to one knee. "As you wish, Master."

"Then open the door." The Master lifted a hand and pointed. "To Belltroll."

The Apprentice stood and set to work.

The Master paced, but not from worry. If an onlooker came, or someone was roaming freely in the night, the Master would take care of it.

That was the fun part.

A Core Cleaner came around the corner, whistling a merry tune. A name tag on his chest said *Harold*.

"Evening," the Master said.

The old man's tune fell silent.

"Evening," he said, nodding. "What're you up to?" His eyes widened as he looked back and forth.

The Master channeled the strength of the Tiles and was able to look through Harold's eyes to see what the old man saw.

The trembling Apprentice, kneeling before the door.

The Master, cloaked, but with a shadow of light cast over a pale face.

"*You,*" Harold gasped. His broom clattered to the floor. "But . . . but it can't be. . . ."

"A shame," the Master said, lifting a single long finger to the air, vision returning to normal. "You were always such an excellent worker."

The Master's body shuddered, just once, as a surge of power came from the two Master Tiles.

Then Harold dropped to the floor, his mouth open in a silent scream.

"Is he . . . ," the Apprentice began.

"Not dead," the Master said. "But not able to speak a word of this. Your slowness ails me." A deep sigh, and the Master stepped up to the door. "I wonder, sometimes, why I even keep you around."

The Apprentice scooted away into the shadows.

With a final push of magic from the Master Tiles, the door to Belltroll swung open with a silent hiss. Dust rained down from the doorway, as if the entrance to the Realm had not been opened for a very, very long time.

"You know what to do," the Master said. "Do not fail me. If Albert Flynn does not arrive and does not die in this Realm . . ."

"The boy will die," the Apprentice promised. "I'll make sure of it."

"No," the Master said, grinning. "I will."

The tunnel beyond the door was beautiful, black like a moonless night, black like the two Master Tiles clinking on their chain. The Master stepped forward.

Albert Flynn would walk through this very tunnel soon.

And once he went inside Belltroll, he would never come back out.

CHAPTER 1

The Tremor

Albert Flynn had faced a lot of dangers these past several months.

He'd flown on the back of a wild Guildacker, and done so a second time once the winged beast was tamed. He'd braved fire and volcanoes and water cold enough to stop a man's heart, and he'd been one-third of a team that had saved the world not once, but twice.

He'd opened a door in the side of tree, crawled through a tangle of roots, and made it to the *core* of the earth. Better yet, he'd lived to tell the tale.

That was all normal for a Balance Keeper. A bit scary at times, but thrilling, too.

But now Albert was in New York City facing the scariest thing yet.

A math test.

Even worse, an *algebra* test.

Albert sat in the back row of his third-period class tapping his pencil on his desk. It had only been a few weeks since he and his friends had saved the Realm of Ponderay from facing a horrible Imbalance, and Albert was already bored.

Pencils scratched around him. The clock ticked closer and closer to the end of the hour. And still Albert's page was mostly blank. He tried to tell his brain to think *math*, but all it would think about was the Core.

It was right under his feet—or rather, hundreds, maybe thousands of miles down— but still, it was there, full of danger, and laughter, and hundreds of secrets yet to be uncovered.

School was full of . . . well, school.

Albert yawned and scratched his head with the eraser side of his pencil. He had never really excelled in school, but since he'd learned about the dangers the world really faced (Imbalances! Two missing Master Tiles, and a traitor! His dog Farnsworth's awful chicken-jerky burps!), school felt less and less important every day.

"Five minutes remaining," Albert's teacher said. Mr. Barnes was bald, and his brown sandals squeaked with each step, like crying mice. Albert looked down at his paper and groaned.

He'd only answered ten of the twenty-seven questions. And not a single one had made sense to him so far.

You're falling behind in classes, his mom had said to him just that morning, on the car ride to school. *You haven't been the same since coming home from your dad's house after Christmas break.*

Albert put the finishing touches on an equation, not entirely sure if it was even right, and set his pencil down.

This was hopeless.

All around him, his classmates scribbled furiously, trying in vain to finish the test before time was up. Mr. Barnes was known for his brain-busting equations, and sometimes, Albert thought the guy expected every sixth grader to be smart enough to solve world hunger. Or the climate change. With *math.*

Albert closed his eyes and told himself what he always did. *I can do this.* He touched the black, rectangular Master Tile that hung on a cord around his neck. How badly he wished he could turn on some of the superhuman brainpower that his teammate Leroy had.

As he touched his Tile, he imagined the Core so vividly, he felt like he was actually there. He could smell the delicious foods that the Whimzies dropped in Lake Hall during lunch. He could hear the sound of the red birds in Cedarfell, singing him to sleep. He could feel the ground trembling. . . .

Wait a second.

Albert's eyes flew open. That wasn't his imagination. It was *real*.

The ground shook again.

He looked around and saw that other students had put their pencils down. Heads turned left and right as it happened a third time. Now the ground shook hard enough that the clock slipped from its hook on the wall and shattered against the hard tile floor.

"What's happening?" someone shouted as the lights flickered. A poster tumbled from its tacks.

Then a big one came. This one rattled Albert's skull, and he shook so much that his pencil hit the desk and snapped in half. The lights went out, and everyone screamed.

"Calm down! Everyone just calm down!" Mr. Barnes tried in vain to stop the screams, but nobody cared.

Albert waited it out, telling himself the tremors couldn't last long.

"It's okay," he said to another classmate, a boy with wide eyes who was gripping his desk with white knuckles.

There was a final tremor, one that shook the room so hard that even Mr. Barnes yelped like a startled poodle.

Then the shaking stopped, just as suddenly as it had started. Aside from the fallen clock and poster, it was like it hadn't happened.

The classroom was deadly silent.

Albert heard the squeal of sirens in the distance, and then the loudspeaker came on. Principal Peters's voice spoke calmly and evenly across the school.

"Please, remain calm. There has been a minor earthquake. Students, stay in your seats while we wait for the authorities to announce that normal activities can resume."

The speaker crackled off. Everyone looked at Mr. Barnes, who was wiping sweat from his bald head. *Chill out, man!* Albert thought. *Your head is dripping so much it looks like you're standing beneath a faucet!*

"All right," Mr. Barnes said, taking a deep breath. "I can see that everyone is a little rattled after that. In light of this, we'll go ahead and resume the test tomorrow." He sat down at his desk and mopped his head with a handkerchief once more.

Albert relaxed. He'd lucked out with the earthquake canceling today's test. But he was worried about something else. Just then, his phone buzzed in his pocket. He pulled it out, careful to keep it hidden. A group text popped up on the screen.

Birdie Howell: Earthquake in NYC. Albert u ok?

Leroy Jones: Albert!?

Birdie Howell: I'm sure he's fine.

Leroy Jones: He could be buried beneath a hot dog stand!

Birdie Howell: Not funny. And not likely either.

Leroy Jones: ☹

Birdie Howell: Imbalance?

Leroy Jones: Hope not . . .

Albert's fingertips hovered over the screen, but he was too busy thinking to type out a response.

Because Birdie and Leroy were on the right track. Earthquakes in New York weren't normal, and when abnormal things of this scale happened, it could really mean only one thing.

His fingertips touched the smooth Master Tile at his neck, and he nodded to himself as he faced the facts. There was an Imbalance.

And that could *also* mean only one thing.

There was someone causing it.

Albert gulped, a mixture of fear and excitement surging through him. He'd be returning to the Core very, very soon. And he'd have to face the traitor.

Albert didn't know why, but he knew that the traitor was out for destruction. And if the Core fell apart, then the rest of the world would fall with it.

CHAPTER 2

The Truth Revealed

The rest of the day flew by, and though the conversation in the halls was of the quake—the stories had morphed into the walls splitting and the floor swallowing people whole—Albert knew his classmates would forget about it soon enough.

But Albert wouldn't forget.

If the Core was in trouble, he needed to get there. *Fast.*

But it wasn't spring break yet. Albert's mom had been lenient enough in the past, letting Albert hop on a plane by himself and fly to Herman, Wyoming, where she *thought* he was staying with his dad in his little home on the edge of the tiny town.

It wasn't entirely untrue. Albert *was* with his dad, but they weren't hanging out in Herman. They were in the

Core of the earth, stopping the worst possible Imbalances from spiraling out of control.

Just a few months ago, Albert had gone to Herman during Christmas break. He'd raced through the snow to the Troll Tree entrance to the Core and joined back up with his Hydra teammates, Birdie and Leroy.

They'd saved the watery realm of Ponderay from an Imbalance just in time for Albert to return back home.

But where *was* home, now? Albert's heart was divided, and with today's earthquake, he was yearning for the Core more than usual.

He looked around at his classmates. *There's a traitor in the Core, causing Imbalances!* Albert thought. *Don't you people know this?!*

Of course, they didn't know about the traitor. Neither did the people he passed on his walk home. Nobody did.

That's why it was so important that Albert stay alert. He had been walking around the city as if the traitor was going to pop out of nowhere and rip the one remaining Master Tile from his neck. The traitor already had the other two. There was no telling what the power of *three* Master Tiles could accomplish.

Albert wasn't entirely sure why the traitor wanted to ruin the Core and screw up the surface world in the process, but he knew that this person, whoever they were, was going to strike again. With today's earthquake, that time had finally come.

It was the only thing on his mind as he sat through a spaghetti dinner with his mom and half siblings and dodged flying noodles as a spaghetti war broke out. It was all he could think about as he brushed his teeth and got ready for bed.

He stayed awake until his eyes grew heavy, studying the Tiles in the Black Book, learning every single one that he could. He had to be ready for the traitor.

He *had* to.

Eventually, at half past midnight, Albert left his dog, Farnsworth, snoring on his bed and tiptoed down the stairs to grab a cup of milk.

Downstairs, the kitchen light was already on, casting a warm glow into the shadows of the hall.

Albert stepped into the kitchen and found his mom sitting at the table. She had her own cup of milk in front of her, though it looked like she'd hardly touched it.

"Albert?" she asked. Her hair was pulled back in its usual curly ponytail, its shade the same chocolaty-brown as his hair. "What are you doing up?"

"Apparently, we had the same idea," Albert said, nodding at the milk. He joined her at the table. "Couldn't sleep."

His mom smiled and pushed the cup of milk toward him. "Go ahead," she said. "You're a growing boy. You need the calcium more than I do."

Albert took a big gulp. Cold milk had always calmed

his nerves, but tonight, it didn't have the same effect. He felt jumpier than a Jackalope. His heart hadn't stopped racing since the earthquake.

And his mind was shouting, *Tell her! Tell her about the Core!*

But he couldn't. He wouldn't. If he could just get ahold of his dad in the Core, then maybe Albert wouldn't have to convince his mom to let him go. His dad would do all that work for him. His dad's phone had been going to voice mail all day, though. As a Professor in the Core, he must have had a lot to attend to today.

"What's on your mind, kiddo?" Albert's mom said.

He sighed and leaned back in his chair. "Not much," he said, because what was he supposed to say?

His mom saw right through it. "You were always a hero," she said. "You know that, right?"

Albert's eyes flitted upward. Where was she going with this? "Um, I guess so," he said. "What do you mean?"

Albert's mom smiled. "When you were only five years old, you nearly got run over by a bicycle messenger because you were so determined to protect a bird that had fallen and broken its wing."

Albert laughed. That sounded more like something his teammate Birdie Howell would do.

"And when you were seven, you got sent home early from school for standing up to a bully who stole all your classmate's crayons. You poked him in the eye with a blue marker! You said you were aiming for his cheek, but . . ." She chuckled under her breath. "My point is, Albert, I've always known that you wear your heart on your sleeve. And right now, your heart isn't here."

Albert nodded. If only she really truly knew where his heart was: deep in the Core of the earth, where he'd left it the last time he was there.

"I don't understand what you're getting at, Mom," he said.

His mom leaned forward and placed a warm hand over Albert's. She took a deep breath and looked into his eyes. "Albert. I know."

"Know what?" Albert said.

He wanted to pull his hand away.

"I *know*," she said again, more insistent this time. Then she said five words that Albert never in a million, billion years expected her to say. "I know about the Core."

He was dreaming.

He was dreaming, and this was all his crazy imagination, making things up as he slept. Probably Farnsworth had let loose another acid fart, and it was messing with his brain.

"Mom," Albert said. "I think it's time for us both to go back to sleep. It's late."

She squeezed his hand gently as he tried to pull away.

"You've done a wonderful job keeping it to yourself. Sure, it wasn't easy, not blurting out that I do know about what you're really doing when you're off with your dad on breaks, but . . ."

"Stop," Albert said. "Just . . . stop."

She smiled reassuringly again. "Albert. A mother always knows who her son really is. And I know, just as I knew about your father and his father, that you're a Balance Keeper."

And there it was.

Two words, two perfect words that explained everything.

Albert tried to speak, but all he really did was look like a fish out of water, opening and closing its mouth. He had so many questions.

"How?" he finally blurted out. "When? Who?"

Albert's mom laughed, the sound warm and light and all too real in this moment. "I was married to a Balance Keeper," she said. "Your dad might have kept the secret from you until the time was right, but I was his wife. And a wife always has a way of prying the truth from her husband. Your dad did *so* love those peanut butter brownies I used to make."

Albert nodded. The brownies were pretty good, but good enough to pull the truth out of Bob Flynn? No way.

"The truth is," his mom said, blowing Albert's mind even further, "he told me about the Core right before we were married. He didn't want me to be married to a man who held back the truth. He wanted me to know that, in the future, there was a chance his Balance Keeper genes would be passed on to our children." She looked at Albert and grinned as bright as the sun. "And they were. To you, Albert."

He swallowed the lump that had been growing in his throat. This conversation wasn't full of accusations, fear, and disbelief like Albert had always imagined should his mom discover the truth about the Core. His mom was smiling. A lot. Like she was *proud* of Albert's other life.

If this was a dream, he decided, he'd better act quickly, before he woke up.

"I have to go to the Core," he said. "I have to go as soon as possible."

His mom ran her fingers through her hair. She nodded, and when she met his eyes again, she looked incredibly sad.

"I already purchased your ticket," she said. "Your father called me this afternoon, shortly after the earthquake."

"You talked to Dad?" Albert blurted out. "Is he okay? Is the Core okay? Is the . . ."

His mom held up a hand. "He's fine, Albert, and he didn't give me any details, because honestly, I didn't want them."

"But you know about me being a Balance Keeper!" Albert said. "That means I can finally talk about everything with you, and not feel like there's this big weight of the secret on my shoulders, and . . ."

"I don't want to know the details," she said. "I don't want to know what dangerous things my son is out there doing. I just know that you need to be there, and so, because I love you and I believe in you, I'm going to let you go."

She stood up and pushed her chair back in place beneath the table. "You leave first thing in the morning. The first flight out."

She turned to go, but before she made it out of the kitchen, Albert leaped from his chair and ran the last few steps to her side.

He flung his arms around her and gave her the biggest hug he could manage.

"Thank you," Albert said as she wrapped her arms around him, too. "Thank you for not being mad."

She laughed again and ruffled his hair. "You might be my son, but you're your father's son, too. You were born to do this, Albert." She pulled away from him and held him at arm's length, so they could look into each other's matching green eyes. "Just do me a favor? Whatever's going on down there, make sure it gets right again. And come back to me. You might be a Balance Keeper, but you're still my little boy."

Albert raised an eyebrow at the "little," but nodded. "I promise."

"You're just like him, you know," she said. There was

a sad look in her eyes suddenly, one full of memories near-forgotten.

"Like Dad?" Albert asked.

His mom shook her head, and the look in her eyes changed suddenly.

It wasn't sadness any longer. Was that . . . *fear*?

"Mom?" Albert asked. "Who am I just like?"

"Get some sleep," she said, shaking her head. "You're going to need it. I love you, Albert. And I always will."

"Love you too, Mom," Albert said.

She sent him on his way back up the stairs with questions lingering in his mind.

But when he fell into his bed, sleep came in an instant and stole Albert away.

CHAPTER 3

The Cavalry Arrives

The plane ride was endless, or so it seemed.

Albert studied the Black Book the entire time, desperately trying to remember all the Tile symbols he'd yet to learn.

There were so many.

PlantGrow (the ability to grow plants without a seed)

BatSight (the ability to "see" in the dark, like bats)

LaughALot (making someone laugh uncontrollably)

By the time the plane landed, Albert's brain felt like mush. He grabbed Farnsworth's crate and walked like a zombie along the moving sidewalks at the airport. But then he saw a familiar shock of white hair at the exit, and his mind cleared. He felt rejuvenated from head to toe.

It was Pap. Maybe Albert would finally get some

answers about the most recent Imbalance in the Core. Because surely that was why he'd been allowed to come, right?

He'd texted Birdie and Leroy, but hadn't gotten any responses from them either.

Why was *no one* answering him?

Pap hugged Albert and helped him carry his bags to the car and let an eager Farnsworth out of his crate and into the backseat.

Pap's driving was enough to give anyone a heart attack, and as Albert strapped his seat belt tight around his chest, they were off.

"So," Pap said a few minutes later, as he swerved right to dodge a turtle in the road, "you're back earlier than I expected."

Albert nodded. He'd clutched his Master Tile the entire plane ride, afraid the traitor was going to somehow use the magic of the two Tiles he or she had to pluck Albert's plane right out of the sky. That begged questions that, after two visits to the Core, Albert had never thought to ask.

Did the power of the Tiles work outside of the Core? Would the Master Tiles hold the same power on the surface? He was always afraid to try it himself, afraid of what might happen if he did.

He pressed his own Tile neatly beneath the collar of his shirt, hiding it away from the world. Pap had been a Balance Keeper once. Maybe he knew the answer to Albert's questions, and more.

"There's a traitor," Albert said. His voice came out rougher than he'd expected. "There's a traitor in the Core, and he or she is causing Imbalances. I'm scared, Pap."

Pap rapped his knuckles on the steering wheel. He nodded, like he was mulling something over in his head. "You're a Flynn," he finally said. "Flynns are strong. Whoever this traitor is, you'll give them a good whipping, I'm sure."

"I hope you're right," Albert said.

He thought about Birdie and Leroy and knew they'd both say the same type of thing. A little flash of longing went through him. They were probably already in the Core, waiting for him to arrive.

Suddenly, Pap placed a hand on Albert's shoulder. He opened his mouth like he was going to say something, but then he shook his head and sped up to near-breakneck speeds.

The car ride was silent the rest of the way into Herman.

The last time Albert was in Herman, the whole town was covered in a thick blanket of snow. Now buds were forming on the trees, and though a cold wind still whipped at the windows of Pap's truck, there was a definite "springness" in the air. Everything felt fresh and light, and Albert's body buzzed with the anticipation of being this much closer to the Core.

Pap whizzed through town, almost blowing through a stoplight. The old tires of his truck squealed as he skidded around a curve, soaring past the square post office. His porch buddies, a group of old men who seemed to never *not* be playing a game of Tiles, were, as always, sitting on the porch, sucking down gallons of sweet tea.

Farnsworth pressed his nose to the window and yipped happily as they passed by.

"Yep," Albert said, scratching Farnsworth's soft ears, "that's where we first met! Where this all started, huh, buddy?"

The road came to a dead end, and usually, Pap took a sharp right. But not today.

Today, he gunned the engine and soared past Albert's dad's house, which was now a blur in the distance. They were heading toward the main entrance to the woods, where just a few months ago, Albert had driven his dad's snowmobile.

"We're not stopping at the house?" Albert asked. Farnsworth's cold nose touched the bottom of his chin as he, too, turned to look at Pap.

The old man shrugged. "I'm under strict instructions. Straight to the Core. No time to waste. And, ahh. There's your welcome party now, I believe."

No sooner had he said it than Albert saw two familiar shapes in the distance. They were standing on the edge of the woods. One tall, with a backward hat on; the other shorter and ponytailed.

Pap slammed on the brakes, and the truck skidded to a stop. Albert practically leaped from the front seat; he knew who those two shapes were.

"It's about time you showed up," Birdie said as Albert rounded the front of the truck. She stood there with her hands on her hips, grinning like the madwoman she was. And she'd changed her hair! Birdie usually had pink streaks in her blond curls, but now she'd added in a few dashes of blue. Suddenly Albert had a craving for cotton candy.

Leroy stood casually beside her, leaning against a fat tree. "Give the dude a break, Birdie," he said, striding forward. Had he grown since Albert saw him last? Albert was sure he'd gained at least another inch in the few months they'd been apart. Leroy smiled and held his long arms out. "Well? Did we surprise you?"

Albert pulled them both into a group hug, then stepped back and scratched his head. "So *this* is why you guys weren't answering any of my texts? I figured you were already in the Core!"

"The cavalry is here," Leroy said, bowing. "Or, at least, two great traveling companions."

Birdie nodded, her eyes wide. "We're sorry! Your dad asked us not to say a word. Something about *being as careful as possible.*"

"He wanted us to be here, so we could all enter the Core together," Leroy added in. "For safety, probably. He was worried about calling you and alerting anyone to your arrival. He thought it would make you feel better if we were all together. Just in case, you know . . ." He lowered his voice to a whisper. "The *traitor* is waiting just inside."

Birdie thumped him over the head. "Don't scare him, you bonehead!"

"I wasn't trying to scare him, I was just being honest!" Leroy said, and Albert laughed.

Birdie and Leroy would have been the perfect siblings.

"You should be on your way," Pap said from behind Albert. He handed him his backpack.

"Thanks for the ride," Albert said. "I wish you could come with us."

Pap chuckled and draped an arm across Albert's shoulders. He smelled like old leather and evergreen trees, and Albert suddenly wished he could stay here, in Herman, where it was safe and sound, and there wasn't a traitor lurking around the corner, just waiting to destroy the world.

Pap sighed. "My time has passed. But yours is just beginning." He gave Albert a good squeeze and lowered his head. "Keep those two friends of yours close. Loyalty is your best asset in times like these."

Farnsworth let out a growl and tugged on the toe of Pap's leather boot.

"And keep that dog under control," he said, nudging Farnsworth playfully.

"I will," Albert said. Pap climbed into his truck, and the old engine sputtered to life.

"Albert?" Pap called out the window. He chewed on his lip for a moment and adjusted his rearview mirror. "Just . . . remember who you are. Remember that the Flynns are the good guys. No matter what anyone else says." He waved good-bye before peeling out, rocks flying behind him.

Albert watched him fade into the distance. That was kind of a weird thing for Pap to say. He shook it away a second later and turned to his friends.

"Farnsworth?" he said. The little dog yipped and circled Albert's feet. "Lead the way!"

Farnsworth howled once. Then he turned and dashed into the woods, a blur of black amid the evergreen trees.

"That dog doesn't understand the meaning of *lead the way*," Leroy said.

"We'll find the path together," Albert said.

Birdie hopped in the middle of them and linked her arms between Albert's and Leroy's. "Another adventure awaits us, boys," she said. "Let's do this."

Together, they headed into the woods.

CHAPTER 4

The Troll Tree

Albert had been in these woods many times over the course of his eleven years. When he was younger, he would imagine the trees were alive and it was his mission to discover their secrets. Little did he know, there *was* life in the ring of trees beyond Herman, and it all centered on the Troll Tree.

Albert knew he'd never forget the first time he came upon it. He had followed Farnsworth through the shadows, determined to deliver a letter to some strange hermit who lived there.

He could still remember the shadows moving through the trees, and the awful, prickly feeling he got when he thought he was being watched. Or followed.

Of course, it had only been Leroy and Birdie making

their way through the woods like he was, for their first visit to the Core. The way they seemed to disappear was the work of the Path Hider, who concealed their paths toward the Core to confuse anyone from the surface world who might have seen them.

Now, on Albert's third time finding the Troll Tree, he was *with* those shadows. And they had become his best friends in the entire world.

"It's really fascinating," Birdie said as she hopped over a fallen log, "that we're finally entering the Core together. Like, totally as a team."

"It would be more fascinating if Farnsworth would slow down," Leroy said. He took his hat off and shook out his sweaty hair.

Albert laughed as they passed by the slingshot tree. Farnsworth was, indeed, doing his typical race ahead. He was a blur of black in the trees, leaping up every so often to snap at a bug.

"I think I've memorized the way by now," Albert said. "We'll be there soon."

What he didn't say was, *what will be waiting for us when we reach the tree? Or even worse*, he thought, as he swallowed a new lump in his throat, *who will be waiting for us?*

Albert pressed his Master Tile closer against his chest, and they walked on.

Eventually they came to the familiar stream, and Albert and Leroy took turns leaping over it. Birdie just stomped through the water.

The Troll Tree would be a few minutes ahead.

Albert let the sounds of his friends' voices distract him from the dread that was gnawing at him.

It didn't help much, though. The gnawing was still there when the Troll Tree came into view.

And then it got worse.

The Troll Tree was as wide as a school bus, so large it should have been impossible that it even existed. It was a magnificent being, full of life and secrets just begging to be uncovered. Or, at least, it *had* been.

The tree was wilting now. The branches hung like tired arms, and where there should have been new springtime buds, there was nothing.

It looked as barren as a tree in the middle of winter.

"It's . . . dying," Birdie said. Her voice was only a whisper.

Leroy shook his head. "It looks like it's already dead."

Albert rushed forward. He circled the tree, searching for some speck of green. Around and around he went, ignoring Birdie's and Leroy's shouts.

It was all so *wrong*. The bark was peeling in places, like flecks of shriveled skin, so different from the rough, thick covering it had once been.

Albert found the door on the side of the tree, and the handle looked rusted and forgotten. He put his hand on it, about to turn the knob, but he stopped.

If the outside of the Troll Tree looked this bad . . . what would be waiting for him and his friends once they stepped inside?

Birdie and Leroy came up behind him. Farnsworth appeared at their feet, his ears droopy and his tail totally still.

It was Leroy who finally spoke. "I'm not sure what happened here, but we have to go in, and we're going to do it together."

He nudged Birdie, who had been standing there staring blankly at Albert. "Right," she said. She stomped her foot and stood tall. "We go in together, and we face whatever we have to face to make it to the Core."

Albert's hand was still on the knob, so Leroy set his over Albert's. Then Birdie stacked hers on top.

On the count of three, they turned the knob.

The door swung open, creaking on its hinges, and Team Hydra stepped inside the lifeless depths.

CHAPTER 5

A Surprise Welcome

N o one had thought to bring a flashlight, but Albert had something even better to cut through the darkness.

Farnsworth was in the lead, his tail wagging like a helicopter blade, his bright-blue eye beams on full blast.

Albert, Leroy, and Birdie crawled along behind him, twisting their way through the roots of the Troll Tree. They went deeper and deeper, and every time Farnsworth turned a corner, Albert felt his heartbeat quicken.

He was half expecting the traitor to leap from the shadows and steal the Master Tile from around his neck. It would be so much better if he knew who he was looking for. He'd gone over and over a list of possible traitors in his mind, but it was a long list. The traitor could be anyone.

Anywhere. At any time.

"We're almost there," Albert said, forcing those thoughts to the back of his mind.

"Good," Leroy said, "because I'm getting too tall for crawling around in this tree."

"Just keep moving, Memory Boy." Birdie giggled from the back of the group.

Finally, the tree opened up. Farnsworth's eyes cast an eerie blue glow on the doorway that led to the Core.

"Here goes nothing," Albert said.

He placed his hand on the sticky lock. Warm goo covered his fingertips—he would never get used to that feeling—and the door creaked open. A glowing orange platform sat waiting like an old friend on the other side.

Farnsworth hopped on, either oblivious to the dangers that could be waiting below, or completely and totally fearless.

Albert, Birdie, and Leroy followed. The platform sank, and Albert closed his eyes and wished—and hoped— that the Core would still be safe when they reached the bottom.

Albert had expected the Path Hider's domain to be destroyed. He'd envisioned pipes split in half, with steam pouring out like waterfall mist. He'd expected the Path

Hider's gears to be scattered all over the floor, and the wires spitting angry sparks like fireworks.

But everything was normal. Fat pipes crisscrossed the large room, spitting out little bits of steam that made the place feel warm and safe. The same old tangled wires hung like vines, and in the distance, the cranking sounds of the Path Hider's gears buzzed and whirred.

Farnsworth ran through the room, sniffing about as if he were searching for the Path Hider so he could say hello. He came sprinting back, his ears drooping.

"I guess the Path Hider isn't here," Albert said as he and his friends hopped off the platform. He knew the Path Hider worked overtime, and was probably somewhere in some hidden part of this room, chugging down mugfuls of coffee, or trying to scrub the grease off his miner's helmet.

"No," Birdie whispered. "But someone else is."

She was right.

Across the room, through the steam, Albert spotted a shadowed figure heading toward them, and it wasn't the Path Hider. This one was shorter, with wider shoulders, and he or she walked with purpose. The person was heading straight toward Team Hydra.

Farnsworth growled, his hair rising on his back.

"Oh man, it's too soon for this," Leroy whispered, leaning down as if he could hide himself. "This is the moment when we run, right?"

Albert's body was frozen. He wasn't sure if he should go forward or backward, and suddenly his mind was running through all the Tiles he'd studied recently in the Black Book. SuperSpeed, and Invisibility, and Gale Force, the ability to soar like the wind.

But then Farnsworth's growl turned to a happy bark, and as the steam cleared, Albert saw the shimmer of an emerald-green jacket. His face broke into a smile.

"Dad!"

He ran, ducking and dodging pipes, and threw his arms around Professor Flynn.

There was the familiar smell of evergreen trees and freshly cut wood as Albert's dad returned the hug. "Hey, kiddo," Professor Flynn said. "I'm glad to see you made it safely. Did you like your surprise?"

Albert stepped back, his smile big and bold.

But when he saw the dark circles underneath his dad's eyes, his smile faded. It looked like his dad hadn't slept in weeks. Then again, Albert didn't think he'd be able to sleep either if he had been the one in charge of the two Master Tiles that were now in the traitor's hands. His dad couldn't be feeling so great about himself right now. And with this Imbalance . . .

"What's going on?" Albert asked. "There was an earthquake back home, and then when we got to the Troll Tree, it was . . ."

Professor Flynn held up a hand. He lowered his voice

to a rushed whisper. "We can't talk here. It isn't safe."

His eyes flitted to and then away from Albert's Master Tile, like it was an angry talisman. Like Professor Flynn wasn't sure if it was safe to be in the presence of it.

Albert retucked it beneath the collar of his shirt.

Birdie and Leroy caught up, and Professor Flynn nodded a greeting to them, broken from his spell.

"Let's move," he said. His eyes fell onto Albert's, and he nodded. "Stay close."

He turned on his heel and marched off, disappearing into the steam.

CHAPTER 6

Lucinda's Silence

The gondola whizzed along its track, carting the group to the inside of the Core. Professor Flynn kept quiet the entire time, shushing them when they tried to ask questions.

Were they in that much danger of being overheard? Was the traitor really so powerful that they could listen in on conversations as the gondola rushed along at top speeds?

Albert guessed that yes, probably the traitor *was* that strong. Causing Imbalances was the height of power. Anything less complicated had to be a piece of cake.

Everything went by in a blur—the Memory Wipers dipping and diving in and out of the open windows, Farnsworth's velvety ears flapping in the wind, tickling

Albert's chin. Everything was the same, but everything was not.

There was a certain stale taste to the air, as if the Core itself knew that there was someone here who didn't belong.

Finally, the gondola slowed and Lucinda's floating platforms came into view.

Just seeing her, standing there looking so *normal*, lifted a little bit of weight from Albert's shoulders.

Until he remembered that Lucinda was on his list of possible traitors.

He narrowed his eyes as the gondola stopped in front of her.

"Back so soon?" Lucinda asked. Her voice wavered as she spoke, and there was a thin line of sweat beading on her brow. She was a large woman, and her hands were covered in giant glittering gemstone rings. Kimber, her black snake, sat on her shoulders. It flicked its tongue and hissed, and Farnsworth growled.

Albert had always found Lucinda to be creepy, in several ways. Last term, when Team Hydra discovered the Book of Bad Tiles and found out Lucinda was behind it, it had sent her creepiness factor up to an eight out of ten.

But then again, Lucinda had given Albert the Counter last term as well, a device that helped Hydra keep track of how much time they had in Ponderay before the Imbalance got out of hand.

Albert enjoyed a good mystery. But Lucinda was one he just couldn't crack.

"What are you three doing here?" Lucinda asked. Her voice wasn't as sugary as usual. *A little on the salty side, actually*, Albert noted.

Professor Flynn answered before Albert could. "I'm escorting Team Hydra back to the Core, for an important meeting."

"Well, not without a gift from Lucinda, right?" Lucinda rifled through a rucksack she had on her ramshackle stand. Her hands shook, and she dropped a small metal orb. It tumbled sideways and disappeared into the abyss below. She giggled, the sound strangled and out of place. "Oh, goodness. Well, I've got other things to do. You should be off, now, shouldn't you?"

She wouldn't look up, and Albert was pretty sure her hands were shaking even harder now.

"Are you all right?" Birdie asked.

Lucinda's snake hissed again, and instead of tightening itself around her neck, it began to uncoil. Lucinda tried to grab it, but it hissed louder. Was it rebelling? It was definitely trying to free itself from her shoulders.

"Perfectly fine, dear," Lucinda said as she gained control and recoiled Kimber around her neck and shoulders. For one moment, her eyes fell onto Albert's Tile. She let out a little gasp, and her face reddened. "Move along, now. Old Lucinda has work to do. No time to talk today."

Birdie's smile was tight. She raised her eyebrows at Albert and Leroy, and both boys shrugged.

"Well, uh . . . see you later," Albert said. He looked at Farnsworth, who let out two barks. The gondola started up again, and they left Lucinda behind.

Leroy let out a huge breath. His shoulders relaxed. "That woman just gives me the heebie-jeebies," he said.

"Nobody uses that phrase anymore, doofus," Birdie said.

Leroy turned to her and laughed. "Nobody says doofus anymore, either."

They argued back and forth, and for once, Albert didn't mind. At least they were acting normal. Between the missing Path Hider, the Troll Tree, Lucinda, and his dad's strange silence, Albert just wanted something to feel the same.

He wrapped his arms around Farnsworth, closed his eyes, and listened to the voices of his friends as the gondola continued on toward the Main Chamber of the Core.

It was only when it finally stopped at the double doors that Professor Flynn finally spoke.

"Remember. No questions," he said, pointing at the three of them, "until we're in a safe place."

He looked over his shoulder at the darkness of the cave. It was as if he was searching for something, or some*one*.

"Dad?" Albert asked.

Professor Flynn snapped out of it, turned away, and pushed open the double doors. They groaned like old spirits whispering a warning to the Core.

Nothing, and no one, is safe.

CHAPTER 7

A Strange Greeting

Normally, the Main Chamber was a sight to behold.

Students were always rushing back and forth, laughing and sharing stories about who had defeated whom in a Pit Competition, or in a friendly game of Tiles in the Library. Core creatures hopped across the pipes, crisscrossing the ceiling space, or swung from the giant chandelier that shed a warm glow on everyone below.

But today wasn't normal.

Albert stepped through the double doors and was shocked at how much of everything there *wasn't*.

The Main Chamber was as quiet as the Cave of Souls.

Strange, Albert noted, *there isn't a soul in sight.*

"Where is everyone?" Birdie asked. Her voice echoed

across the empty room, and Albert flinched. This wasn't right at all. One word echoed in his mind.

Danger.

Where was the laughter? Where was the chaos that, to some, was a big fat headache, but to Albert felt like *home?*

He stole a glance at his dad. Professor Flynn just stood there, his arms pressed neatly to his sides, staring across the Main Chamber.

"There you are!" a voice said from across the room. A familiar tall, spindly figure was heading toward them. It was Trey, the Apprentice for the Calderon Realm, and one of Professor Flynn's most trusted friends.

"We need to get moving," Professor Flynn said, ushering Albert, Birdie, and Leroy forward. They met Trey halfway, on one of the arched bridges that stood over a glittering silver stream.

Albert stopped to greet Trey, but Trey shook his head and motioned for them to keep moving.

"We're late as it is," Trey said. "The entire Core has been waiting for your arrival."

"Arrival for what?" Albert asked.

"You'd think you three were First Termers, the way you keep asking questions," Professor Flynn said, chuckling.

His voice was *just* light enough to make Albert feel a little bit safer, for the time being.

They walked quickly, disappearing into one of the tunnels. Blue flames on torches lined the walls, but as Albert passed by one of them, the flame flickered, and a sickly greenish tinge took its place. When Albert looked back, the flame was blue again. *Strange.*

"We're heading toward the Pit," Albert said. "What's everyone doing in there?"

"Save the questions, kiddo." Professor Flynn waved him off, speeding up so that he and Trey could speak in hushed voices up ahead.

"This is totally weird," Birdie said as she ran her fingers through one of the cool blue flames. "Everyone's acting like we're in the middle of a war."

"We are," Leroy answered. "A war with hunger. I haven't eaten in hours."

"*Leroy,*" Birdie growled.

Albert grinned despite how on-edge he felt. Leave it to Leroy to always make light of situations that were way too dark.

"Let's just see what everyone's up to, and then we'll decide if it's time to worry or not," he said.

They followed Professor Flynn and Trey down the tunnel, all three of them wondering what would be waiting in the Pit.

It was *everyone.* The entire Core.

People were packed in the stands, pressed tightly

together so everyone could fit, and some were even standing or sitting around the edges of the Pit. Professors were all gathered on the far right, talking in hushed voices. Albert's dad and Trey headed straight for the Professors, their faces tense.

"Is this like a meeting or something?" Birdie asked.

Albert shrugged as he took it all in.

The last time he saw the Pit, it was a smoking heap of rubble after the traitor had destroyed it. Now it was covered with a thick black tarp, which probably meant the repairs still weren't done. A rush of heat went through Albert as he thought of all the Balance Keepers who wouldn't be able to train because of this. Including his team.

Professor Bigglesby, a tiny dwarf who was hundreds, perhaps thousands of years old, took his place in a crane-like machine by the side of the Pit. He fired it up and it extended, lifting him in a little cage into the air, so that he hovered over what used to be the Pit.

"Please, find a spot and settle down." Professor Bigglesby spoke into the MegaHorn, a device that amplified his voice so that it echoed loudly through the room. "Quickly, quickly!"

Albert nudged his friends forward, and they went to find a seat in the stands.

The bleachers were packed with lots of familiar faces, including one dark-haired boy who rose from his seat and waved so frantically he slapped a Core Cleaner in the face, sending his glasses flying into the crowd.

Birdie giggled. "I see Petra hasn't changed since we last saw him."

"We should go over there, before he accidentally starts a fight," Leroy added.

As they walked, people laughed and reached out their hands to pet Farnsworth's soft head. A group of girls on the front row called out his name and petted his tummy as he rolled onto his back, his tongue lolling out of his mouth.

"He's more popular than we'll ever be," Leroy added.

When they were all seated, Petra leaned over and said hello. "I'm glad you guys made it okay. It's been rough down here."

"How so?" Birdie asked.

"You want the honest truth?"

They all nodded yes.

Petra glanced left and right, then leaned in when he was satisfied that no one was listening. "Well, since the Pit was broken, they've been working around the clock to fix it. But every time they seem to get ahead, it breaks all over again. It's like someone's sabotaging it."

"But that's terrible!" Birdie whispered.

Petra nodded. "They've even had people guarding the entrance at night! Nobody goes in or out, but in the morning . . . the Pit's broken. Like a ghost went in there and destroyed it."

"But how is that even possible?" Albert asked.

Petra shrugged. "They put cameras in there, but they don't show anything. You know what I think?" He lifted a finger and tapped Albert's Master Tile.

Everyone nodded, understanding perfectly.

"And that's not the worst of it," Petra exclaimed, a little too loudly. Birdie held a fingertip to her lips, and Petra nodded and lowered his voice. "Some of the Core workers have disappeared."

A little shiver raced through Albert's veins. That was something he wasn't expecting to hear. "Disappeared? Like, out of thin air?"

"Kind of." Petra frowned. "Cleaners are working in the halls at night, cleaning up while everyone's out of their way. I used to help my mom do it when I couldn't sleep. Nightmares, you know?"

Leroy nodded.

"There's been three of them. Two Core Cleaners and one Core Historian—some old dude who's usually hanging around the professors' lounge in the Tower."

"Where are they disappearing to?" Birdie asked. "Maybe they just left. Got scared."

"That's what the Professors thought, but they left their possessions behind. The weirdest part is that all three of the disappearances happened in the Main Chamber. At night." Petra shifted in his seat and looked each of them in the eyes before continuing. "The Core Cleaners' brooms and trash bins were just sitting there left behind, and the Core Historian's glasses and book were lying on the floor like he'd dropped them."

Albert felt like he was going to be sick. This was too creepy. Too *not* okay. The Core wasn't safe.

It seemed Petra wasn't done yet. "But the strangest thing is that all three of them disappeared in the exact same spot."

"Where was that?" Leroy asked. He leaned forward with his hands on his knees. Albert leaned in, too.

Petra's face paled. "Right by the door to Belltroll."

Eeeeeeeeiiiiiiiiiiiiiiiiiiiiiieeeeeeeeeeeeeeee! A piercing screech split the half silence.

Albert's heart raced in his throat, and he whirled around, thinking it was a scream. But it was only Professor Bigglesby, tapping the MegaHorn.

It squealed loudly again, and after Farnsworth and several other companion creatures stopped howling or hissing or cawing, the crowd fell silent. If Petra had anything else to say, it would have to wait.

"Balance Keepers, Core workers, Professors, and Apprentices," Bigglesby said into the MegaHorn. "Thank you all for gathering on such short notice. I'll get straight to the point."

Suddenly, the door to the Pit swung open and Lucinda shuffled in. She was dragging an old, rusted TV on wheels behind her, the screen flickering in and out.

Bigglesby swung his cage around. "Nice of you to join us, Lucinda. We're just getting started."

Lucinda's snake hissed and flicked its tongue, and two Core workers rushed forward to help her haul the TV around to the stands.

"What's that all about?" Albert whispered to his friends.

Leroy pointed. "The Path Hider's in there, dude. Like a live video feed or something."

Sure enough, when Albert craned his neck, he saw the Path Hider's face, with his strange different-colored eyes, staring back at the room from the TV screen. Albert could barely make out hints of the entryway to the Core, the big fat maze of pipes. He wondered where the Path Hider had been when they'd arrived just an hour before.

"I guess they're letting him watch the meeting from his domain," Birdie said. "So he can still guard the paths. That's cool."

Finally, once Lucinda was seated, Bigglesby cleared his throat and began again.

"As I was saying, before the interruption . . ." Bigglesby's tiny, dark eyes flitted toward Lucinda. "I will get straight to the point." He stopped and took a deep breath before speaking again. "The door to the Realm of

Belltroll has been opened, by force. We are afraid that an Imbalance is imminent and could quite possibly be the worst Imbalance the Core has yet to face."

Murmurs carried across the room like a sudden gust of wind. Lucinda gasped dramatically and pressed a hand to her chest.

But Hydra wasn't surprised in the least bit. They'd been waiting for this to happen for months.

"The doors are never to be opened, unless a Realm is in dire need. But someone found the power to open the door and used it just yesterday morning." Bigglesby looked around the room, his head turning very, very slowly as he took every face in. "This has not happened since . . ." His voice trailed off, and his eyes flitted toward the Professors.

Professor Flynn shook his head, just once. But Albert caught it. What didn't his dad want Bigglesby to share?

Professor Bigglesby cleared his throat. "This has not happened in centuries."

All around him, Albert heard snippets of questions and conversations, and though he knew he should be asking questions, too, he just couldn't.

It was obvious that an Imbalance was on its way. It was even more obvious that if the door to Belltroll had been forced open, meaning someone probably went *inside* the Realm, on the very same day the earthquake happened in New York . . . well, it had to be the traitor. There was no other logical answer.

From the corner of his eye, Albert saw Hoyt Jackson and the rest of Team Argon. They sat with their heads pressed together, no doubt asking the same questions everyone else was.

Albert shifted in his seat so he didn't have to look at Argon. Slink and Mo were all right, but seeing Hoyt made the hair rise on the back of Albert's neck. He still hadn't forgiven the guy for nearly destroying the world last term, with his little stunt in Ponderay.

Professor Bigglesby held up a tiny hand, and the crowd stilled.

"Fear is a very real thing, but I must urge you not to give in to it. Not now, when the Core needs bravery the most." He scanned the crowd again, more quickly this time. "The other Professors and I have come to an agreement. We need to act *now*, before the Imbalance escalates, and we need the very best team of Balance Keepers to lead this mission."

Albert thought he saw Bigglesby look directly at him, but there were so many people, he couldn't be sure. He sat a little taller, and beside him, Birdie and Leroy did the same.

"Today, we will perform the first Team Election the Core has had in centuries. There is no time for a competition to see who will enter the Realm. We will vote. Every member of the Core, not just the Balance Keepers, will get a say on who will train to save the Realm of Belltroll."

Birdie leaped to her feet in an instant. "But how will they train, Professor? The Pit was destroyed months ago."

It was a good question. People throughout the stands called out to second it, but Bigglesby held up a hand to calm the crowd.

"This has all been taken into account," he said. He was so tiny, yet he spoke with such authority. It calmed Albert a bit. Of course the Professors already had a plan in place. Bigglesby continued.

"This, perhaps, will be our most dangerous mission yet. Not simply because we do not know who opened the door to Belltroll, and how he or she was able to do so, but because we don't yet know the damage that has been done to the Realm. The Core Watchers have been working around the clock to decipher what's been causing the quakes, but all we know is that they originated from the Belltroll Realm. Since the door was opened, there has been . . ." His voice trailed off and he looked to the other Professors.

Professor Asante and Professor Flynn nodded in unison, and Bigglesby continued on.

"We don't know the state of the Realm at this moment in time because there has been a strange interference with our instruments."

Leroy leaned over to Albert and Birdie. "The traitor,"

he whispered. "What if this person is messing with the readers and stuff? What if the Imbalance is *already* in full swing?"

Birdie shook her head. "If it was, then wouldn't the surface be in way worse condition?"

Albert nodded. "That's true. But I think the traitor's not going to attack that fast. They want my Tile, remember? I think they're going to take this slow."

"What do you mean?" Leroy said.

"I think . . . ," Albert began, but Bigglesby was still talking and Albert didn't want to miss a thing. "I'll tell you later, okay?"

"There's no way for us to know what it's like in the Realm right now," Bigglesby continued. "This is why we must build a team today," he said, "and enter *tomorrow*."

The reaction from the crowd was immediate. Someone shot up, an older shaggy-haired boy who Albert recognized from last term as one of the Pures. "We can't just throw a team into the Realm without the proper time and environment to practice!"

Several others shouted their agreement to this, including Albert. Going into a Realm without any training seemed not only dangerous but stupid. How could they battle whatever was wrong in the Realm and come out alive if they hadn't trained for it?

Bigglesby raised both his hands this time and the crowd eventually fell silent. Bigglesby looked annoyed, like he'd expected all of them to get on board with the Professors' plan right away. But everyone was eerily silent. If they were feeling like Albert, Bigglesby's speech hadn't inspired them; it had only highlighted the direness of the situation. Going into the Realm without even knowing what they were dealing with . . . it was a desperate move.

Bigglesby cleared his throat. "So now, we will take a vote."

Professor Asante and Flynn both rose from the crowd. Asante crossed to the right of the stands near Lucinda, and Professor Flynn to the left, closest to Team Hydra and Petra. Albert had a feeling he knew how this vote was going to turn out, and he didn't like it, not if he was right about the traitor's plan.

"First, we will ask for nominations," Bigglesby continued. "Does anyone wish to nominate a team of Balance Keepers, based on previous acts of bravery and accomplishment?"

A hand immediately shot up, in the very front of the crowd.

"I nominate Team Hydra," Lucinda said. She stood, and as she did, Kimber slid from her neck and slithered off into the crowd. "They clearly are the most prepared unit, as they've saved the Core twice now from a terrifying fate."

She turned, her eyes scanning the crowd for Albert,

Birdie, and Leroy. When she found them, she gave her biggest smile.

Albert felt Birdie's hand grasp his. He held on tight, like it was an anchor.

They didn't trust Lucinda. Not after last term. And her eagerness to nominate Hydra only added to Albert's theory about the traitor's plan.

"Something's fishy about this," Leroy whispered.

Albert couldn't have said it better himself.

"Hydra is in the running," Bigglesby said into the MegaHorn. "Do we have any other nominations?"

Another person stood. This time it was a tall, wiry woman with long dark curls, someone Albert hadn't seen before. "I nominate Team Argon as well. Particularly the captain, Hoyt. After all, he has been training for this moment his entire life."

"As have several other Balance Keepers," Professor Bigglesby said. The woman gave Bigglesby a scowl that looked oddly familiar to Albert, though he couldn't quite place it. "But Argon showed extreme bravery last term in the Realm of Ponderay, and so I think it wise to add Argon to the running."

Petra leaned forward and whispered, "That's Hoyt's mom. Of course she wants him to be the big hero."

Figures, Albert thought.

Other teams were nominated, but in the end when the voting took place, it was indeed Hydra and Argon

that took the lead. The two teams' previous wins in Ponderay had obviously made an impression on the rest of
the Core.

"In Ponderay, it was a necessity to have two teams.
But this term, we must be discreet. Six Balance Keepers
is far too many to send in at once," Bigglesby said. "We
will now decide between Team Hydra and Argon."

Professors Flynn and Asante both nodded in agreement.

"Now . . . all those in favor of Team Hydra as our First
Unit?" Bigglesby asked.

This is happening too fast, Albert thought.

All around, hands shot up. One after the other, until
almost every single hand in the stands was held high.
There were only a few hands that didn't go up.

And of course, Hoyt's was one of them.

"Team Hydra it is," Bigglesby said. But he didn't sound
pleased. "Argon will be our backup unit, should we need a
second one to enter the Realm. But I do think, possibly"—
he tapped his fingers on his chin—"that a fourth Balance
Keeper should be added to this team. A final member,
from Team Argon, to enter the Realm with Hydra and
begin training alongside them. Should the backup unit
need to enter, it will be beneficial to have their captain
with some previous experience."

He looked around the crowd until his dark eyes landed
on Hoyt's.

"Mr. Jackson," he said, nodding. "I heard you were a very hands-on member of the teams in Ponderay last term."

Leroy let out a very Farnsworth-like whimper.

"Oh, he was hands-on," Birdie hissed. "He nearly killed us all."

"You will join Team Hydra as the fourth and final member. Each night when you return, you will debrief Team Argon on the Realm, and help prepare them, should their time come to enter." Bigglesby looked back at the rest of the crowd. "Do we have any objections to this?"

"Oh, I have objections," Birdie muttered under her breath. She had her arm halfway up when Albert and Leroy both reached for it and pulled it back down.

"Be the bigger person," Albert whispered.

"If you start a fight now, it'll only make it worse in Belltroll," Leroy added.

Birdie rolled her eyes and set her hands in her lap. "Fine," she said. "But after what that little worm did in Ponderay . . ."

"He won't do it again," Albert said. In his mind, a vision appeared of Hoyt standing on the final pillar in Ponderay, plucking the last Tile from its spot and then purposely *dropping* it at the very *last* second, nearly destroying the Realm in his failed attempt to be the savior. "I'll make sure of it."

Hoyt's eyes were wide as saucers, all the fight from last year seemingly leached from him.

Albert remembered the fear Hoyt had the night before they went into Ponderay. And as he watched Hoyt sink deeper and deeper into his seat in the stands, Albert realized . . .

Hoyt didn't want to enter the Realm. Deep down, Hoyt was still afraid. Albert couldn't blame him—he couldn't remember ever being this afraid himself.

"That settles it, then," Bigglesby said. "Tomorrow, Team Hydra, including Mr. Jackson, will enter the Realm of Belltroll." Bigglesby pushed a button and the crane-like thing started lowering him back down to the stands.

The crowd began to disperse, but Albert felt glued to the bleachers. Tomorrow they'd go into Belltroll, which meant tomorrow . . .

I could face the traitor, Albert thought, with absolute clarity.

He knew it like he knew his shoes were on the right feet, and the grass was green, and the sky was a bright Farnsworth's-eyes blue.

He knew it like he knew Leroy was hungry, and Birdie's fingers were about to reach up and tighten her ponytail in a silent show of determination.

But now that it was real, Albert wasn't sure he had what it would take.

"Leroy?" Albert said.

"What's up, bro?" Leroy sat back down. Birdie and Petra did too.

"What I was saying before . . . ," Albert said. His gut told him he needed to let his friends in on what his mind didn't want to admit was true. "I think us going into the Realm is only going to speed things up." He glanced around, but Leroy didn't seem to be following. He'd just have to say it. "The traitor wants my Tile, right? And sooner or later, that means the traitor and I are going to face each other, and the Realm is the perfect place to do that. Us going into the Realm, *me* going into the Realm, it's playing right into the traitor's hands." Albert glanced at Birdie, whose face had gone pale. At least it was sinking in now. "I know I have to do this, but . . ."

"Albert," Petra said, and put a hand on Albert's shoulder. "You aren't alone in this. You aren't expected to do anything on your own. That's what teams are for." Birdie and Leroy nodded their agreement.

The words were simple. But in this moment, they were the perfect reminder, music to Albert's ears. He would go into the Realm and face the traitor and his friends would be there to support him, to help him—

His thoughts exploded, as the world lurched forward and back.

Albert grabbed the bench—it was like déjà vu of yesterday in math class, only the shaking was ten times worse. His friends grabbed on, too. People all around

them who had been climbing down the bleachers strug-
gled to find a seat, like a game of musical chairs from
some wild nightmare.

There was a quick moment when the trembling faded
completely and Albert exhaled. At least that one hadn't
lasted as long.

Then all at once, the shaking came back with a ven-
geance. An explosion rocked the entire Core.

CHAPTER 8

The Traitor's Message

Albert could hardly see through the dust, but he could hear the screams. People were *freaking out.* Professor Bigglesby was shouting, trying to calm everyone down, but once the dust settled, Albert didn't stay to listen.

He sprinted from the stands, his lungs burning, and raced around the Pit and out the doorway that led to the orange platform.

He chased after his dad's retreating figure as Professor Flynn and Professor Asante ran down the Pit path back toward the Main Chamber.

The explosion had only lasted a moment, perhaps even only a breath of a second, but with each step he took, the silent alarm in his head blared at top volume. *Traitortraitortraitor!*

"Albert! Slow down!" Birdie and Leroy shouted from behind him.

Below, Professor Flynn and Professor Asante raced through the door that led back into the tunnels. Albert slipped through the door just before it closed and chased after them.

With each stride, his Master Tile bumped against his chest, reminding him that he was a target, and he always would be, until the traitor was captured.

Finally, his dad and Professor Asante slowed.

The Main Chamber came into view as the tunnel opened wide. The giant chandelier was dark and the Chamber was creepy enough to be a setting for a horror movie. Professor Asante grabbed a flickering torch from the wall and held it aloft.

The blue flames had faded to a pale, sickly green. And this time they didn't flicker back to blue.

"Dad!" Albert said, breathless, as he finally reached them. Birdie and Leroy skidded to a stop seconds later.

Professor Flynn turned around and held out an arm at the mouth of the tunnel. "You three shouldn't be here," he said. "*Especially* you, Albert. Go back to the Pit with everyone else, and stay there until it's safe."

"I have to see what happened!" Albert said. "I have to know."

"Plus, it's safer if we stay together," Birdie said beside Albert.

"Yeah, we could get jumped on the way back," Leroy added. "You know, like, by the traitor and his gang."

The corner of Professor Flynn's lip curled up, and he sighed heavily as if he knew this was a battle he couldn't win. "Stay close. If you see anyone, you run." Then he took a green torch of his own and turned to Professor Asante. "Let's go."

Slowly, they stepped into the Main Chamber.

It was strange, so dark and empty. The room seemed smaller, as if it were closing in around them. The green torches cast an otherworldly glow on the silver streams, so that they resembled a witch's brew. Albert shuddered. Witches had always creeped him out.

The bridges were still intact.

Professor Asante and Professor Flynn went first, crossing over the middle one.

Albert could feel Leroy's warm breath on his neck, close behind.

"What happened?" Birdie whispered. "I don't see anything damaged."

"Shhh," Albert said, because in this moment, silence seemed key.

They took a few more creaking steps across the bridge.

A *whoosh* sounded from below, just as they hit the halfway point.

Leroy screamed like a Hexabon and practically threw himself against Albert, who then smashed into Professor Asante's back.

"We're going to die!" Leroy yelped.

"Chill out!" Birdie thwacked him across the forehead. She pointed past Albert and Leroy at the water below. "It's only that silly CoreFish. Glad to know he's okay, though."

Albert saw a flash of golden yellow swimming beneath the surface, just a few feet below. His heart rate settled as he watched the CoreFish swim along the side of the stream, until it disappeared into the depths. Everything looked normal, save for the darkness, but then something caught Albert's eye.

Something that sent a chill racing up and down his spine and caused a cold sweat to bead on his brow.

"Dad," he heard himself say. "Look."

Professor Flynn turned, his torch shedding its creepy light across the stream, toward the door to Belltroll.

The torch tumbled from his hand, landing in a sizzling heap on the stone floor of the Main Chamber.

"This can't be," Professor Asante said. She whispered something, words in another language that Albert couldn't understand, but he didn't need to.

What stood before them was proof of how dire this situation really was.

Birdie and Leroy gasped as they too saw what everyone else saw.

The door to Belltroll was cracked down the middle. One large, jagged crack—as if lightning had struck the door—gave way to endless darkness on the other side.

It was a message from the traitor, Albert knew. And he had to admit it was impressive.

How had they done it?

And more importantly, *who* had done it?

CHAPTER 9

The Realm of Belltroll

L unch in Lake Hall was unusual, to say the least.

When Hydra arrived, the turtles that usually escorted them to their docks were nowhere to be seen. Everyone had to trudge through waist-deep water to get to their tables.

To make matters worse, the Whimzies were lethargic, only dropping a few light baskets full of sandwiches instead of their usual big, mouth-watering meals. They perched at one side of the cavernous room, resting their wings on the outcroppings of rock. And once everyone was done eating, instead of arriving with desserts, the giant birds simply disappeared into the darkness high above.

"This feels all wrong," Birdie said as she picked the crust off of her sandwich.

"I'm soaking wet, I'm starving, and I would literally befriend Hoyt right now for a slice of chocolate pie," Leroy added. "What's going on with this place?"

"*Everything* is off," Albert said.

Lake Hall was full of buzzing voices all around. It reminded Albert of the atmosphere at his school in New York City after the quake just yesterday.

But Albert could feel it. Even with the dire circumstances at hand, there was something here in the Core that people on the surface didn't always have in the face of disasters like this—hope.

Unlike people on the surface, Albert and his Balance Keeper teammates had the power to stop this destruction, even if they didn't yet know how to do it. That alone lifted the tiniest bit of dread from Albert's shoulders as he sat up in his bed later that night in the boys' dorm of Cedarfell.

Still, with Farnsworth beside him, his little blue eyes shining just enough that Albert could read without waking Leroy, Albert was having trouble concentrating on the Black Book in front of him. He'd spent months poring over the images—hundreds, thousands of Tiles—learning skill after skill. All he had to do was focus on the symbol with all his might, and the Master Tile responded with a rush of power.

Elasticity (the ability to stretch one's body in an unnaturally extreme way). Albert had used that once in

Ponderay, to stretch out his arms and save Hoyt from the Hammerfins.

Size Shift (the ability to manipulate one's body size). That Tile image was two circles side by side, one much larger than the other.

There was Animal Control, and Healing, and Ice Manipulation. All these Tiles, all these symbols to memorize and learn, and the only thing Albert could think about was the fact that the traitor had the other two Master Tiles. No matter what, they would always be stronger than Albert ever could be.

The traitor had already created two horrible Imbalances, and a third was well underway. Albert had stopped the Imbalances in Ponderay and Calderon, sure, but he hadn't done it alone. He'd had Birdie and Leroy in Calderon, and even though Hoyt almost ruined everything in Ponderay with his selfish move, nearly allowing the Imbalance to destroy the world because he deviated from the plan, Hydra *still* couldn't have stopped the Imbalance without Team Argon's help.

But only Albert could face the traitor. Only he had pulled a Master Tile from the Waterfall of Fate. How was he supposed to face the traitor and actually *win*?

Farnsworth let out a big, heavy sigh, and his eyes began to droop.

"You can get some sleep, buddy," Albert said. "Thanks for staying up with me."

The dog's eyes shut, and in seconds, he was snoring almost as loudly as Leroy.

Albert closed the Black Book and lay down, too, but sleep wouldn't come, no matter how hard he tried *not* to think about anything.

Could the traitor be Lucinda? Another Balance Keeper, or maybe a Core worker who had Balance Keeper blood?

Could it be, Albert hated to think, a *Professor*?

Everyone had been in the Pit when the door to Belltroll was broken.

But was there some sort of Tile symbol that could do things from far away? Or would it have been possible for the traitor to be wearing the two Master Tiles but keep them hidden? It's not like someone was walking around with two jet-black Master Tiles dangling from his neck.

There were too many thoughts. Too many questions, and Albert was getting a headache.

Enough was enough. Albert nudged Farnsworth awake. "Go wake up Leroy," he said.

Farnsworth yawned, then crossed the tent and licked Leroy from chin to forehead.

"KILLER SASQUATCH!" Leroy suddenly shouted and sat up straight in bed, his arms held out in front of him in a ninja pose. His hair was sticking out in every direction, and without his glasses, he looked wild-eyed as a cornered animal.

When he noticed Albert and Farnsworth, he blinked a few times, like he'd just realized he wasn't dreaming.

"Killer sasquatch?" Albert chuckled. Farnsworth wagged his tail.

Leroy yawned and wiped the slobber from his face. "Look, I have crazy dreams after I eat ham sandwiches, okay?"

Albert nodded and tossed Leroy his hat and glasses. "Whatever you say, dude. Sorry to wake you up, but I'm going to get a closer look at the door to Belltroll while the Main Chamber is empty. You coming with me?"

Leroy popped out of bed like it *wasn't* three o'clock in the morning. "If you tell Birdie about this, I will personally shave your eyebrows off in your sleep."

Albert laughed and held open the flap of their tent. "Not if the sasquatches get you first."

It turned out Birdie had the same idea. When Albert and Leroy tiptoed into the Main Chamber, following the light from Farnsworth's eyes, they saw her kneeling by the river that led to Belltroll, a fat notebook in her lap.

"I figured you'd be showing up here at some point," Birdie said. She had a little copper lantern beside her, casting just enough of a glow on her notebook to see that she had already been writing before they'd arrived.

She'd scribbled a long list of names. In fact, when

Albert leaned in, it appeared Birdie had already listed half the Core.

"Is that your list of possible traitors?" Albert said.

"But that's, like . . . everyone," Leroy said, crossing his long arms over his chest.

"There's a few I've checked off," Birdie corrected him. *Professor Flynn, Trey,* and *Petra* were all crossed out. They knew those three weren't guilty.

"It's true," Albert said, sighing. "It could be anyone."

Farnsworth licked the paper, and Birdie rolled her eyes. "Whatever the case, we've got to be vigilant. We have to start narrowing this down before—"

A clang sounded from a tunnel to their left.

Birdie quickly doused her lantern. The three of them rushed into the shadows of one of the arched bridges and waited as a Core Cleaner shuffled past, sweeping the floor with an old, worn-out broom. Albert held his breath.

For one moment, his imagination went wild. He pictured the traitor, using two Master Tiles for Invisibility, somehow sweeping the Core Cleaner off his feet. Stealing him away to some unknown lair.

But if the traitor was taking people, what was the point? And were those people okay?

Albert put everything he had into hoping that they were.

"You know, statistically speaking, we're overdue to

get caught for sneaking out," Leroy whispered.

"Let's hope that doesn't happen for a while," Albert whispered back. "We can't afford to waste time in a detention right now."

Farnsworth's tail thumped across Albert's ankles as if he agreed wholeheartedly with this.

A few long minutes later, the Core Cleaner had swept his way down one of the tunnels and Albert let out a long exhale. At least that Cleaner was safe. They walked back to the Belltroll door to examine the destruction.

It looked like it had been through battle. The jagged crack down the middle was peppered with sharp splinters of wood where the door had broken apart. Albert noticed that the door didn't have hinges.

He thought back to the first time they'd passed through one of the doors, into the Realm of Calderon. The river leading to the door had turned into a great wave, splashing into the face of the door. Then there was simply a giant empty hole where the ancient wood used to be.

How would they enter Belltroll tomorrow if the door was broken?

"What if this prevents us from going inside?" Albert asked, moving closer to where Leroy and Birdie were standing near the right side of the door.

Leroy shook his head. "I don't know, dudes. But I do know that wasn't there yesterday, before the door was broken." He knelt on the river's edge and pointed at the far right corner of the door, closest to the water.

"What is it?" Albert asked. "I can't see anything."

Farnsworth turned on his brights, illuminating the door in blue.

"There's a smudge," Leroy said. "It's hardly notice- able . . ." He reached down and lifted his Synapse Tile with his fingertips. "But I can't help but notice. I defi- nitely didn't see that before."

"We just walked past the door for, like, two seconds when we got to the Core," Birdie said. "And you saw the *absence* of a smudge?"

Leroy shrugged. "The Tile does what the Tile does, Guildacker Girl."

Albert leaned in for a closer look.

Leroy was right. Sure enough, at the middle right of the door, where a handle would have been, was a small black smudge.

Albert reached out and skimmed his finger across it. It came away a little sticky, like paint still only half dry.

"Think that means something?" Albert turned to show Birdie and Leroy the smudge on his pointer finger.

Birdie scribbled something into her notebook, not looking up when she said, "Definitely."

Birdie split from the boys soon after, and Albert, Leroy, and Farnsworth quietly made their way back down the tunnel that led to Cedarfell.

"You know, this is starting to really feel like home," Leroy said as they passed the Frog Man statue. Albert remembered the way Leroy used to angle the bill of his hat over his right eye as they passed the Frog Man when they'd first arrived in the Core. Now he marched past it like a soldier, eyes wide.

"You're right," Albert said. "Which is why this traitor stuff feels all the more personal. This is our home. Someone can't just come in here and . . ."

Just as the tunnel turned right, Albert saw a tiny, yellowish glow.

He grabbed Leroy by the arm and yanked him backward, just in time for Professor Bigglesby and Professor Asante to come walking around the corner.

Invisibility, Albert thought, squeezing his eyes shut. He held on to Leroy's arm and felt the warmth of his Master Tile working through both of them. When he opened his eyes, he couldn't see his body *or* Leroy's.

They backed slowly up against the wall, careful not to make a sound.

"The point is this situation is amiss," Professor Bigglesby was saying. He held a tiny, flickering candle, and in the dancing light it made the frown on his wrinkled face look far deeper than normal. The Professors were getting closer to them than Albert was comfortable with.

"There's no point to see," Professor Asante said. "We're in the middle of a crisis, and we must act with vigilance."

They stopped walking mere inches from Albert and Leroy.

Albert gripped Leroy's arm tight, hoping Leroy would stay quiet. If they could do that, they'd get away just fine.

That was when a realization hit him like a punch to the chest.

He'd forgotten to Invisible-ize Farnsworth!

The little dog sat beside them, stone still in the darkness, his eyes faded to a normal-dog blue. If he moved, or scratched at his collar, or let out a typical Farnsworth burp . . . they'd be caught in an instant.

Please, buddy, Albert thought. *Don't mess this one up for us.*

He focused instead on what the Professors were saying.

"Vigilance is good, yes," Bigglesby said. The candle flickered with the force of his words. "But the dangers far exceed anything we've yet to face. Imagine, Milena, if we run into someone we don't want to see."

"What are you getting at?" Professor Asante asked.

Bigglesby lifted a hand, then dropped it in frustration. "Festus," he said. "I'm talking about Festus."

Professor Asante hissed between her teeth, like Albert's mom had that time Albert used a different four-letter word to describe Farnsworth's poop. She'd made it clear he'd be changing his little brother's diapers full of that word if she heard it from him again.

Festus? Albert didn't know who that was. He looked to Leroy, but only saw the stone walls of the tunnel. At least he knew the Invisibility was still working.

Professor Asante took a step closer to the dwarf and lowered her voice even more. "That's not a possibility, and you and I both know it." Her whisper was so fierce it made the hairs on the back of Albert's neck stand on end. "You've been entertaining that notion for years, and it's one that needs to go. Festus has been handled. There are other, far more important worries ahead."

"Like the Flynn boy," Bigglesby growled.

Albert had to fight to keep in his gasp. Beside him, he felt Leroy stiffen.

Even Farnsworth looked up.

The Professors took several steps forward, their voices fading away. Albert had to use the Hearing symbol, fast, to catch their words.

"Think of the situation. Think of the similarities . . . ," Bigglesby said. "He's a danger to us all, Milena. I don't like the idea of him entering a third Realm, specifically one as pivotal as Belltroll, and with that Master Tile of his, it's only a matter of time before he does what . . ."

"I won't allow you to speak ill of him," Professor Asante snapped, fire in her voice. "The boy did well in the other two Realms, and many will stand by that. Myself included. He is *good*. Down to the very beat of his heart."

"But the past," Bigglesby started. "The past will—"

"*Not* repeat itself," Asante finished for him. "Not this time. The boy won't fail in Belltroll."

"And if he does?"

They moved on, but Albert still heard Professor Asante's final, haunting words float down the tunnel like ghosts. "If he fails, the Core could cease to exist."

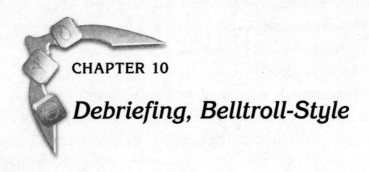

CHAPTER 10

Debriefing, Belltroll-Style

Morning came all too soon.

Albert's head was thick, as if someone had stuffed his ears full of cotton balls while he slept.

What had he ever done to Professor Bigglesby? He'd never really spent time with the dwarf other than during a class or two during his First Term in the Core, when Bigglesby taught the students about Calderon.

So why did Bigglesby not trust Albert?

He tried his best to lock that thought away and make it *stay* there.

But it wasn't easy, because today, Bigglesby was debriefing Hydra and Hoyt on the Realm of Belltroll.

Albert and Leroy met Birdie in the hallway just outside

the little dwarf's office. Hoyt was already there, standing awkwardly beside Birdie.

When he saw Albert and Leroy, he perked up. "Hey!" he said and pushed off of the wall where he'd been leaning. Leroy scrambled backward and almost tripped over his own feet. Hoyt, mercifully, ignored the opportunity to make fun of him. "I haven't had a chance to talk to you guys. I'm, uh . . . looking forward to working with you again."

Birdie, who obviously still hadn't forgiven Hoyt since the incident in Ponderay, rolled her eyes. "Sure you are, Hoyt."

"Look, you guys, I just . . ." The smile fell from his face. "Never mind. I'll see you guys in there." He turned and went inside Bigglesby's office, his shoulders drooping as if he were a dog who'd just been scolded for stealing the meat off the table.

"Maybe he meant it," Leroy whispered when Hoyt was out of earshot.

Albert shrugged. "I want to believe that. But he's going to have to show us that he really has changed. He could have gotten someone killed last term."

"No," Birdie said as she yanked her ponytail out and began feverishly raking her fingers through her curls. "He could have gotten the entire *world* killed by letting the Imbalance come that close to its breaking point." She took a deep breath and leaned back against the cool wall of the tunnel. "Anyway, enough about him. It looks like you guys had a rough night."

Leroy bit his lip. "Don't. Even. Ask." He gave Albert a sideways look, the kind he'd been giving him all morning.

"What happened?" Birdie asked anyway.

Albert filled her in on the conversation that he and Leroy had overheard.

Birdie's forehead creased so deeply her eyebrows threatened to touch in the center.

"If Bigglesby doesn't trust *you*," she said, flicking her fingertips through a green torch on the wall, "then I don't trust *him*."

Albert was about to say something to try and calm her down, but Leroy took that into his own hands. "That's exactly what we can't be thinking right now. He's obviously going to be our biggest asset in Belltroll. We'll just have to prove to him that he's wrong about Albert." He nudged Albert. "Right, dude?"

Albert swallowed hard and forced away thoughts of last night. "Right."

"Festus," Birdie said, testing out the strange name. "Who do you think that is?"

"No idea," Albert said. "We'll have to read up on it later, see what we can find. Maybe Petra knows something."

Just then, Professor Bigglesby appeared. He stopped

before the trio and lifted a hand toward his classroom door. "Standing around chittering like Moxenmice, are we, Balance Keepers? Time is of the essence, or rather the essence is of time! Onward!"

He shuffled past.

"That dude is so strange," Leroy said.

"Strange doesn't even begin to cut it," Albert answered. "Let's go."

Birdie and Leroy entered, Albert and Farnsworth trailing behind them.

Belltroll was *definitely* the most curious Realm of them all.

Albert, Birdie, Leroy, and Hoyt—and Farnsworth, who was so thrilled to be allowed in class that his tail hadn't stopped wagging for the past half hour—sat in chairs across from Professor Bigglesby.

Because he was no taller than a yardstick, Bigglesby's desk was larger than most, acting as a sort of stage for the dwarf in the front of his office. There were the usual gleaming swords, old wooden crossbows, and strange spiked balls on chains that Albert had seen before in medieval video games and movies.

But there was something else today. To the left of Bigglesby's desk was a smaller table. There was a row of smoking, bubbling potions on top.

"Potions!" Albert pointed them out to his friends.

Professor Bigglesby sauntered past them all and

climbed on top of his old oak desk. He looked like a little figurine, full of pride.

He waved his arms wildly, his beady eyes lighting up like hot coals as he began to explain the Realm of Belltroll.

"You've been to the other Realms before, and as you know, Calderon and Ponderay are quite the opposite of each other," Bigglesby said. "Calderon can get rather fiery, and Ponderay is full of water. But Belltroll is another thing entirely, perhaps the most beautiful of the three." He had an old projector set up, with a hand-crank battery on it to keep it running. Bigglesby moved toward it. "Now, if my assistant were here . . ."

Suddenly the door burst open, and Petra shuffled in.

"Sorry I'm late, Professor!" Petra squeaked. He was always squeaking, no matter the time of day, and Albert smiled at the sight of his poor, frazzled friend.

"No matter, Petra!" Bigglesby squeaked right back.

It was like watching two mice have a conversation about fresh cheese.

Petra waved a quick hello to the group and rushed past them to the projector. He pulled down a wall screen, cranked up the motor, and stood there turning the wheel while Professor Bigglesby got started with his speech.

A picture appeared, in black and white. Professor Bigglesby wasn't exaggerating. Even from the grainy image of Belltroll, it looked like it really could be the prettiest

Realm of the three.

There were, as always, several Rings. The Ring of Entry, the Ring of Emerald, and the Troll Mountain Range in the very center.

It suddenly struck Albert how much the Realm looked like a giant painting of Scotland that his mom had in their apartment back in New York. Flat marshlands leading into big rolling hills, which then turned into three fierce mountains in the very center.

He imagined how green it all must be, in real life.

"That looks beautiful," Birdie said. "Just imagine Jadar, getting to spread his wings and soar all over the place."

"And Geoff," Leroy said, mentioning the Jackalope he'd gotten last term, in Ponderay. "She'd hop those hills like a boss."

Farnsworth, too, would love Belltroll, from what Albert could see. But Albert could already tell the Realm was too dangerous for the little dog. He'd be swallowed up by the swamps in a second. Albert looked sideways at Hoyt and realized he didn't have a companion creature. For one second, Albert felt sorry for Hoyt, missing out on that small bit of joy.

But when Hoyt looked over at Albert and raised a brow at him, Albert looked away. Last term, Albert had saved Hoyt's life in Ponderay. That very same day, they'd decided to put their issues aside and work as a real unit.

Together, they blazed up the Ten Pillars, leaping across them to plug in Tiles and stop the Pillars from spinning out of control.

Albert had seen a shining chance at a new friendship there, and when Hoyt betrayed him, and everyone else, it *stung*.

Had Hoyt just *pretended* to like Albert, to get his help in solving the Imbalance? If Hoyt's plan had worked, instead of screwing everything up, Hoyt would have been the one to plug in the final key to saving Ponderay.

Albert didn't realize until just now how much Hoyt's move had hurt. To go back on your word of friendship so soon after giving it . . .

But now wasn't the time to dwell on Hoyt. Albert sighed and turned back to the projector.

"Indeed, Belltroll is beautiful!" Professor Bigglesby was saying. "But don't let her good looks trick you. Belltroll is a wicked Realm, and she uses her beauty to fool even the smartest and strongest of Balance Keepers. She is the most pivotal Realm to keeping the Balance of all three."

Albert thought that sounded a little like his mom's fresh brownies. Sometimes, they looked and smelled so good that he'd snag one right off the cooling rack, only to yelp and toss it away when he realized how hot it was.

"I'm confused," Hoyt said.

Professor Bigglesby nodded. "It's tough to explain, Mr.

Jackson. Perhaps a visual aid will do the trick." Professor Bigglesby snapped his fingers, and Petra handed him three books. Bigglesby stood the first book upright on his desk, then leaned the other two against it at an angle, almost like a teepee.

"We have Ponderay and Calderon on the sides, and Belltroll in the center," Bigglesby said, pointing at the three books. "With both Ponderay and Calderon leaning against Belltroll"—he pointed at the two books on the sides—"they are able to stay upright. But remove the perfect Balance of Belltroll . . ." Bigglesby ripped the center book away, and the other two came crashing down against each other, unable to stay upright. "The other two Realms will fall into chaos as well."

"Well, this changes things," Leroy said.

The traitor is a genius, Albert thought. *Destroy Belltroll, destroy the Core, destroy the world.*

"The goal is still the same," Bigglesby continued as Petra cranked the projector and changed the slide. "We solve the Imbalance before it reaches its splitting point, and in turn, stop the fall of all three Realms."

He was making it sound so easy. *Forget a math test*, Albert thought. *Fail this test and the whole world fails to exist.*

"We will enter Belltroll through the Ring of Entry," Bigglesby continued, diving right in to the plan for the day.

According to the drawing of the Ring of Entry, it was

basically marshlands. They were low and watery, and Albert imagined it might smell a bit like a swamp. "Since you four have already entered a Realm before, I won't spend long explaining the way it all works. I feel it is best to learn by experience, and so today, I will simply give you a quick overview of the Realm itself. We'll learn as we go, beginning tomorrow."

He surveyed Albert, Birdie, Leroy, and Hoyt, who all sat quietly, soaking up his words. At least they had one more day to prepare than Bigglesby had said they would during the meeting in the Pit. Albert was about to ask why the change of plans, but Bigglesby plowed on.

"The real trouble here is that we don't yet know the cause of the Imbalance in Belltroll." He waved a hand at Petra, who changed the image again. Sweat was beading up on Petra's brow, but he wiped it away and cranked the projector like he was a conductor driving a train.

"In the center of Belltroll stands three mountains, with Troll Mountain in the middle," Professor Bigglesby said, his voice growing more excited by the minute. The image switched to the very center ring of the Realm.

This mountain wasn't shaped like any normal mountain.

In fact, Albert wondered if it was truly a mountain at all. Jagged and fierce-looking, it was more like a giant rock that stretched high into the sky, with lethal crags and divots all across its sides.

At the very top of the mountain was a prominent split, almost like a giant had taken a knife and carved out a solid chunk from the center of the peak. It looked like the tuning fork Pap's porch buddies used to tune their banjos, or like it had been split into two halves. In between them was a gap, just wide enough for a golden, floating . . .

"Is that a *bell* dangling in that gap?" Albert asked.

The mountains all had the same shape, with the same giant golden bells floating in the middle of their strange splits.

Bigglesby winked. "Indeed it is, Mr. Flynn, but I'll cover that in a moment."

"It's called Troll Mountain," Birdie said, cocking her head. "Why?"

Professor Bigglesby grinned. "Because, Miss Howell, the lower portion of the mountain is home to the Trolls of Belltroll."

"Trolls?" Hoyt practically shouted the word. "Like the giant ones?"

Bigglesby nodded. "Very giant indeed." He waved his hand at Petra again.

All four Balance Keepers gasped as a sketch of a Troll came into view. Calling the Troll ugly would be an understatement.

"It's hideous," Hoyt whispered.

For once, Albert totally agreed.

It was just as Albert imagined the creature to look: humanlike, and as tall as a four-story building. Its arms and legs, as wide as tree trunks, were coated in awful-looking bumps and warts. The Troll's head was the size of a boulder, and its eyes were as large as pumpkins. It wore what looked like a giant loincloth, and when Petra switched the slide again, they saw a sketch of a Troll bending on one knee, handing a tiny flower to a baby deer.

"It's actually kind of adorable," Birdie said. "Once you get past all the bumps and lumps."

"One would think so," Bigglesby responded. "But should the Trolls wake at the wrong time of day . . ."

The slide switched, and Birdie clapped a hand to her mouth.

The image on the screen was a full-color drawing, and it was horrific. The Troll, who had looked ugly but peaceful before, had transformed into a giant green monster.

Its face was frozen in a horrific roar, its fists gripping trees, yanking them right out of the ground like blades of grass.

Leroy leaned over. "Birdie, you might have spoken too soon."

She nodded, her face frozen in a mask of horror.

"Normally, the Trolls are peaceful," Professor Bigglesby said. "Should you see them in shades of green, though, you must *run*."

"Curse my incredible memory," Leroy said with a groan. "I will never forget that image."

The picture switched again, thankfully. This time, it was a drawing of Troll Mountain. The artist had drawn this sketch so that the bottom half of the mountain was see-through, like a 3D rendering. Inside, Albert could see there was a strange, spiral-like shape leading from the center of the mountain down deep into the ground beneath.

"The Trolls sleep most of their lives," Bigglesby explained. "They only wake once a day, to do their job in Troll Mountain."

"And what's that?" Leroy asked.

Professor Bigglesby paced back and forth on top of his desk, like a little toy soldier marching to a beat. "It's all about the center of the range. Troll Mountain sits on a massive spindle. You see it there, depicted in half the drawing."

So that's that spiral thing, Albert thought.

"Think of it as a screw buried deep in the ground of Belltroll. The mountain naturally grinds downward, deeper and deeper into the Realm. Troll Mountain sits right on top of a set of tectonic plates. If it grinds too deep . . ." He held his arms out. "Boom! We experience a quake. A few minor ones are all right, but in large quantities and proportions, disaster is imminent."

"Well, that sure makes me want to take a vacation

there," Leroy mused, and Albert muffled a laugh into his fist.

"I will pretend I didn't hear that unfortunate attempt at humor, Mr. Jones," Bigglesby said, and went on. "Now, this Realm is not without a defense against disaster, of course. Inside Troll Mountain is a massive wheel, impossible for humans to turn. This is where the Trolls come in. The next slide, Petra, if you will."

Petra, who was looking incredibly close to passing out from keeping the crank turning, switched the slide.

Another drawing of Troll Mountain appeared. This one was zoomed in on the top of the mountain, so that they got a really good closeup look at that strange peak. It wasn't at all like the mountains Albert had seen in documentaries, where big mountain sheep leaped from one rocky crag to another.

That strange split was much larger than Albert originally thought, perhaps a car's length wide. Dangling in the center, held aloft by *nothing* at all, was the Bell.

It looked very nearly like the Liberty Bell that Albert had always seen in his history textbooks—big and old and full of ancient stories. "What's that for?" he asked. It seemed pretty random, but if Albert had learned anything about the Core, it was that nothing was random here. Everything had a purpose.

"Once a day, by magic, the Bells of Belltroll ring. There are two more, on the smaller mountains on either side of this one. The Bells ring at just the right frequency to wake the Trolls, who rise, march down to the wheel in the center of the mountain, and spin it counterclockwise."

"Which, I'm guessing, turns the mountain *up* and *away* from the ground of the Realm," Leroy said, adjusting his glasses.

"Precisely!" Professor Bigglesby said, clapping his hands. "The Trolls turn the wheel, pulling the mountain's spindle up and out of the ground, thus preventing it from digging too deep. The Core Watchers and I are assuming, at this point, that the quakes are happening because the Trolls aren't doing their job. Now, whether it's because they aren't waking, or because the wheel is broken, or because of some other unknown reason . . ." He held his empty hands out before him. "The cause of the Imbalance has yet to be seen."

Birdie raised her hand and waited for Professor Bigglesby to acknowledge her before she spoke up. "So how do we find out, then?"

Professor Bigglesby smiled at this, his tiny face lighting up as if he were standing before a ray of sunlight. "We go into the Realm itself, Miss Howell." He looked at the drawing of Belltroll. "And we discover the truth with our very own eyes."

Everyone watched as Professor Bigglesby reached around his desk to a shelf where a leather tube was resting. He lifted it gently, sweeping dust from the top.

"This was delivered to me just this morning," Professor Bigglesby said, handing the scroll over to Hydra. "It's been considered a Core artifact, and therefore not for public use, but . . . a dwarf always has friends in high places."

He took the top off the tube. Inside was a rolled-up map, which spilled out onto the desk. It was made of ancient parchment, much like a pirate's treasure map, colored with shades of faded black and brown ink. There was the Realm, in circular layers like an onion.

Professor Bigglesby allowed them a moment to look before rolling the map up and placing it back into its leather case. "This will show you the best route from the Core to the center of Belltroll, so keep your eyes on it, Balance Keepers. Learn it well, pay attention. The map will change according to the Realm's conditions."

"How?" Albert asked, because this was too cool not to know.

Professor Bigglesby winked but didn't answer Albert's question. Instead, he signaled for them to stand up. Class was over, and Albert yawned as he realized how exhausted he really was.

"Get some relaxation in, Balance Keepers," Bigglesby said. "Go to the Library, enjoy a candy or two. Tomorrow, we'll enter Belltroll, and with any luck, we'll stop this Imbalance before it gets out of hand."

"And if we can't?" Hoyt asked. He'd been pretty silent this entire time.

Professor Bigglesby didn't smile at this. "Then we'd better hope the Core is strong enough to hold itself together."

CHAPTER 11

Entering the Realm

Hydra was on their way to Lake Hall when the green torches flickered.

Farnsworth let out a hair-raising howl.

"What's wrong, buddy?" Albert asked, stooping to pat him on the head. "You okay?"

Farnsworth's hackles raised, and it was then that Albert noticed the trembling beneath his feet.

"You guys, I think—"

BOOM!!

It was as if the Core itself exploded.

Albert was flung sideways into the hard tunnel wall. Birdie cried out as Leroy knocked into her. Screams echoed down the tunnel, and dust rained over Albert's head.

Then all was silent.

"Everyone okay?" Albert scrambled to his feet. Torches had tumbled from their spots on the wall, and up ahead, a door hung from a broken hinge.

There was a screech and a pop as the speaker started up. Professor Asante's rushed voice rang through the Core. "Students, please report to your dormitories at once. Report any injuries or fatalities to the hospital wing."

"Fatalities?!" Leroy squawked.

"Professors, Core Watchers, and teams Hydra and Argon, please report to Lake Hall immediately," Professor Asante finished. The speaker cut off.

Albert looked to his friends. Dust clouds still hung in the tunnel, and for one moment, he felt like he was standing in the middle of a war zone. But other than Birdie's bloody nose, they were all okay.

"Let's go see what they want," Albert said, brushing the dust from his pants.

"Odds are, it's nothing good," Leroy said with a groan.

Farnsworth raced away, the glow of the torches flickering across the surface of his smooth coat.

A small crowd had gathered outside of the doorway to Lake Hall, and as Hydra arrived, Albert heard the news.

"It was only a matter of time," Tussy, Professor Asante's Apprentice, was saying to her mentor. "I mean, sure, the glass was thick and supposedly lava-proof, but . . ."

"What happened?" Birdie asked.

"There you are," Tussy said. She held an arm toward the open doorway. "Professor Bigglesby and Hoyt are just inside."

Albert looked back at his friends and shrugged. Then he led the way, shuffling past Tussy and Professor Asante, into the dark stone stairwell that carried them down to Lake Hall.

They didn't get far before the heat came.

And then the glow of orange as the tunneled stairwell opened up and Lake Hall came into view below.

It was . . .

"Lava," Leroy gasped. His face was a mask of horror, reminding Albert of the face of a woman he had once seen at the site of a bad car crash near his apartment in New York.

What used to be a shimmering dark lake, with floating docks scattered across its surface, was now a pool of bubbling, bright-orange and yellow lava.

"The glass wall shattered," Birdie said, pointing across the lava pool to where there *used* to be a big wall blocking off a space full of swirling liquid rock.

The lava behind the wall was the light source for Lake Hall, and a major conversation piece when newbies arrived each term. And now it had spilled through with the quake. The Whimzies were nowhere to be seen, and

Albert hoped they were far away, up in the highest part of the cavern.

"The turtles!" Birdie gasped. "What happened to them?"

"Animals can sense things," Leroy said. "Maybe that's why they weren't here yesterday, because they knew something was coming. I hope they're somewhere safe."

Professor Bigglesby and Hoyt stood a little farther down the stairs, staring out at the chaos below.

"Gather around, Hydra," Professor Bigglesby said. "Glad to see you weren't injured too badly in the quake." He waved them over. "We're going to need your strength now more than ever. This area is off-limits to students, but you needed to see the destruction that Belltroll is capable of."

"There have been quakes before, right?" Albert asked.

"Not of this magnitude," the dwarf said sadly. "I'm afraid the Imbalance is worse than we originally suspected."

Albert could feel the heat from the lava stealing his breath away. Down below, it bubbled and popped like an angry, boiling sea. "What about the surface world?" he asked. "If this is happening here already, what's happening up there?"

Bigglesby shook his head. "We'll know more tomorrow when we enter the Realm. But look down at the chaos, Balance Keepers. Let it fuel you forward, with the hope that we can stop this."

Three Core Watchers arrived, carting big bags full of their strange scientific instruments.

"Impossible," one of them said as they shuffled past Hydra to head farther down the stairs and investigate.

"And yet, possible," answered another.

Professor Bigglesby looked out at what remained of Lake Hall and sighed. "Such a shame. We'll be eating bagged lunches for the rest of the year at this rate."

Leroy gasped, and Birdie leaned over to console him.

Hoyt just stared at the mess, his eyes wide in shock.

And maybe a part of Albert was in shock, too. At any second, Belltroll could send up another quake.

Nowhere, and no one, was truly safe.

After a sleepless night, Albert and Leroy met Birdie in the Main Chamber the next morning. Birdie's hair was a mess of curls piled on top of her head, and Leroy still had remnants of sleep in his eyes.

But, as unnatural as it was waking this early, it seemed the entire Core had come to see Team Hydra off. After the news of Lake Hall, everyone needed to witness the physical act of four brave Balance Keepers heading into the wild Realm to try and save the day.

Hope, Albert thought. *I have to believe we can give it to them.*

The rest of the Balance Keepers were all packed to the left of the door. They wore their own team shirts—Alpha, Ecco, Blaze—but there was a look about them that spoke of silent unity. Albert appreciated their show of solidarity, but the quiet was freaking him out. The first time his team had entered a Realm, everyone had cheered and sung the Core song. It had given Albert the boost of confidence and energy he needed to bravely enter the Realm.

Today, the room was full of only whispers. The countdown clock from last term was back on the wall, a giant 6 blazing bright red on the screen.

"I can't believe we're doing this a third time," Birdie said.

"I can't believe we've survived two Realms," Leroy added. "If you want to know the odds of it happening *again* . . ."

"Maybe keep those to yourself," Albert said, trying to shake his nerves away.

A roar broke out, and Birdie's Guildacker, Jadar, swooped in from one of the tunnels, landing on the big copper chandelier overhead. It creaked and groaned. A few First Termers looked up warily, but everyone else was used to Jadar by now. Geoff, Leroy's Jackalope from Ponderay, hopped in next, and Albert felt his shoulders relax a little. He already felt safer with Jadar and Geoff in the Main Chamber. Farnsworth was glad to see the great beasts, too, evidence of Hydra's success in the other two Realms. He barked a greeting, his blue eyes flashing bright as day, and suddenly all the other companion creatures joined in, hooting and howling and hissing.

Professor Bigglesby emerged from the crowd and approached Hydra, his tiny frame covered in a thin leatherlike armor.

"Hydra, Hoyt. You will wear this, too," Bigglesby said. He clapped his hands, and Petra appeared, hauling a huge rucksack behind him, his forehead damp with sweat. He'd probably dragged the thing all the way from the dwarf's office. Albert exchanged a look with Leroy. Since when was Petra Bigglesby's servant?

"What's up?" Leroy asked, helping Petra haul the bag the last few feet.

"Professor Bigglesby's Apprentice chose life on the surface," Petra explained as he set the bag before Albert, Birdie, and Leroy. "I guess with all the fear that's going around, it makes sense people would want to get out."

"Better here, fighting against the darkness, than up on the surface, not knowing when it's all going to end!" Birdie said, her face flushing red.

Petra dug through the bag. "It's true, Birdie, I agree. But in any case, things are probably going to get worse before they get better. That always seems to be the way things go."

"Not if we have anything to do with it," Hoyt said as

he, too, made his way through the crowd of people. He at least looked like he'd slept last night. His eyes were bright, and he didn't look as scared as he had yesterday in Lake Hall. "You guys ready?"

Albert nodded. "As ready as we'll ever be."

He knew he should talk to Hoyt about what happened in Ponderay. But Albert just couldn't bring himself to do it yet, not without losing his temper. He turned his attention back to Petra.

Petra lifted a leather vest out of the bag and tossed it to him. "You'll be wearing this at all times in the Realm. Bigglesby says it's made of dragon skin, from the dragons that used to be in Belltroll before they went extinct. Anyway, it's super tough but super light."

Birdie grinned as Petra handed the rest of them similar vests. Then he produced helmets, wrist guards, and shin guards.

"For the quakes," he explained.

As all three Hydra members and Hoyt strapped on their gear, the little dwarf sauntered over.

"Vigilance is key, Balance Keepers!" Bigglesby's voice was shrill as ever. "We stay close together, and we work as a team. Pay attention, and if one boy falls behind—"

"Or girl," Birdie said.

"Or girl," Bigglesby corrected himself. "If any boy or girl falls behind . . . we move on without them! We blaze forth like a mighty scalding fire!"

He turned to the crowd and began to shout about bravery and camaraderie and something that sounded a little like *weapons* and *death*, and the crowd silenced, everyone leaning in to listen to the crazy old dwarf as he went on his epic pump-up rant.

Albert turned to Leroy, whose face was practically snow white.

"Did anyone else hear the whole *moving on without the fallen* part of his speech," Leroy said, "or was it just me?"

Right then, Albert caught sight of his dad's face in the crowd. Professor Flynn and Trey were standing on the other side of the stream, deep in conversation with Professor Asante and Tussy.

"You haven't talked to him much yet, have you?" Birdie asked.

Albert shook his head. "He's distracted, I guess. Understandably."

"No worries, bro." Leroy leaned in, the bill of his hat knocking Birdie in the forehead. "I'm sure he's doing his best to help us out in his own way."

Albert knew his dad was probably up late into the night, trying to figure out who the traitor was. Professor Flynn hadn't meant to lose the two Master Tiles, of course, but that didn't stop him from trying to fix things.

He caught Professor Flynn's eye and smiled and waved. His dad waved back, gave Albert a quick thumbs-up, and turned back to Trey.

"Albert!"

A voice rang out through the crowd, and a familiar round, dark-haired woman wove her way toward Hydra.

Lucinda's snake, as was usual lately, was trying its best to unwind itself from her shoulders.

"Wretched thing!" Lucinda hissed, and wrapped Kimber back around her neck like a living scarf. "I don't know what's gotten into him." She held out a small black cuff with a little screen on it. "Your Counter, from last term. Professor Bigglesby requested I deliver it to you myself. It's already set."

"Oh, thanks," Albert said.

Lucinda's smile was tight as she helped Albert clasp it around his wrist.

"Best of luck to my favorite Flynn!" She wiped sweat from her brow. Her eyes flitted down toward Albert's black Tile. "Such a beautiful color," she said. "Just like my Kimber."

The snake hissed, finally uncoiling himself from her neck. He fell to the ground, then slithered away at lightning speed. Lucinda yelped and shoved her way into the crowd, disappearing without a good-bye.

That was creepy, Albert thought. He didn't want to trust Lucinda.

But the Counter had worked last term. And if Bigglesby himself asked her to deliver it . . .

"Albert!" Birdie shouted and waved him over. "Let's go!"

They were about to enter Belltroll. He'd need whatever help he could get.

And for all Albert and his teammates knew, the traitor could be waiting just inside.

The tunnel that led to the Ring of Entry was dark and silent, a combination that chilled Albert to the bone.

They'd only climbed through the wreckage of the broken door a few minutes ago, if Albert was correct, and already he felt trapped.

He wished they would all walk faster, get to the light sooner. Every step, he wondered if a hand would glide from the darkness, unseen, and grasp his Master Tile, tear it away from its cord around his neck, and then use it to burn the world to ashes.

The ground trembled every few seconds. The shaking wasn't enough to knock anyone off their feet; it felt more like the Realm had a pulse. A heartbeat. It was like a living, breathing being.

And it wasn't happy.

The only indication that anyone else was there with him were Hoyt's footsteps behind Albert's back, and Birdie's, Leroy's, and Professor Bigglesby's in the front.

Finally, a light appeared in the distance.

It grew bigger, and brighter, until Albert's boots hit

soft green grass, and the tunnel spit them out into the Ring of Entry. A light breeze tickled Albert's nose and cheeks.

"Wow," he said.

It was truly the only word that came to mind in that instant, because Belltroll literally stole his breath from his lungs.

It was as if Albert had walked into an oil painting, one that was so green and so bright, he had to squint his eyes to truly take it all in.

Professor Bigglesby wasn't joking when he'd said Belltroll was the most incredible Realm of the three.

"I can't believe this is real," Birdie said.

"My eyes hurt," Leroy said. "It's so . . ."

"Green," Albert finished for him.

"You can say that again," Hoyt added. "Man, I wish Slink and Mo could see this."

It was like someone had spilled a roll of perfect emerald fabric across the entirety of the Realm.

Green and green and more green. The Ring of Entry sat before them, the patches of land and water just down at the bottom of a sharp, grassy hill. Beyond that, as the water thinned out and more grass took its place, the landscape climbed upward into the hills that made the Ring of Emerald.

Albert wanted to close his eyes and feel the breeze dance across his skin. There were no birds singing, but he imagined how lovely they would have sounded here.

Or maybe the singing voices of the centuries-old drag-ons that used to soar across these glittering skies.

Beyond the hills, in the distance, was the ghostly form of the jagged mountain range. Troll Mountain stood in the center, as tall and beastly as ever. It was so far away, Albert wasn't sure how they'd ever make it there.

He also didn't see a single thing wrong with the Realm of Belltroll.

"I'm not sure what the problem is, Professor," Albert said. "It just seems . . . fine. Doesn't it?"

No sooner had he spoken the words than the Realm groaned loudly. A quake rumbled beneath his feet. Albert tumbled sideways into Hoyt, whose hard head conked against his. It felt like being in a car on a bumpy country road with Pap as the driver.

The shaking stopped as suddenly as it began.

"*Not* a normal quake," Professor Bigglesby noted. He stood off to the right of the group, surveying the land with a look of fatherly affection. "Typically, the grinding of Troll Mountain makes a rumble so slight you'd hardly notice. We'll need to keep track of the frequency of the quakes. If another one like that happens this hour, it's much too soon. Now, onward! Let's explore the face of our beautiful mistress, and hope she's kind to us today!"

He marched forward, his arms swinging and his little legs carrying him with surprising speed down the hill that led deeper into the swampy moors of the Ring of Entry.

Hydra stood there staring at one another with amused expressions on their faces.

"That guy," Leroy said as he flipped his hat backward, "is one of the strangest people I have ever, and will ever, meet."

CHAPTER 12

The Ring of Entry

It had been weeks since Albert, Birdie, and Leroy had practiced in the Pit.

Sure, they'd helped save the world in Ponderay just last term, but for the past several weeks, Albert had been sitting behind a school desk, his feet bouncing up and down beneath it, desperate to run. To *move*, or do something actually worth doing.

Trudging his way through the Ring of Entry, in the swampy part of Belltroll, wasn't worth doing.

Even Birdie didn't think so.

"I love water," Birdie said. She grabbed her Water Tile to clean it off but couldn't find a sludge-free piece of clothing to wipe it with. "This, though, is NOT water. This is, like . . . totally disgusting."

They'd been making their way across the moor for the past two hours. The ground was like a puzzle with missing pieces.

The area was mostly a sludgy mess of water and mud and algae and floating sticks, though there were mossy islands every couple of feet, like stepping-stones—mossy islands that sometimes weren't mossy islands but just extra-large clumps of mud and algae and floating sticks masquerading as mossy islands. Albert would know. He'd stepped on one too many non-islands.

The Ring of Entry was *much* larger than it looked on the map, and Albert wondered if they'd ever make it out. He leaped from one moss-island to the next, passing Leroy, who lost his footing and splashed into the moor, taking Hoyt down with him. Each island was only large enough for a single person, so the Balance Keepers and Professor Bigglesby were spread out like a chain across them all.

"Isn't there some kind of creature we can use to bypass the moor?" Albert asked Professor Bigglesby, who was a few islands ahead of him, currently leaping with a strength Albert didn't know the man's small legs possessed. "Those dragons would have been pretty useful right about now."

"Indeed they would be. Long ago, the Realm was also home to a herd of Pegasi," Professor Bigglesby said. Birdie squealed and jumped up and down behind them, her boots squelching in the mud.

"Flying horses?" Leroy called out from the back of the pack. "Now that's cool."

"It was *wonderful*," Professor Bigglesby said loudly enough so everyone could hear. "But the Pegasi have long since become extinct as well. So, alas, we must make our way on foot."

That was depressing. It would have been so easy to hop on a Pegasus's back and soar over all this muck and mud.

Albert could imagine using the Jackalope symbol to leap away from here, but one look at the rest of Team Hydra, and he just knew he couldn't do it. He couldn't leave them in the dust, even if Professor Bigglesby's speech in the Main Chamber suggested he actually very much *could*.

"What's the point of this anyhow?" Hoyt shouted somewhere behind Albert. "We aren't going to find any clues here about the Imbalance. Nothing would last in this mess. Not even a footprint, if there was someone who came through here before we did."

He was right. Twice, the swamp had nearly sucked Albert's boot right off his foot.

Professor Bigglesby's voice carried back to them from the front of the pack. "We must push forward to get to the center. No shortcuts in Belltroll, I'm afraid, just like in life. Now keep your eyes open. We're nearly at the halfway point."

"Oh, *come on*!" Leroy shouted.

For what felt like five hours, but according to Albert's Counter, was really only two, they hopped and leaped and crashed into the water and came up shivering despite the brightness of the Realm. On and on they went, until Albert began to notice a change in the ground. It was becoming less boggy, more solid, with larger moss-islands.

Soon, he was able to see the end of the Ring of Entry. Fresh, endless grass sat waiting for them, not half a mile away.

"Bridges," Leroy said, groaning, from the very back of the group. "There were bridges in Ponderay, but *nooooo*, there couldn't be bridges in Belltroll, could there?! I never thought I'd say this, dudes, but I actually miss that Realm!"

"I miss Slink and Mo," Birdie said, hopping onto an island large enough for two people. "I wonder what they're . . . Oh!"

Professor Bigglesby stopped in front of Albert and they both turned in time to see Birdie wobble a bit. Then she started to topple sideways.

"Birdie!" Albert cried out.

Hoyt leaped across and caught her as she tumbled to

the ground, her eyes closed.

"What's happening?" Leroy shouted. "Is she dead? ARE WE ALL GOING TO DIE?!"

"She's asleep! And she's getting heavy!" Hoyt shouted.

"Be quiet!" Albert hissed. He whirled back to Professor Bigglesby, needing answers, fast. "What's going on?"

"The toads," Professor Bigglesby murmured. "Someone has tampered with them."

There was a great burp from the back of the group. Albert was about to ask Leroy why he'd burp at a time like this when he spotted the real source of the noise.

It would have been impossible to see, had the creature not moved.

Sitting just beneath the surface of the water, the top of its head and eyes the only things visible, was a massive toad the size of a basketball. Its color made it perfectly camouflaged, a muddy greenish brown like the water.

The toad was just a few inches away from Hoyt, who was starting to tremble under Birdie's unconscious weight. Albert started toward them, but Bigglesby threw out an arm to block him.

"Hold it! Don't move!" Bigglesby stared at the toad, who was now staring back at Bigglesby.

"Interesting," Professor Bigglesby said.

The toad let out an explosive burp, and a slimy black tongue shot out of its mouth, connecting with Bigglesby's neck.

"That's not normal," the dwarf said, yawning.

His eyelids fluttered.

Then he collapsed, landing in a heap on his island, just inches from the swampy water. He looked perfectly content, sound asleep and dreaming.

"Professor!" Albert shouted. He whirled around to look at Leroy, who was standing frozen about twenty feet away on his own island.

"Don't look at them," Leroy said, his voice steady and calm. "Eyes to the sky, dudes. I think something's wrong with them. If you look at them, and they notice, they attack. Assuming I'm correct," he added.

"Their necks," Albert said, pointing at Birdie and then at Bigglesby. They each had a small red mark on their skin. "What did it do to them?"

"Definitely not something I've read in a book before," Leroy answered. "But we need to get them back to the Core and to the hospital wing."

Albert checked his Counter. Only three hours had passed since they'd arrived, and already they'd lost two members of their team.

Hoyt spoke up. "And we can't move forward with two unconscious people!"

Another burping noise sounded from the back, and this time, Leroy blurted out, "Uh, dudes?"

Albert turned to Leroy. His friend was completely surrounded by Poison Toads.

Leroy stared at the sky, his whole body shaking like a leaf in the wind.

"Leroy. Don't move an inch," Albert said.

An idea sparked to life in his mind. Hoyt could potentially get them out of this situation. But could he be trusted?

Albert's face must have betrayed his doubts, because Hoyt spoke up.

"I'm not the same guy I was last term, Albert," Hoyt said.

"Yeah, I know," Albert said. Because he did. Or at least, he knew Hoyt was trying to be different. Still, Albert couldn't seem to shake the lingering hurt from Ponderay. How selfish could one person be?

But that was then, this was now. He took a deep breath. "You feel like using that Speed Tile a little, Hoyt?"

Hoyt nodded, still struggling to hold Birdie up.

"Okay," Albert said. "You have to distract them, provoke them, and then while Leroy goes back to the beginning of the Ring of Entry, I'll use my Tile to get Birdie and Professor Bigglesby to safety. You'll have to move quick enough that they can't hit you with their tongues."

A new spark ignited in Hoyt's eyes. "If you need speed, I can give you that."

Albert nodded, then turned toward Leroy, careful not to look down in the process. "Leroy! Sound okay to you?"

"There is literally *nothing* okay about this!" Leroy shouted.

"All right, Leroy's good to go," Albert said, turning back to Hoyt. "Hold Birdie steady. I'll come to you and then you can go."

It wasn't easy, navigating across the moor without being able to look down, and Albert was afraid the toads might somehow catch on if he used the Double Vision symbol. But Hoyt guided Albert across, and they were side by side in only a few minutes. Albert pulled Birdie's unconscious figure into his arms.

"Okay," he said to Hoyt. "You ready?"

Hoyt gripped his Tile, nodded, and turned to Leroy.

"Ready!" Leroy shouted, despite his *not* looking ready at all.

"Here goes nothing," Hoyt said.

He turned away, and his shoulders moved up and down as he took a deep breath. Then he looked a toad right in the eyes.

It happened so fast Albert wondered if what he'd seen was really true.

Hoyt moved like a bullet. The toad's black tongue shot out to hit Hoyt in the neck, but he dodged it in a blur. He leaped from island to island, looking at toads, provoking them, even poking them with a stick he'd scooped up in a flash.

Toad burps sounded as black tongues shot out left and

right, but Hoyt dodged them like a master. Leroy, who was screaming at the top of his lungs, hopped furiously back toward the very beginning of the Ring of Entry, not stopping for a second.

Albert had to move, too. He summoned the Strength symbol, then boosted Birdie up over his shoulder. She was feather-light, thanks to the power of his Master Tile.

He needed to move faster, though. He pictured the Merge symbol, one he'd used long ago in Calderon, and imagined the Speed symbol merging with the Strength one. The two Tile symbols became one, and suddenly Albert was blazing across the moor, with Birdie slung over his shoulder like a rag doll.

He soared past Hoyt, who was doing some sort of bop-the-frog-on-the-head game, and past Leroy, who was hopping so fast he could give Jemima a run for her Jack-alope money.

They got back to the beginning of the Ring of Entry in a mere fifteen minutes with the Speed symbol doing its thing. Albert gently placed Birdie down on the grass, then turned right back and headed for Professor Big-glesby. The dwarf was so light it was like Albert was clutching air. Still, his legs were getting tired, and Hoyt's must be, too. He did seem to be losing a bit of his edge.

"Look out!" Albert yelled as Hoyt nearly got a tongue to the neck. Hoyt dodged and sped off in the other direction. The toads were in a burping, tongue-flicking fury.

Fifteen minutes later, Albert got Bigglesby onto dry land next to Birdie. His legs were officially jelly. Some sort of weird sludge-flavored jelly. Leroy was still making his way across the moor.

"Come on, Leroy!" he shouted. "Use those long legs and hop faster!"

Leroy crashed down into the water, and Albert groaned, then pulled his last ounce of willpower to use both Speed and Strength to go after him.

He made it to Leroy and together they forged their way back to the others. Seconds later, with Leroy and Albert cheering him on, Hoyt leaped onto solid land at the start of the Ring of Entry.

"Should we pick Birdie up between the two of us?" Albert said, turning to Leroy. "Hoyt can grab Bigglesby."

"You got it, bro," Leroy said. "And if we walk backward up the hill, physics will work in our favor and it won't be so hard."

As they headed backward up the hill that would take them to the tunnel to the Core, Albert stared out toward the Troll Mountain Range and adjusted his grip on Birdie. The mountains would have to wait for another day. His gaze followed Troll Mountain back down to the Poison Toad bog, and he started thinking about symbols that might be helpful for the next time they had to cross it. He was just trying to remember the Animal Control symbol when he spotted it.

A glittering red thing, probably about the size of a Ping-Pong ball, was stuck in some moss floating on the surface of the moor, not too far out from where they were, but far enough that it was in toad territory.

"Look!" he shouted. "There's something in the moor!"

Leroy didn't even look up. "Whatever it is, leave it, bro," he said. "We have to get these two back to the Core."

Albert knew he should listen, but there was something inside of him, a tugging, whispering voice that said, *That's important! You can't leave it!*

"Go without me," Albert said. "It's a clue!" He set Birdie down as gently as he could, then took off running back down the hill. He'd use his Speed Tile and grab the thing real quick. No problem.

A voice piped up from behind him.

"If I let you do this alone, you'll get all the glory," Hoyt said, catching up with Albert.

Seriously? It was like Ponderay all over again. Albert turned to give Hoyt a piece of his mind, but saw that Hoyt was smiling.

"It was just a joke, man," Hoyt said.

Albert nodded. "Right. Yeah, okay." He shook his head and turned back to the moor. "Let's go get that thing."

Albert closed his eyes and put all that he had left in him toward imagining the Speed symbol. He ran and hopped like his life was on the line, like he was a character in a video game being chased by a giant, fire-breathing dragon. Hoyt distracted the toads.

Finally, he reached the moss and his fingers closed over the red ruby. It was heavy, like a paperweight.

"Got it!" Albert shouted. "Let's head back."

They were almost to dry land again when Hoyt shouted, "ALBERT, DUCK!"

"TOAD!" Leroy yelped from up on the hill.

Hoyt tackled Albert and they skidded to a stop on the shore, grass filling Albert's mouth.

Leroy ran down and dragged both boys away from the bog. When Albert rolled away from Hoyt, he turned in time to see Hoyt's eyes flutter closed.

"Saved you," Hoyt said, yawning. "Just in time." He passed out on the green grass, a smile on his face.

"Well, that was heroic," Leroy said. "Did you get it?"

Albert looked down as he uncurled his fingers. He'd been clutching the ruby so hard it cut the palm of his hand. But it was there, bright as blood despite all the dirty mucky mess.

"I hope that thing was worth it," Leroy said. "Because we've got three unconscious people to drag up this hill before dark."

Albert stood up and looked at Birdie, Hoyt, and Professor Bigglesby, all asleep on the hillside.

"We screwed up bad," he said.

But though he knew it was the truth, he couldn't help but feel they'd found *something* in the jewel.

The ground rumbled, gently at first.

Then all at once, Albert was thrown from his feet, knocking heads with Leroy, as the entire Realm shook.

Albert gripped the jewel, and when the quake faded, he and Leroy both had the same exhausted, hopeless looks on their faces.

"Come on," Leroy said, looking out across the Realm. "If there's another one of those, I don't wanna be around for it."

Albert nodded. He tucked the gem safely into his pocket, then helped Leroy haul his friends up the hillside and out of the Realm of Belltroll.

CHAPTER 13

Another Day, Another Danger

After they'd waited at the hospital wing for hours, the cyclops nurse finally gave them an update.

"The poison that the toads produced was an incredibly powerful antihistamine," she said, her one eye glaring at Albert, like somehow he was the one who had caused it. "It was in such a high dose that it immediately put them to sleep. They'll wake tomorrow, I'm sure. But you must know, I've never seen such a thing happen with those toads. It seems as if they've been tampered with."

No kidding, Albert thought. *This has traitor written all over it.*

"You'll keep an eye on their vitals until they wake up,

right?" Leroy asked the cyclops nurse. "No pun intended, really."

Albert couldn't help it. He snickered, and the cyclops nurse shooed them out the door and locked it behind them, promising to knock them out, too, if they came back.

The two friends walked back to Cedarfell, wondering how mad Birdie would be that she missed all the action. When they passed through the Main Chamber, the countdown clock still read 6. *That's a good sign*, Albert thought. *I hope.*

"We'll figure this out," Albert said aloud, because he needed to hear it to believe it.

When they got to their tent, a letter was waiting for Albert. It was sitting on his pillow beside Farnsworth, who wagged his tail in greeting.

"Hey, buddy," Albert said. He sat down, relaxing a little as he scratched Farnsworth behind his velvety ears. "It was a rough day in there. Be glad you were here, doing whatever you do when we're not around."

Farnsworth just kept on wagging his tail, and for a second, Albert was jealous of his dog. It would be nice to be able to lie around all day, chewing on blue bones and old shoes without a care in the world.

Albert turned to the letter, hoping it was from his dad. But when he flipped it over, he recognized the curling, looping handwriting in pink gel pen. It was from his mom! Albert's fingers trembled as he tore open the envelope and pulled out the letter.

It didn't say much, but that was okay. Just holding the letter was a sign that, despite what was happening on the surface, his mom was fine.

> *Albert,*
>
> *It's getting worse up here. I know you're in good hands with your dad and the other Professors, but . . . be careful, son. Please. Say hi to your dad for me, and make sure you're getting enough to eat. I know you're not going to listen to me about this—but don't do anything too dangerous. I need my son to come back to me in one piece when this is all over!*
>
> *Stay safe. I love you, always.*
>
> *Mom*
>
> *P.S. Give Farnsworth a pat on the head for me!*

Albert read the letter twice, a smile on his face, even though his mom said things were getting worse. He imagined his mom sitting at the kitchen table in their apartment, her hair up in a bun, a pot full of spaghetti on the stove behind her as she wrote to him.

She'd also included a newspaper clipping. Albert smoothed it out on his bed. His eyes widened as soon as he saw the headline.

Superquakes Sweep the Country: New York to Yellowstone

"Leroy," Albert said, waving his friend over. "Check this out."

They read the article together.

"Scientists have captured an alarming amount of seismic activity since last Friday, when an earthquake struck all the way from New York to Yellowstone National Park in Wyoming, stretching nearly 2,000 miles."

"That's 1,919.6 miles, to be exact," Leroy said.

Albert kept reading. *"Yellowstone National Park, underneath its pristine beauty, is home to the Yellowstone Caldera, a vast supervolcano beneath the earth's surface."*

"Sounds like Calderon to me," Leroy said.

Albert nodded and read on.

"Peggy Whitman, the head of scientific research at Yellowstone National Park, sat down with one of our reporters and expressed her concerns. 'Earthquakes aren't uncommon, even in Yellowstone. But this many, so frequently? Should they rise in magnitude, the Yellowstone Caldera could wake. And that, I'm afraid, could be the end.'"

Albert set down the article and turned to Leroy.

"The end?" Leroy said, his eyes wide. "Like, *the end,* the end?"

"I know Bigglesby was right about Belltroll being the balance between all three Realms," Albert said. "But seeing this . . . it just feels all the more real."

"It's felt real since day one," Leroy said. His stomach rumbled, and he grimaced. "And it feels even more real every time they serve us those awful sandwiches. When we solve this Imbalance, item number one on my list is to fix Lake Hall."

Albert smiled, despite the news he'd just received.

Tomorrow, they'd have to do better in Belltroll.

The next morning, Albert felt a little hopeless when he and Leroy arrived in the Main Chamber. It was time to go back into the Realm and be the team that everyone was counting on them to be. But without Birdie . . .

"She's up!" Leroy yelled.

And Albert's hopelessness melted away in an instant.

"Birdie!" Albert and Leroy cried out, racing across the cave to pull her into a hug.

"You two are worse than my mom." Birdie giggled and broke away from the hug. Her eyes were bright, as if she'd just had the best sleep of her life.

"Are you all right?" Albert asked. "Are you going to be okay to go into the Realm today?"

Birdie nodded and did a little spin for them. "No injuries. Perfectly fine. In fact, I feel like I could take on the traitor *right now* and totally kick him into the next Realm!"

"Something tells me you might actually be capable of doing that," Leroy said. "Is everyone else awake?"

"Hoyt is," Birdie said, pointing over her shoulder as Hoyt walked into the Main Chamber. He waved, and he, too, looked like he was ready to rock and roll.

But then Professor Bigglesby came into the Main Chamber—in a wheelchair.

"Oh . . . crud," Leroy groaned.

A group of students were clustered around the old dwarf. The wheelchair was tiny, seemingly made for a child, and Bigglesby had a big strip of gauze wrapped around his head. His shock of white hair nearly blended in with the bandage.

"What happened?" Birdie asked as they pushed their way to the front of the crowd. "He was still sleeping when I left the hospital wing this morning, but he looked totally fine to me."

"I can't believe this," Hoyt said.

Professor Bigglesby gingerly lifted an arm in greeting when he saw them.

His other arm was in a cast.

Albert stopped dead in his tracks.

Professor Bigglesby's arm was fine yesterday. And had he even hit his head when he'd landed in the soft mossy area on the moor? Then again, everything had happened pretty fast. It *could* have happened without Albert noticing.

"I won't be joining you any longer," Professor Bigglesby said. His voice wavered. "I'm afraid the Realm proved to be too much for an old man like me."

Hoyt sidled up next to Albert. "He didn't seem to be an old man yesterday, when he was giving that speech."

Albert had to agree with that.

"So we're going in without you?" Leroy asked. His face had gone as pale as paper.

Professor Bigglesby nodded. "I'm afraid the time has come for you young Balance Keepers to carry the burden. A terrible mishap. Brittle bones, you see, and it's lucky for our in-Core nurse. Otherwise, I may not have survived." He coughed into his non-broken arm. "Sleep. That is the best thing for me now. I do, however, have a gift for you all before you continue on."

Just then, Petra came sprinting around the corner, carrying a small black box. "I've got it, Professor!" he shouted, and set the box down on the floor in front of Bigglesby. Albert, Birdie, Leroy, and Hoyt crowded around it.

It was full of potions. Four strange little triangular glass vials full of a lavender liquid. Petra passed them out, one to each Balance Keeper.

"What is this?" Albert asked.

"Knockout Serum," Petra explained. "It'll take care of the toads for you guys. I made it myself, just this morning!"

Leroy clapped Petra on the shoulder. "I had no idea you could do this stuff, dude."

"A bright future for this one, I should think," Professor Bigglesby said weakly.

"Well, there's loads of books in the Tower." Petra's cheeks flushed, and he beamed. "Just empty a vial into the moors. It lasts only an hour, so you'll have to dump another bottle on the way back."

"Thanks, Petra," Albert said. "This is really great."

"I just wish I'd known before you guys went in last time," Petra said. "Good luck today."

"We'll need it," Albert said. "But we'll do better today with this stuff." Petra was such a constant supporter, loyal down to his bones.

There were a few other people there to see them off, but most were still in their dorms, hiding out in case of more quakes. Lucinda shuffled past, mumbling to Kimber. "Stay *on*, you awful beast!" she hissed. She headed in the direction of the exit doors that led toward the gondola.

"Going to visit the Path Hider?" Leroy asked.

Lucinda stopped, her face reddening. "That's none of your business!" But then she leaned close to Birdie and whispered, "How do I look?"

"Fine," Birdie said stiffly. Albert knew Birdie didn't like Lucinda anymore, not since they found the shopkeeper studying that awful Book of Bad Tiles last term.

"Good luck today," Lucinda said without her usual gusto. She smoothed her hair down, tugged Kimber back up onto her shoulders, and shoved her way through the doors, into the darkness beyond.

"That's odd about her snake," Birdie mused. "I thought those two were practically inseparable."

"I wouldn't sit on her shoulders if you paid me to," Hoyt said.

Albert chuckled. He went to place the vial into the pocket of his protective vest and suddenly remembered the gem that was already in there. He pulled it out and showed Professor Bigglesby.

The little dwarf's eyes widened. "These are Troll symbols," he explained, and pointed out the old markings on the gem. "I'm afraid I'm not sure exactly what this is though. I myself have never been to Troll Mountain, and there's rumor of caves within its depths. I've studied the Trolls' symbols over the years, from what little documentation we've been able to gather, but the language is nearly impossible to decipher. Curious beings, the Trolls. Keep it with you. Perhaps it will come of use once you make it to the mountains."

He yawned and rubbed his head.

The cyclops nurse arrived, tsking and swatting at everyone. "Pests, the whole lot of you," she said. "Can't you see he needs his rest?" She unlocked the brake on the wheelchair and slowly backed Professor Bigglesby away.

Birdie rushed after them. "But Professor! How are we

supposed to continue on without you?"

"We don't even know if there are other creatures in there," Leroy added. "And there's a *traitor* in there, for crying out loud!"

"The Realm has chosen its protectors," Professor Bigglesby said, without turning around. "This time, I'm afraid I won't be one of them."

The cyclops nurse pushed him along faster, and then he was gone.

Hoyt threw his hands in the air. "Well, that's just great. First Poison Toads, now this. Next it's gonna be velociraptors running rampant in the Core."

Leroy wrung his hat in his hands. "Dude. If that's the case, I'm out of here."

"And with only five days left," Hoyt said, gesturing to the countdown clock near the broken door to Belltroll, "there's no way we can do this on our own."

Albert thought of his mom, and the article she'd sent, about the Yellowstone Caldera. It was too close to Herman. Too close to another place that felt like home.

Time was moving quickly. The surface needed saving, and Albert needed his team to be in their right minds.

"We'll handle it just fine," he said. "We've never had a Professor with us in the Realms, and we don't need one now." He thought of the conversation he'd overheard two nights ago and how Bigglesby seemed to have a problem with Albert. "We especially don't need him."

It was Birdie who finally stepped up to the plate and said the final words to get them all going. "I'm certainly not afraid," she said. "And you boys shouldn't be either."

Hoyt puffed up his chest. Leroy slid his hat back onto his head.

Birdie winked at Albert as they all stepped forward and headed through the door into Belltroll.

The potion worked as Petra promised it would. One vial dumped into the water of the moors, and it spread throughout, dousing the giant toads.

They were able to pass through the bog in just under an hour, and that small victory alone gave everyone a dose of new energy.

As they walked across the final stretch of the moor, hopping from landmass to landmass in a very frog-like way, Albert studied the gem he'd found.

"Maybe it belongs to one of the Trolls," Hoyt suggested. He hopped over a toad, which was snoring even louder than Leroy and Farnsworth combined. "In stories, don't trolls like to collect and guard things? Maybe the caves in Troll Mountain are full of treasure. And whoever came in here before us stole something, and the Trolls are mad, and that's why the Realm is out of Balance?"

"Dude, that could be true. Maybe the Trolls are on strike," Leroy added.

"That doesn't even make sense!" Birdie snapped from

the back of the group. "Especially what Hoyt said."

Hoyt whirled around. "What did I ever do to you?"

"Seriously?" Birdie threw her arms up in the air. "Ponderay! That's what you *did*, Hoyt! You nearly got us all killed in there."

"I screwed up," Hoyt said.

"You betrayed us all," Birdie said. "We agreed to work together, and then you just turned your back on that!"

Albert jumped in between them, and Leroy placed his hands on Birdie's shoulders and pulled her gently back.

"Look, guys," Albert said. "We've all got our issues here, but now is *not* the time."

"Albert's right," Leroy said. "Every second we waste fighting is another second we lose on figuring out the Imbalance and who the traitor is."

Birdie scuffed her toe on the grass. Hoyt gave a curt nod.

"So here's the question," Leroy said, stretching out his arms as they started walking again. "Anyone else think Professor Bigglesby's faking it?"

Albert didn't want to say it earlier, but he totally agreed. "Something is off about him. And with the broken-arm thing . . ."

"I've already added him to our list of possible traitors," Birdie said with a nod.

"There's a list?" Hoyt asked. "Can I see it?"

"It's only for the people we trust," Birdie growled.

Albert threw her a look, and Birdie sighed. "Well . . . I guess. When we get back. But you have to promise not to tell anyone a thing about it."

"Scout's honor," Hoyt said.

Albert knew she'd calm down after a while. And Birdie being that upset just showed Albert he was further along toward forgiving Hoyt than he thought. Hoyt had already saved Albert in this Realm, and honestly, Albert didn't have the energy to be upset with Hoyt any longer.

People made mistakes, and there was something about the imminent threat of death that made forgiveness feel a lot more important.

"Can we get back to the velociraptors thing?" Leroy asked Birdie. "Because if those are here, dude, I'm gone."

"Leroy Jones, if you call me a dude one more time . . . ," Birdie warned.

Their talking trailed off as the moors ended and their boots finally landed on solid ground. They had reached the Ring of Emerald.

It was stunning, like a land made out of dreams.

The hills rolled on and on ahead of them, with Troll Mountain Range just barely in view beyond what looked like a cloudless sky. Everything was still so green, and Birdie clapped her hands and hopped up and down like a kid on Christmas morning.

"I just love this Realm," she said.

As if in response, the ground trembled, and Hoyt yelled, "Hold tight!"

A quake split through the Realm. Hydra locked arms, waiting it out, as Belltroll rebelled.

The moor sloshed like a wave pool, and overhead, the very sky seemed to darken. Even from this distance, Albert could hear the mountain grinding deeper and deeper into the ground. This really wasn't good.

As if on cue in response to Albert's thoughts, a tiny, half-inch-wide tear snaked its way across the ground, sweeping right in between Albert's feet. He hopped sideways to avoid it. When the quake ended, Albert bent down to get a closer look.

"Uh . . . guys. This isn't a good sign." The crack went deeper than Albert could see, and as far as he could see in either direction.

"Five days might not be long enough," Leroy said as he looked around at his teammates.

Hoyt gripped his Speed Tile, eyes widening. "Five days is all we have."

Birdie tightened her ponytail, and they all looked to Albert.

"We'll just have to make it work," Albert said. "Like old times, right, guys?"

They walked on, the tall green grass like a sea of swaying silk all around them.

*   *   *

The Ring of Emerald was no joke. Half the time, they were hiking *uphill*, which wasn't exactly a walk in the park.

Without the Pit, and at the rate this Imbalance was worsening, the Balance Keepers hadn't been able to train. Even Hoyt, who was usually bouncing off the walls thanks to his Speed Tile, looked ready to drop by the time they made it halfway through the ring of hills.

"Are we there yet?" Leroy asked from the back of the group. They'd stopped in a small clearing at the bottom of a hill, and he was busy massaging his sore legs.

"I need water," Birdie said as she dug through her backpack. "Hey, look! I forgot we had this! Though I don't remember putting it in here . . ."

She pulled out the old map of the Realm and spread it across the grass. A little purple-and-black ladybug landed on it, which she promptly swept away.

"Professor Bigglesby said it would give us the best route to Troll Mountain," Albert said. He leaned in even closer to take a look.

"We're here," Birdie said. She tapped the left side of the map, and Albert could see that they were only a little ways into the Ring of Emerald, with lots of hills still to go. "We can go through this little valley here, though," Birdie said, "which seems to be the fastest way to the mountain range." She looked at Leroy and raised a brow in question.

"You're on track," he said, and nodded. "That's about three quarters of a mile, if I'm rounding up. If we walk at a constant speed of four miles per hour, we should make it there in about eleven minutes."

Hoyt whistled in approval. "You've got enough brains for the lot of us."

"It's the Tile," Leroy said, tapping his Synapse Tile.

It struck Albert how strange this was, standing here with Hoyt. Two terms ago, Hoyt had pushed Leroy in the Library, and Albert had snapped.

Now the two were chumming it up in Belltroll as if nothing had ever happened.

I guess dark times bring people together, Albert thought. Then he remembered what a mess Lucinda had been lately. *Or, they can tear people apart.*

He promised himself he wouldn't let that happen to any member of his team.

"Take a few minutes to catch your breath," Albert offered. "Then we'll move on."

Leroy ate a snack while everyone else tightened their laces and checked the straps on their leathery armor. So far, today had been easy. Effortless, almost.

And Albert knew that was always too good to be true.

CHAPTER 14

The Trundlespikes

Though Birdie's map had said it was a straight shot up the hill and through a bit of trees into the valley, it turned out things had shifted in the Realm due to the quakes.

Trees were overturned. Cracks in the ground—some as wide as the pipes in the Path Hider's domain—threatened to, at best, trip them, or at worst, suck them down to the underworld, as Leroy had mentioned several times already.

But as they walked, the map changed. The ink morphed to show them a new path. Birdie shouted out commands for where to turn, and Leroy, alongside her, helped decipher whether the routes would work out as expected.

Hoyt just walked in silence, his eyes on the horizon. Albert was focused on finding clues that could lead them to the identity of the traitor.

They searched left and right, for any sign of anyone having passed through here before them. But there was nothing. No footprints, no fallen Tiles, no signs that anyone had been here before them at all. Unless Albert considered the dire state of the Realm, and the surface world above, he wouldn't have known they were in any danger at all.

As they walked, Albert kept an eye on his Counter. The little screen still read *5 days*. It felt like plenty of time, but adding in trips back to the Core to get some food and rest would take big chunks out of that.

"We've targeted twelve hours today, to make it back by dark, and we're already at the five-hour mark," Albert said aloud. "We're making good time, but I think we need to move faster. We've got to get to the mountain range. My gut tells me that's where we'll find a clue of who did this."

"The Imbalance is our clue," Hoyt said. "It's someone who's trying to kill us all."

"Dude. A little positivity wouldn't hurt!" Leroy whined like Farnsworth from the back of the group.

"I think the other side of this hill is the end of the Ring of Emerald!" Birdie shouted. "We'll be in the center of the Realm in no time." She stopped and turned her map around so the rest of them could see it. They were standing at the bottom of another steep hillside, the green grass looking like a perfect emerald tidal wave stretching up. Albert imagined going to the top and rolling all the way down like he was a little kid again.

"It looks pretty accurate," Leroy said. "But I don't see the boulders on there."

He pointed at the map, where the hillside was simply green and empty. When Birdie moved it and they looked in front of them at the actual hill, it was covered with large lumpy boulders all around.

"Those are weird," Birdie said. "Think it's possible they came down from one of the mountains, during a quake?"

Albert shrugged. "Could be. But if that's the case, we'll need to be quick. If there's another quake, there's no telling how fast those boulders might move."

Birdie nodded and carefully rolled the map back into its case, tucking it into her pack for later.

"Race to the top?" Hoyt asked as he chugged water from a canteen. "It can't hurt to have a little fun, right? And it'll get us there quicker." He tossed the canteen to Albert. "Come on, it'll be just like old times in the Pit."

"Those old times weren't exactly fun, Hoyt," Birdie growled. But then she held a hand to her mouth, like the words had slipped out of their own accord. She looked down at her toes. "Sorry."

He held up his hands. "It's cool, I get it. I was just kidding."

"Let's just get to the top," Albert said. "And if you want to race, Hoyt, then let's just go old school. No Tile powers. Just normal, surface-level climbing."

"Deal," Hoyt said with a grin.

The hills in Belltroll weren't exactly small hills, so after Leroy estimated a twenty-minute hike to the top, they began.

It felt good to move fast, after having walked most of the day.

Hoyt went straight up, then forked left between two large boulders. Leroy, whose long legs were an advantage, followed Hoyt at a pretty even pace. Birdie and Albert both went off to the right, zigzagging between boulders as if they were playing a game of chase.

"He's quick even without his Tile!" Birdie shouted from behind Albert.

They both watched as Hoyt zipped left, hopping over a smaller boulder, then landed on his feet and zipped right.

Albert laid on the speed, doing his best to pull ahead. He could see flashes of his friends behind him, and hear everyone breathing heavily as they began to tire, but he wanted to win. Even though Hoyt was acting fine this term, Albert still didn't think he could stomach a loss to the guy.

They weren't even halfway up the hill when Albert

decided to change tactics and hop along the tops of the boulders like stepping-stones. The first boulder his feet hit was no problem, and Albert leaped hard, aiming for a second that would put him ahead of Hoyt.

But when his boots hit the second boulder, it began to move. It was a strange sort of feeling, as if the boulder were alive. Albert leaped off—there must be another quake going on.

But then his eyes saw something incredibly strange. Something that couldn't possibly be real.

The strange lumps on the boulder began to unfurl. There were hundreds of them, slowly rising up out of the surface of the boulder.

"Spikes," Albert heard himself say.

He stumbled backward as what he'd *thought* was a boulder turned into a beast. Four short, stubby legs appeared beneath the main body of the boulder. Then a head, with mouselike ears, and a weasellike nose.

The beast turned, its large dark eyes set on Albert. There were spikes spread out across its back and sides, almost like a giant hedgehog . . . if hedgehogs were the size of ponies.

"It's a Trundlespike!" Hoyt said as he came up beside Albert, forgetting the race. "Oh, man, these things are super rare! I've only heard about them in stories! I wonder if there's more of—"

He didn't have a chance to finish his sentence. The

Trundlespike suddenly let out a screech that had Albert clapping his hands to his ears.

The other boulders around the hillside began to move.

There were popping and hissing noises all around, and suddenly all the boulders had uncurled themselves. There had to be at least fifteen Trundlespikes, all of them with their spikes out, their big eyes shifting left and right.

"Awww," Birdie said. Albert agreed that they were kind of cute—giant and cute—but something in the back of his head was also shouting *No way, not good in an Imbalanced Realm!* But before he could say anything, Birdie rushed forward, hand held out to touch one.

"Birdie, don't!" Leroy shouted.

It was too late.

There was an earsplitting screech, and the Trundlespikes curled back up into their boulder-like shapes.

"What are they doing?" Leroy asked. Albert was wondering the same thing. Two seconds ago he thought Birdie would come away with a bloody hand. Albert wasn't looking forward to that. But this made him uneasy, too.

"We scared the poor things," Birdie said.

"Nuh-uh," Hoyt said. "We need to run." He said it casually, but when none of them moved, he turned to Albert, Leroy, and Birdie, his eyes wide with fear. "You guys, this isn't a drill! RUN!"

Leroy took off after Hoyt, but Birdie looked like she wasn't so sure.

"Let's go!" Albert shouted, grabbing her hand.

They turned and sprinted down the hill as a line of Trundlespikes tumbled down the hillside, headed straight for Hydra.

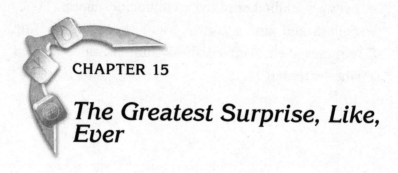

CHAPTER 15

The Greatest Surprise, Like, Ever

I f there was any time in Albert's life to be grateful for having trained in the art of staying alive, it was now.

All four Balance Keepers sprinted down the hill, desperate to escape.

The Trundlespikes gained speed.

It was like that story Albert's mom used to tell him about the tortoise and the hare. But in this case, slow and steady did *not* win the race.

Giant and spiky and angry did, and Hydra was about to be smashed.

Hoyt, who had used his Speed Tile, was standing at the bottom of the hill, screaming, "RUN FASTER! RUN FASTER!"

"We're trying!" Leroy yelped as his feet nearly slipped out from under him.

To Albert's left, Birdie was slowing down.

Albert knew if he didn't act fast, his team would be annihilated. Desperation took a hold, and the need to survive had Albert begging his Tile to give him the power of Leroy's Synapse Tile.

All it took was the image of Leroy's symbol, an outspread tree, and it was as if Albert's mind expanded. A perfect mental image of the Black Book appeared. One symbol stood out in bold, clear as day: it looked like a tornado, a big spiraling gust of wind. He'd seen it only once, but with Leroy's memory powers, the image was perfectly there.

I need the power of the wind, Albert thought, harnessing the Tile symbol. Time seemed to slow as he felt the magic of his Tile wash through him, and suddenly he was soaring.

Not flying, but *spinning*. It was as if Albert himself had become a human tornado, powerful and faster than a strike of lightning. He was on the far right side of the group and as he spun to the left, his body gained momentum. With a force that only a storm could bring, he knocked into Birdie and Leroy and swept them off the ground.

All the air in Albert's lungs rushed out as they landed in a heap, nearly twenty feet away. Not a second later, the Trundlespikes rolled past, barely missing Birdie's left foot with their spikes. The ground thundered beneath their power, and Albert's hair blew back from his face as they zipped by.

The Trundlespikes continued on, up over the next hill, before fading into the distance.

That was too close for comfort, Albert thought.

His chest throbbed, and for a few moments, he felt as if he could hardly breathe.

"Dude," Leroy said, when he finally caught his breath, too. There was grass covering his vest and stuck in his hair. His hat was nowhere to be found. "First of all, my hat's gone. Second of all, you are a freaking beast."

Birdie spat out a mouthful of grass. "Albert, I've seen you do amazing things, but . . . what symbol even *was* that?"

Hoyt stood there, openmouthed, staring at Albert like he'd just seen a ghost.

"It was Gale Force," Albert said. "The power of the wind, I guess." It was like he had stopped being Albert for a moment and had *become* the wind. Albert knew his Master Tile had immense power, but this was something else entirely. If he could become the wind, what could the traitor become with double the power Albert had? The very thought made Albert's heart jump into his throat.

But it didn't help to think of that now. Albert stood

up, brushed off his pants, and turned to his friends. "We should get moving. No telling if those guys are going to be back."

"Hold on," Birdie said as she stared across the Realm, the wind blowing her curls from her face. "The map. Who put it in my bag?"

Albert didn't answer. Neither did Leroy or Hoyt.

"It led us across the Realm, right to the Trundlespikes, and I'm starting to feel seriously afraid."

"How come?" Hoyt said.

Birdie's hands trembled a little, and she tucked them into her front pockets. "Because, I thought one of you put it in there, or maybe Petra, though I don't know when he would have done it. But if it wasn't from you guys, and it wasn't from Professor Bigglesby . . ."

"The traitor," Albert said. He looked over his shoulder, afraid that someone was watching them even now. "They must be closer than we thought."

"I'm so sorry," Birdie whispered. "We almost got killed because of my mistake."

Leroy patted her on the back. "Hey, it's not a big deal. Albert's crazy wind-ninja move saved us."

"We have to be more careful," Birdie said. "We can't trust anything or anyone but each other." Her eyes softened when she looked at Hoyt. "Thanks for the heads-up. You saved us back there."

"We're a team," Hoyt said with a shrug.

They gathered themselves and headed up the hillside. They left the map behind, crumpled in a ball that blew away with the breeze.

The Realm spread out before Hydra, three massive mountains towering high into the sky. They were tall enough, even, to make Calderon Peak and the Ten Pillars of Ponderay look pathetic by comparison. In the very center was Troll Mountain. Its peak was serrated and brutal, full of rocky crags. Troll Mountain, when Albert watched carefully enough, was spinning.

It was steady and methodical, like a merry-go-round in super-slow motion.

And Albert could just barely hear the sound of the mountain grinding into the Realm, deeper with every second that went by. Like metal grinding against metal, the sound made chills run up and down his spine.

Beneath that sound was something else. A constant, slow rumble.

"Is that snoring?" Birdie asked.

"It must be the Trolls," Hoyt said.

"They are totally in hibernation mode," Leroy added.

As they listened to the Trolls snoring from their caves, the Realm began to shake.

"It's coming!" Hoyt called out.

They all dropped to their stomachs, lying flat on the hillside. Albert's teeth chattered, and he felt like his brain was knocking around inside of his skull.

He counted the seconds. Thirty.

Thirty-five.

Forty-five.

At fifty-seven, the quake finally ended.

Albert stood up and looked around. "Everyone in one piece?"

Hoyt nodded, and Leroy readjusted his glasses on the bridge of his nose.

"You're keeping track of these, right, Leroy?" Birdie asked.

Leroy tapped his head. "Got it on lockdown."

"Let's move, then," Albert suggested, "before another quake hits."

They set off down the hill, into the wide, emerald valley that led into the mountain range.

The walk was quick and, thankfully, uneventful, until they came to the trees.

It was a small, forested area, just before the mountains rose into the sky. But it was darker here, the canopy overhead blocking out the Realm's strange, sunless source of light. Albert felt like he was in the woods in Herman . . . if those woods also possibly contained a dangerous traitor who could jump out from behind a tree at any minute. He paused to consider the best way to proceed.

Birdie stopped next to him. "I don't like it here," she whispered.

"It's the perfect place for a traitor to hide," Leroy said.

Hoyt balled his hands into fists, as if he were looking for a fight with whoever might pop out of the trees.

Albert looked into the darkness. It wasn't Herman, but he could pretend it was.

"We have to keep going," he said. "The mountains are just ahead, and if we don't get a chance to look around before nightfall, we'll be way behind. We have to summit those mountains and get a look at the Bells."

They walked through the trees for a few moments when Leroy froze several feet in front of the rest of them.

He lifted a fist, like a soldier leading a battalion. Albert, Birdie, and Hoyt froze.

Leroy cocked his head and pointed ahead of them, where the trees thickened.

There was a noise coming from the shadows. A *crunch, crunch.*

Albert held his fists before him like a martial artist.

Please, he thought. *Don't let it be the traitor. I don't think I'm ready for this yet. Not now. Not so soon.*

Fear struck through him, but he forced it down. "Stay here," he whispered. He took a few steps forward.

"If you die, I might as well go down with you," Leroy said. He reached up to turn his hat backward like he always did, but his shoulders drooped when he remembered he'd lost it in the Trundlespike attack.

Birdie joined Albert and Leroy, and Hoyt, surprisingly,

stepped up without any hesitation.

"Let's get them," Hoyt said, with a determined grin.

As one, with Albert in the lead, Hydra went forward to face the traitor of Belltroll.

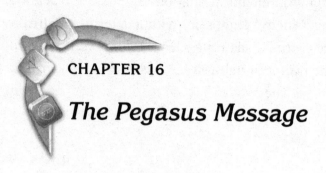

CHAPTER 16

The Pegasus Message

Birdie was going to scream, Albert knew it.

But it wouldn't be from fear.

She'd scream from excitement, because what was waiting for them beyond the trees wasn't the traitor.

It was, without a doubt, truly incredible.

The trees died away, and a small, grassy pasture sat at the very bottom of the mountain range. Standing in the center of the pasture, straight out of a storybook, was a herd of horses.

Not just any regular horses, either. These were *winged* horses.

"A Pegasus herd," Albert whispered, testing out the word on his tongue. "I thought they were extinct."

Albert stared. There were only four of them, but they

were sleek and beautiful. Two of them were black and shimmery like the night sky, the others as pure white as untouched, fresh-fallen snow. Their wings were made of thick, shiny birdlike feathers, some of them longer than Albert's legs. They were tucked into the horses' sides, but Albert knew when they spread them wide, they'd look magnificent in the light.

The crunching noise wasn't a traitor at all. It was the herd of Pegasi, happily munching away on fresh grass.

"Whoa. Birdie's going to lose it, bro," Leroy said to Albert, a huge grin lighting up his face.

"Oh yeah," Albert said. "Totally."

The Guildacker from Calderon was amazing. The Jackalopes from Ponderay were a close second, and Farnsworth was pretty cool, too. But a *Pegasus*? A whole *herd* of them? Albert's mom used to read him stories about them, and he'd seen them in movies and TV shows. Back in New York, his little half sister's room was full of winged horse dolls and stuffed animals.

Pegasi existed here. And that alone made today totally worth it.

Leroy and Albert turned to watch as Birdie and Hoyt came through the trees.

Birdie froze.

Her mouth opened and closed like a fish. Her eyes widened. Then she blinked a few times, and then, finally, Albert, Leroy, and Hoyt covered their ears as Birdie squealed like a newborn pig.

"Omigosh," she said, over and over. "Omifreak-ingosh!"

The Pegasi jumped, startled, and Albert gasped as they spread their wings. They spanned at least eight feet on each side.

"If only Slink were here," Hoyt said, glancing at Albert. "He could talk to them, and see if they could give us a ride."

Albert smiled even bigger. "I can take care of that."

He didn't know much about horses, but Leroy did.

"Move slow," Leroy said. "Keep your arms at your sides, and don't make any sudden movements. Let them come to you."

Albert nodded. Birdie almost let out another squeal, and Albert wondered if she was literally going to sponta-neously combust from the excitement.

He mustered up the image of Slink's Creature Speak Tile.

Then, slowly, he stepped into the pasture.

The Pegasi watched him with their soft, dark eyes. They didn't look evil. That was unusual in an Imbalanced Realm. One of the black horses stamped his hooves and blew air out his nostrils. He was the tallest and by far the most muscular of the herd. He pranced a little closer, and Albert could see that he even had little feathers lining his legs, just above his giant hooves.

Albert focused on the power of the Tile symbol.

We aren't here to harm you, he said. But it wasn't exactly words he said. His voice came out as a whinny. Albert almost laughed at how silly he sounded.

He thought the words, and the whinny came out. *We're Balance Keepers, from the Core, here to protect the Realm. We need to get to the top of the mountains.*

The black horse walked forward, his wings held high above his back. *You are small ones. Perhaps you are lost?*

Somehow Albert understood the Pegasus, as the power of his Master Tile did its work. He thought for a second on how to explain to the Pegasi what they needed.

The Realm is in danger, Albert said. *We need to get to the mountaintops to check on the Bells.*

The Pegasi do not work for free, their leader said with a huff. *Especially Spyro.* He bowed in a show of pride.

Albert turned and released the Creature Speak power. "They don't work for free," he told his friends.

They were all staring at him like he'd just sprouted a second pair of eyes on his forehead. Leroy reached into his pocket and pulled out an old, broken peppermint. "How 'bout this?"

Albert nodded. "Sure." Then he focused on the Creature Speak Tile again.

We have . . . this mint. As payment. And we can bring you more later, if you want, if you'll give us a ride to the Bells.

For one strange second, Albert thought, *I'm talking to a*

horse with wings. This isn't weird at all.

It took a while for Spyro to come forward, huffing and sniffing. His soft muzzle landed in Leroy's outstretched palm. He sniffed the peppermint, and then, in one second, slurped it off of Leroy's palm and devoured it in two big, crunchy bites.

Birdie giggled as Spyro began to bounce his head up and down like he was listening to rock music, his mane tossing in the wind.

MORE! Spyro shouted. *NEED . . . MORE . . . MINTS!*

All the Pegasi began to whinny and stamp their hooves.

We'll bring you more peppermints, Albert promised. Spyro nodded in agreement and called the other three horses over.

The Pegasi lined up side by side, and before they knew it, each member of Hydra was picking out their own flying horse to ride.

Birdie and Leroy approached white ones, and Birdie danced with delight as her Pegasus knelt down so she could climb on. Spyro, who was still shouting *MORE MINTS,* knelt down for Hoyt to climb on.

That left the other black horse for Albert.

He'd never ridden a horse before, but with Leroy's coaching, Albert was ready to climb on.

But every time he approached his Pegasus, it pranced away, tossing its head in the air, flaring its nostrils.

Your blood! the Pegasus complained. It wouldn't let Albert get close to its side, fear in its big, widened eyes. *Your blood smells like the last one who came this way! Evil!*

"It keeps saying my blood smells like the last one who came this way," Albert said as everyone settled on their Pegasi. "It keeps saying I'm evil!"

"Maybe he just means another Balance Keeper," Leroy said. "That could be a clue. The traitor has to be a Balance Keeper."

"But he isn't saying that about any of you," Albert said, and it was true. The Pegasus didn't have an issue with anyone else. Just Albert.

Its eyes! the Pegasus whinnied. *Its eyes were horrible!*

"Whose eyes?" Albert asked. His head was reeling. He was confused, but this had to mean *something.* He tried to ask the Pegasus, but it was beyond consoling. It galloped away, screaming about bad blood, and took off into the air. Albert was forced to join Hoyt on Spyro's back.

"I promise, Albert," Hoyt said. "I'm not going to screw it up this time." He looked over at the nervous Pegasus as it disappeared into the sky. "It's probably just a crazy old horse anyhow. I wouldn't worry about it."

But Albert didn't agree. Hoyt hadn't heard the fear in the wild horse's words.

If Albert had the same blood as someone who had been here, the Pegasus had to be talking about someone in his family. *The one who came before* couldn't be

Professor Flynn, because he hadn't come here in ages. Pap had never trained for Belltroll. It certainly wasn't Albert's mom, because she wasn't a Balance Keeper, and had never been to the Core. Hadn't Pap mentioned that his father had been a Balance Keeper too? Could the Pegasus be remembering a great-grandparent of Albert's who wasn't all good?

Albert was called out of his thoughts by Leroy shouting commands telling everyone where to hold on to the mane and how to stay balanced on the Pegasi's backs. Albert awkwardly wrapped his arms around Hoyt's middle so he wouldn't fall off.

He tried to be excited and pay attention to Leroy's words.

But he couldn't focus.

The traitor had been here, recently. The horse was terrified of Albert because it thought they shared the same blood. And if Albert and this person, whoever they were, smelled similar . . .

How was that even possible?

And after that, Albert wondered . . . *why me?*

CHAPTER 17

Troll Mountain

The flight was exhilarating.

Spyro's great, feathery wings beat against the wind with a *whoosh, whoosh*, and as Spyro rose higher and higher, all of Belltroll spread out below like a living map.

Despite the setbacks, Albert knew at once that this was his favorite Realm of them all. It was beautiful and so full of life.

Or so Albert thought, until he saw the cracks.

They were everywhere, like scars on the surface of Belltroll. The Pegasi swooped closer to the mountains, rising near the tops. The jagged cracks started at the mountain range, cutting through the pasture, zigzagging across the wooded area, all the way into the Ring of Emerald and beyond.

When Albert was younger, he'd dropped his mom's favorite vase. It didn't shatter right away, but cracks like tiny strikes of lightning appeared, until eventually it fell to pieces.

Belltroll was going to do exactly that, and Albert finally understood what Professor Bigglesby meant by the words *splitting point*.

If they didn't solve the Imbalance in time, Belltroll would shatter. Its chaos would travel to the other two Realms, throwing off the Balance of all three. Eventually, it would hit the surface world, and who knows what would happen after that.

"I see the Bells!" Hoyt shouted, above the howling of the wind and the whooshing of Spyro's great black wings.

Albert leaned past Hoyt's shoulder to get a better look.

They were closing in on the peak of the left mountain, the smallest of the three. That strange, double-pronged peak caught his eye. The Bell hung in the center of the gap between the prongs, dangling in midair. It glowed in the daylight.

Even from here, Albert could sense the magic in it.

The Bell looked golden from a distance, and the shape was eerily similar to the Liberty Bell. Though it rocked slightly back and forth in the wind, Albert couldn't hear a sound.

"Do you hear it ringing?" Hoyt shouted. "Maybe it's not working at all!"

Albert remembered the small lesson they'd had on Belltroll in Professor Bigglesby's classroom. The Bells of Belltroll chimed at a frequency that only the Trolls could hear. But maybe that wasn't working, either. Maybe *that* was why the Trolls were still asleep.

They needed to get a closer look.

Albert shouted directions to Spyro. The Pegasus suddenly swooped lower, and Albert felt like he was on a roller coaster.

They circled the mountaintop twice.

Leroy passed by, his white Pegasus a blur as he screamed, "YEEEEEHAW, BROS!"

Birdie followed, laughing, her arms in the air like she was completely and totally fearless.

"They're nuts!" Hoyt shouted as Spyro spread his wings out, catching the wind so that they came to a sudden stop. With each powerful beat of his wings, Spyro kept them afloat just beside the Bell.

Up this close, the Bells were massive.

As Hydra gathered around the left mountain, their Pegasi hovering in midair, Albert had the sudden mental image of the Bell falling on him and crushing his bones to nothing but dust. He shivered as the wind raged around them.

Albert leaned as far out toward the Bell as he dared so he could search for clues. From far away, even with the little bit of magic Albert had sensed, the Bell seemed simply that: a bell. Nothing spectacular, just a giant golden bell, one that Albert thought was likely to ring a sad, mournful tone.

But here?

The magic was intense.

"Troll symbols," Birdie said, pointing at the Bell.

The golden surface was covered in them, so many symbols that they all seemed to blur together into one giant pattern.

"I wonder what it all means," Albert said.

If only there was a Tile symbol for reading the Troll language. But Albert knew that some types of magic weren't strong enough to harness the powers of others.

Spyro got close enough that Albert was able to reach out and touch the Bell. He skimmed his fingertips across the cool, slick surface. This Bell was ancient. That much he could tell, and it wasn't the symbols or the way the gold was muted in some places, like an old, used penny, that told Albert that.

This was more of a feeling, the kind that hushed the breath in his lungs. The kind that made Albert want to whisper his words instead of speak them.

The gap that the Bell hovered in was only wide enough for one Pegasus to pass through at a time, with their wings slightly tucked. Albert and Hoyt went first on Spyro.

They flew slowly past the Bell, searching for any clue that the Traitor had been here.

"It's just hanging here," Hoyt said. "Sometimes, the magic in these Realms blows my mind."

"I can't find anything that looks abnormal," Albert said.

The front of the Bell had nothing out of place. Not a crack, nor a stray hair from a previous observer.

"See anything, Leroy?" Albert yelled over his shoulder, as Spyro moved out of the way so Leroy's Pegasus could get close.

Leroy's Pegasus was younger, and its wings weren't as steady as Spyro's. He wasn't able to get a close enough look before the horse had to pull away and soar into the sky, where it could fully spread its wings.

Birdie didn't have much luck either. "You guys look one more time!"

Spyro flew them back through the small gap, and Albert leaned past Hoyt to get a closer look at the backside of the Bell.

And there it was.

The second clue.

It was just barely there at first glance, but from the

right angle, it was obvious. A large fingerprint, human-sized, but too big for any Balance Keeper Albert's age.

"Hoyt, look!" Albert shouted. "You see it too, right?"

Hoyt leaned out, squinting his eyes. "Looks like we found our clue."

Minutes later, Leroy and Birdie had both gotten a look at the fingerprint. All three Pegasi clustered together in the sky, just outside the gap beside the Bell.

"It's exactly zero point eight inches," Leroy said. "The average human fingerprint is . . . about half an inch."

"So you're saying the traitor isn't human?" Hoyt asked with a gasp.

"No way, bro," Leroy chuckled. "I'm saying the traitor is a large human. But not actually giant like Professor Asante. Her fingers are larger than this. Someone big. But not too big. An adult, for sure."

"So what are we supposed to do?" Birdie asked, running her hands through her horse's mane. "Just walk around the Core and demand that we measure every-body's fingerprint?"

"We don't even know *what* finger it is!" Hoyt said.

They were right. It wasn't much.

But it was something. And that was more than they'd had all day.

It was then that a thought registered in Albert's mind. If someone left a fingerprint on the Bell, it meant they'd had to touch it.

But what for?

He felt like a caged dog. If only he could fly, and get a little more space . . .

He practically smacked himself on the forehead.

"Stay here," Albert told Hoyt.

"What do you *mean* stay here?" Hoyt asked, his eyes widening. "It's not like there's anywhere else I can go!"

Albert laughed, and with a quick but focused thought of the Float symbol, he slipped sideways off Spyro's back.

Birdie gasped. "Albert! What are you doing?"

"Investigating," Albert said.

It was freaky, floating this high off the ground, and he knew he didn't have the strength to focus on the symbol for long. But Albert slowly thought of moving forward and his Tile responded. It was as if an invisible hand was pulling him toward the Bell.

He could just *feel* it, that something more important was close.

He allowed himself to drop a few feet, on instinct, until he was floating just beneath the Bell. He looked up into its belly.

It looked like there was a hook at the very top of the inside of the Bell, where something should have been attached, but the Bell was as hollow as the Troll Tree.

"Isn't there supposed to be something inside here?" Albert shouted. His voice rang back to him.

"What's he saying?" Leroy asked from above.

"It's hard to tell when you can't hear!" Birdie said back.

"If he falls . . ." Hoyt's voice trailed off.

Albert could feel his concentration slipping, so with one final *shove* against his mind, Albert floated himself back up to Spyro. The Pegasus slipped effortlessly below him, and Albert sunk against Hoyt, feeling like he weighed a million pounds.

"What did you see?" Birdie asked.

"It's empty," Albert said when his mind cleared. "Isn't there supposed to be something inside of the Bell? You know, like . . ."

"The striker!" Leroy shouted, so suddenly that his Pegasus jumped a little, and Leroy had to grab hold of its mane to keep from tumbling overboard.

"The striker, dudes!" Leroy said again. He snapped his fingers, like he'd just remembered the details to a forgotten dream. "Every bell has one. It's the little arm that makes the bell ring!"

Birdie tilted her head, the way Farnsworth did when Albert told him to roll over. Not that he ever *had* rolled over on command.

Leroy explained further. "You know, it's like something has to *hit* the bell, to cause the vibration that makes the sound? This bell is empty."

"There's a hook, where it looks like the striker should be hanging!" Albert added.

"Without it," Hoyt said, catching on, "the Bell can't ring. Which means the Trolls can't wake up."

"Which means they can't go and turn the wheel inside the mountain," Birdie added with a little gasp.

"And then they can't help crank Troll Mountain *out* of the ground! That's what's causing the quakes!" Albert exclaimed. "So all we have to do is put the striker back in!"

Leroy nodded. "Assuming we're correct, of course. But . . . dudes. If we're right, then we've just discovered the reason for our Imbalance."

"And the Means to Restore Balance," Birdie added.

They all had huge grins lighting up their faces. This was it, the answer they'd been looking for.

Albert almost laughed at how easy it had been.

Then he remembered Calderon.

Their first term, they'd gone into the Realm of Calderon to search high and low to find the Means to Restore Balance. It was a trio of silver eggs, nestled deep in the trunk of the Tree of Cinder.

It had been difficult to find the Means with a Realm as large as Calderon. And they'd had weeks to solve that Imbalance, only doing so on the final day, at the final moment.

They had four days left in Belltroll after today.

"We don't have enough time," Albert said as he held up his Counter. "And besides, we've already been searching

the Realm. Even if we weren't looking for it, we would
have seen a striker this size, hiding somewhere."

"We'll keep looking," Birdie said, the determination
like a fire blazing in her eyes. "We'll find what we need,
Albert. We always do."

"But should we be looking for one striker or three?"
Hoyt asked. "Are we assuming the other two bells are
fine? Shouldn't we check those too?"

It was a smart idea, and soon, the Balance Keepers
were soaring to opposite peaks to see if the other two
bells were missing their strikers.

Birdie and Leroy went to the far right mountain,
while Albert and Hoyt went to Troll Mountain itself.

Albert had a sinking feeling he knew what they'd all
find.

That didn't make it any better, though, when he and
Hoyt discovered their striker was missing.

That didn't make it any easier when Birdie and Leroy
found the very same thing.

"We should go home," Albert said when they all met
back up. The Pegasi were starting to get jumpy, as if they
could sense the negative energy from the news of three
missing strikers. "We'll talk to Professor Bigglesby and
report what we've found. Maybe he'll be able to give us
some sort of direction."

*   *   *

It was nearly dark when the Pegasus herd dropped them off at the entrance to the Core. Albert's legs were sore from their earlier hiking as he dismounted. He was relieved they hadn't had to cross back through the Realm on foot.

Mints tomorrow, Spyro said, and Albert nodded his promise. The Pegasus flapped his wings and soared into the sky like a dark rocket, his mane and tail shimmering like stars.

"I'm so desperate for a big, greasy cheeseburger," Leroy said as they walked back up the hill, heading for the tunnel that led to the Core. "Every time I think about Lake Hall, it sort of feels like I lost a comrade in war."

"I just want to take a shower," Birdie said.

Hoyt was already unstrapping all his safety gear, ready to be back for the evening.

They were almost to the tunnel when Albert saw something gold and shimmering.

"Stop!" he shouted.

It was sitting right at the entrance to the tunnel, as if someone had set it down and forgotten it.

"Is that . . ." Birdie's voice trailed off as Albert rushed forward.

"A striker," he said.

It was just *sitting there*, all by itself, a golden striker the length of Albert's arm. He was about to stoop down and pick it up when Leroy clamped a hand onto Albert's shoulder.

"There's a note," he said. "Albert . . . I don't like this at all."

Leroy was right. A small piece of rolled parchment was tied to the striker.

"I don't think you should touch it," Birdie said. Her voice shook, and she actually didn't complain when Hoyt leaned over her shoulder to get a better look.

"What if it's, I dunno, poisoned or something?" Hoyt said.

The wind whistled past, the only sound to be heard across the entire Realm.

Albert didn't know what to do. But they couldn't just stand here. One of the strikers was here right in front of them, exactly what they needed.

"I have to see what the note says," Albert said, his voice strangely calm. He quickly bent down and untied the twine. The note tumbled to the grass and unfurled in the wind.

There were only five words. Five *simple* words, scribbled in jet-black ink.

A gift, for Albert Flynn.

Albert hardly heard his teammates as they questioned him and argued with one another in hushed voices. He barely felt his feet moving as they headed back down the dark tunnel to the Core.

The striker was tucked safely in Albert's pack, and he had the strange sensation that he was literally carrying the weight of the world on his shoulders.

A gift, for Albert Flynn.

He forced himself to keep walking, keep moving. He was a Balance Keeper. He was a Flynn, and he could do this.

Except . . . *could* he do this? Being a Flynn used to be a good thing. But today, it seemed that to be a Flynn was to be responsible for all that was wrong in the world. Albert kept walking, but it was like with each step, the striker on his back got heavier and heavier. He didn't know how much longer he could bear it.

Birdie put a hand on Albert's shoulder as they arrived at the door to the Core. There was just enough light here that they could see one another in shades of black and gray.

"We'll keep it quiet," Leroy said. "We'll call a meeting with your dad. If we don't know who to trust . . ."

"No," Albert said. The only word he'd spoken since finding the striker. "I want the entire Core in the Pit. I want to see their faces when I show them the striker and the note. I want to see how they all react."

"Albert, you'll scare everyone if you do that," Birdie said. "Think of the First Termers."

"I don't care about scaring them!" Albert barked out, wheeling to face her, as heat surged through him. "This striker is on *my* back! This note was addressed to *me*! The traitor wants me dead, Birdie." Albert turned away from them, suddenly furious with the world, with himself, with everything. His next words were only a whisper. "The traitor wants my Tile, and they don't care who they have to hurt to get it."

This was happening too fast. Albert was dizzy with anger. The Master Tile had never felt heavier around his throat. It felt like it was choking him.

He wanted it off. He wished he'd never plucked his Tile out of the Waterfall of Fate.

"Albert," Leroy said, stepping forward in the darkness.

Albert turned, ready to snap. No one knew how he was feeling right now, not even Leroy.

But then he saw the looks in his friends' eyes. They were scared, all of them. A tear slid down Birdie's cheek, and she wiped it away quickly, then crossed her arms in a show of defiance. Hoyt's lips were pressed tightly together like a clothespin, and Leroy looked like he'd been slapped across the face.

"I'm . . ." Albert was ashamed of his outburst. "I'm sorry."

Hoyt stepped forward. "You don't have to apologize. We get it. We've all said some things we wish we wouldn't have. . . ." He rubbed his forehead, sighing deeply.

"Hoyt's right," Leroy said. "It's hard for us, too, to

watch our best friend go through this. We're scared for you. But we're not going anywhere."

"We're with you in this, Albert," Birdie said. "But right now we have to figure out what we're going to do when we walk through that door."

"I agree." Hoyt nodded, looking Albert in the eye. "And really . . ." He swallowed hard, like he was afraid to say what was really on his mind, then turned to Birdie and Leroy. "This note thing could make him look guilty. It makes him look like he's in cahoots with the traitor."

"What?!" Birdie screeched, but Hoyt held his hands up.

"Whoa! I'm not saying Albert's guilty," Hoyt said. "I'm just saying, we've got to be smart with this. We have to make sure nobody blames him, because we all know the truth. The traitor is messing with him to get under his skin."

Leroy agreed. "Hoyt's right. We'll talk to the Professors only."

"And Petra," Albert said. Petra was the only person who'd been on their side since day one, always cheering Hydra on, always jumping up to help at a moment's notice.

"Petra too," Birdie said. "Sure."

She turned to Leroy and Hoyt, and Albert saw a look pass between the three of them, something silent and strange. Like they were afraid he'd snap again.

I'm fine, he told himself.

Albert turned and headed through the door, back into the Main Chamber.

He'd never been more grateful for the light.

CHAPTER 18

The Secret Meeting

Albert's head throbbed the entire emergency meeting. He couldn't look at his dad as he spoke, because he was afraid of the fear he might see in Professor Flynn's eyes.

Albert repeated the story of the day's events twice over, and then listened as Birdie, Leroy, and Hoyt repeated their versions of the same story, too. Professor Asante scribbled notes onto a pad, and Petra gasped at all the right places. Professor Bigglesby glared at Albert the entire time, his beady eyes as black as coal.

It went on for hours, and though Albert was grateful for the feeling of having more people on his side, he needed to stop staring at the traitor's note and the striker, which both sat on Professor Bigglesby's desk, a constant reminder that everything was not okay.

As the meeting bore on, Birdie brought up the map in her backpack, and Professor Bigglesby promised he had nothing to do with it. "I turned it over to your care," he said. "You must have placed it in your bag and forgotten about it. Exhaustion does things to the mind. I'm suffering from the same forgetfulness. Why, just this morning, I forgot to take my pain medication. If it weren't for our dear cyclops nurse, I may not be here with you today."

He still had his head wrap on, and his arm cast . . . and Albert wasn't buying it.

He kept that to himself, though. By the time the meeting was over, Hydra was ready to drop.

But they weren't given the chance. The rest of the evening was spent in the Core Watchers' Cavern as two replacement strikers were made.

Hydra sat on the rocky ground and Professor Bigglesby sat in his wheelchair across from them, assisting with the task.

"I'm with you, dude," Hoyt said to Albert as they watched Leroy and the Watchers babbling away, talking about the measurements and dimensions that the replacements should be. Leroy's glasses fogged up in the heat of the room, but he was so animated and full of life, despite the fact that it was well past midnight.

"He'll be a Core Watcher someday," Birdie said. "Don't you think?"

Albert yawned, but nodded. He could totally see Leroy joining these strange, riddle-speaking workers in the future. Leroy would be an incredible Core Watcher and scientist.

"I think that symbol needs to be more to the left," Leroy said, pointing at the replacement striker they were working on. Professor Bigglesby joined in, and though his voice was still weak, Albert thought he noticed the dwarf's voice coming back at random moments to its full strength.

"Faker," Hoyt said under his breath.

"You think so?" Albert asked, casting him a sideways glance.

Hoyt nodded. "He isn't even acting like he's in pain. My arm broke last year, and the second day, it was still throbbing pretty bad."

"He's right, you know," Birdie said. Her hair was puffed up like a cotton ball from the steam in the Watchers' Cavern. "I went down to the hospital wing today, just to check on some of the people who have been injured in the quakes, and I happened to pass by the medicine log."

Albert's eyes widened. "Birdie!"

"So I might have spent a few extra seconds looking it over." She waved a hand as if swatting a fly and carried on. "It doesn't *fully* qualify as snooping."

Hoyt laughed and held up two thumbs. "I'm starting to think you're pretty cool, Birdie."

"*Anyway,*" Birdie continued on, the ghost of a smile lighting up her face, "I noticed there's no medicine on there in Professor Bigglesby's name. He's not even pre-scribed anything for pain, or inflammation, or any of the things that a broken bone causes. And unless he has some magical dwarf healing powers, which he doesn't, because I looked it up, then I'm thinking something is fishy about all of this."

"And you'd know all this medical stuff *how*?" Albert asked.

Hoyt's mouth was hanging open.

Birdie's cheeks reddened, a rare occurrence. "I'm interested in nursing," she said. "Well, veterinary school, actually. Maybe someday I can get a job here, caring for the Core creatures. Oh, and you, Albert, would make a great Professor, and Hoyt, based on what I've seen from you in the Pit, you could train newbies as a great Appren-tice. . . ." Her eyes lit up as she dreamed of the future. Albert nudged her, and she came back to the present. "Anyhow, that's beside the point. What matters is that *he*," she said, nodding her head in Professor Bigglesby's direction, "is faking it."

Almost as if in answer to this, Professor Bigglesby reached up and scratched his ear . . . with the injured hand, the one that was covered in purple and black bruises.

"There!" Birdie said, after he'd lowered his hand

again. "It's makeup. He's wearing makeup on his hand!"

"What do you mean?" Albert asked.

"There's a little blue smudge on his ear where he used that hand to scratch it," Birdie said. "Look."

Albert squinted to better see Bigglesby's ear, and it looked like Birdie might be right. "How can you be sure?"

"I am a *girl*, Albert," Birdie said. "Geez."

"Oh, right."

"The bruises aren't real?" Hoyt said.

Bigglesby was a fake! If the bruises weren't real, then Albert was pretty positive his injury wasn't either . . . which meant Bigglesby was perfectly fine to go into the Realm with them.

So why wasn't he?

Hoyt stood as if he was going to march over to the dwarf and give him a piece of his mind. But Birdie and Albert pulled him back. They rushed quickly into the shadows, just out of view of Professor Bigglesby and Leroy.

"If he's faking his injury, he could be the traitor," Albert whispered. "Maybe he even came into Belltroll after we went in yesterday, and left the note for me to find."

"He probably removed the striker forever ago, before we ever went into Belltroll!" Birdie whispered back. "It makes perfect sense! But . . . it also doesn't. Why him? He's a Professor."

"I've been here my whole life," Hoyt added. "And I've never known Professor Bigglesby to be the type of guy who'd want to destroy the Core. But then again . . . he's always been a strange man. I guess it's possible."

"Maybe he wants more power," Albert said. "I heard him the other night, saying how much he doesn't trust me. He voted for us to go into the Realm, though. Why would he do that, but admit he doesn't like me when nobody else is around?"

"Because if he's the traitor, he wants your Tile," Birdie said. "Getting it in the Realm would be the most discreet way of doing it."

Hoyt shook his head and tried to pull away. "It doesn't matter why, you guys. What matters is me going over there and knocking out his teeth. I can do it so quickly he won't even notice."

Albert tightened his grip on Hoyt's shoulder.

"We need to take it slow. We're all in a rush, and that could be clouding our judgment."

"It's not clouding anything for me," Hoyt said.

Birdie blew out a puff of air. "We need to be absolutely sure before we decide it's him. And what if he has somebody helping him? We need all the facts first."

"Plus, we need to solve this Imbalance," Albert said.

Hoyt chewed on his lip, seeming to mull it all over in his head. "We don't tell him anything else from here on out. Okay? Whatever we find in the Realm. We don't tell the dwarf."

Albert and Birdie agreed, and in that moment, the three of them shared a secret.

Albert felt the rift between them closing, little by little. They were in this together now, whether they liked it or not.

When they slipped back out into the Watchers' Cavern, Professor Bigglesby was staring at them with his dark eyes.

Albert had the sinking feeling that the dwarf had heard every word.

There was a hand on Albert's shoulder.

It was the traitor, coming for his Master Tile! Albert reached out, ready to defend himself, and . . .

"Bro!" Leroy's voice woke Albert from a dead sleep. "Wake up!"

Albert's eyelids flickered open.

Petra and Leroy were standing over him, both boys breathing hard like they'd just come sprinting over. Farnsworth raced into the tent and yipped a greeting.

"What's going on?" Albert asked. "What time is it?"

Leroy looked at his watch. "It's three a.m. Sorry to wake you, but you should come with us."

"Why?" Albert asked. "What's up?"

Petra swallowed hard. "I've been on the night shift lately, in the Tower, and . . . the Professors are having a secret meeting," he said. "You're probably going to want to hear what they're saying."

Albert was up in an instant. "Let's go."

All three boys rushed from the tent. They were almost out of Cedarfell when a dark figure emerged from the trees.

Leroy screeched like a cat and fell backward into Petra, who fell backward into Albert like they were in some slapstick comedy routine. Farnsworth wagged his tail.

"Where do you three think you're going?" the figure asked. Hoyt stepped from the shadows. "We're supposed to stay here in the dorm, where we're safe from the quakes." He crossed his arms over his chest and stepped forward, blocking their pathway.

"Look, Hoyt, we don't really have time for a fight right now," Leroy explained as he brushed off his pants. "So go ahead and tell on us. We know you want to."

"Leroy, you've got it all wrong," Albert said.

They had just patched things up with Hoyt—taunting him wasn't going to help keep it that way.

Hoyt apparently felt the same because he let his arms drop to his sides. "Guys, how many times are you going to make me explain myself for my mistake in Ponderay?"

"It's not just that," Leroy said. He took a deep breath

and looked Hoyt in the eyes. "You bullied me, our First Term. All of us, really. Don't you remember that?"

Hoyt's shoulders drooped. He paced back and forth for a second and kicked one of the giant acorns that Cedarfell was famous for. "Look . . . it's always been Hydra in the light, and I've been here my entire life, waiting to go into a Realm and save the day. Then you newbies from the surface come, and suddenly you're the next big thing?" He sighed and ran a hand through his hair. "I screwed up, bad. So many times I can't even keep track anymore. But I've been sitting here, hating myself for it for the past few months while you were gone. And I'm not going to be that way again. I'm sorry . . . okay?"

Leroy scratched his head like a monkey. Petra didn't say anything at all.

"I'm sorry," Hoyt said again. He looked back and forth between Leroy and Albert.

Albert nodded. "It's all good between us, Hoyt. No more apologies needed." He glanced sideways at Leroy, who was quite pointedly staring at his toes. "Leroy?" Albert asked.

Leroy looked up at Albert.

Come on, man, Albert tried to say with his eyes.

Finally, Leroy conceded. "I forgive you, Hoyt. It's over and done."

Hoyt loosed a breath. "Thanks, guys." Then he smiled, as bright as the sun. "You know . . . if you're going out in the halls, then you should probably roll with me. Petra knows the Core pretty well, but I know how to break the rules."

That much was true, Albert knew.

And tonight, maybe it was finally time to let Hoyt take the lead.

He was a master sneaker-outer.

He introduced the boys to side hallways that even Petra didn't know about, tiny dark tunnels that weren't even lit by the sickly green torches.

"How did you find these?" Petra whispered from the back of the group.

"I get bored at night," Hoyt answered from up ahead. "Exploring cures that for me."

The walk to the Main Chamber from Cedarfell usually took about ten minutes. But in just under three, the boys popped out in a hidden hole in the wall behind a statue. *Right* by the mouth of the Main Chamber.

Albert gulped as he saw the bright red numbers of the countdown clock above the door to Belltroll. Just over four days left.

Tussy, Professor Asante's Apprentice, sat before the door with a book in her lap. Her eyes scanned the Main Chamber, searching for anyone out of bed. Or the traitor, probably. *They should have been guarding this door the entire time*, Albert thought. But then again, that could have meant more people disappearing.

Hoyt pulled a tiny copper bird from his pocket. It looked like an origami bird, but when Hoyt tapped it twice on the head, the bird's wings snapped out. Then it soared off of his palm and silently flew into the Main Chamber.

"Get ready," he whispered, and Albert, Leroy, and Petra all nodded their response.

Hoyt leaned out of the dark tunnel, slowly, so Tussy wouldn't see. They all watched as the little copper bird flew past Tussy's head, landing halfway across the Main Chamber near Calderon's door.

"Any second now," Hoyt whispered.

The little bird exploded into a flash of purple flames.

Tussy yelped and leaped up, then sprinted across the cave to investigate.

"Go, go go!" Hoyt hissed.

They all raced in a line, like thieves in the night.

The meeting was in full swing when they got to the Tower.

Leroy, Petra, and Hoyt all pressed together up against the closed door, listening in as best they could. Albert used the power of the Hearing symbol.

The Professors were having a heated argument. Albert's heart sank at what he heard.

"He must stay out of the Realm!" Professor Bigglesby's

voice carried through. "He cannot be trusted!"

Leroy gasped beside Albert. They all leaned in closer, their ears touching the wooden door.

"He's a boy," Professor Asante said next. "He's not an evil mastermind!"

"Why else would they leave a note for him?" Professor Bigglesby snapped back.

"Because they want his Master Tile!" Professor Asante said. "They want to lure him back inside the Realm so they can take it!"

"Albert Flynn is . . ."

"Is *what*?" another voice said. Albert leaned in even closer, straining to hear what his dad was saying. "My son is not working with the traitor, and he never will."

"Festus," Professor Bigglesby said.

Leroy turned to Albert and mouthed, *Festus? Again?*

"Who's that?" Albert whispered to Petra.

"No idea," Petra said. "I've been here my whole life, and I've never heard of that person."

Hoyt shook his head. "I haven't either."

"Festus." Professor Flynn spat out the name. "Festus is long gone. We must look elsewhere."

"Why are you staring at *me* like that?" Professor Bigglesby said. "The boy is your son! Your legacy! We should all be looking at *you*, Bob."

"Your injury seems to have passed," Professor Flynn

said. "I haven't seen you around much. Perhaps you've been in your study composing notes for my son and his friends to find. . . ."

A fist pounded on hard wood. "THAT IS ENOUGH!" Professor Asante shouted. Her voice practically shook the closed door, and all four boys flinched, imagining her standing tall and strong and looking positively terrifying. "We must look at this with sound minds. We cannot let fear get in the way of our trust of one another!"

Albert heard Professor Bigglesby mutter something, but he couldn't make out the words.

"Perhaps this is just what the traitor wants," a new voice chimed in. Trey. "Perhaps we should turn a blind eye. Let the Balance Keepers go back inside and give them something more to help protect them."

"The sword," Professor Flynn said. "It's time to uncover it."

"After all these years?" Professor Asante asked.

"Not with him," Professor Bigglesby said. "Not with . . ."

"Speak ill of my son one more time," Professor Flynn said with a growl, "and I will knock you into—"

Suddenly, Leroy sneezed.

It was a giant, explosive, Troll-sized sneeze, loud enough that his forehead banged against the door.

Oh, no, Albert thought. The boys all froze.

There were hushed whispers from behind the door.

Then, footsteps came their way.

"Run," Hoyt whispered, shoving Albert along. "Hurry!"

They turned and sprinted away into the darkness.

CHAPTER 19

Cave of Fire

This was turning into the longest night ever. The boys spent the rest of it in the Library, poring over books.

But there was nothing to find. No mention of anyone named Festus, or any*thing*, on the off chance that it wasn't actually a person's name.

After they took a short break to slide down the zip line in the front of the Library, Hoyt suggested they go and ask Lucinda about Festus. She'd been there for decades, after all, longer than any of the boys had even been alive. And even though Albert didn't trust the creepy woman, she did seem to have a taste for Core gossip.

But even Lucinda didn't know who Festus was.

"I've never heard of such a person," she said. Kimber

writhed around her, doing his best to escape, his tongue flicking at rapid speeds.

"That's enough of you," she said to him. She'd taken to wrapping a leather leash around his neck so he couldn't slither away. "You're welcome to look through my books as long as you'd like. Perhaps try the Core Family Document? It has the most prominent bloodlines of the Core's history. Professors, Apprentices, Pures, and the most successful of our workers. Back left room in the Library. I won't even charge you to look it over."

She tossed them an old golden key.

They checked the Family Document, a giant painting framed in gold. It was at least two stories tall, so they had to drag a wheeled ladder over to climb high enough to read every spot.

There were hundreds of names dating way, way back to times when the world didn't even have phones or cars.

"Look!" Leroy said. "You're on here, Albert!"

He pointed to a spot farther down the painting, toward the ground. Sure enough, there was Robert Flynn (Pap), Bob Flynn, and at the very bottom, Albert's own name in freshly printed black ink. Someone must have added it a few terms ago, when Albert first came to the Core. There were even a bunch of female Flynn Balance Keepers listed.

"That's pretty cool," Albert said, touching his fingertips

to the massive frame. "But no Festus anywhere on here. So if this guy or girl was here, they weren't a Professor or Apprentice."

"Or a Pure," Hoyt said.

He tapped a little to the left, where the Jackson family line was. And then, beside it on another section, was Petra's family.

"Petra *Prince?*" Leroy said.

Petra's face reddened. "Yeah. It's . . . kinda embarrassing."

"Royal, more like," Leroy said, chuckling. He bowed low to the ground and said, "Prince Petra."

"Knock it off, Jones." Petra swatted Leroy away, but he laughed nevertheless.

They moved on from the Family Document and continued their search. But after an entire night of examining dusty books, family trees, and crumbling documents in the archives section, they couldn't find a single thing on Festus. Albert was sure he'd never heard the name before, but something was tugging at him, from the very back of his mind.

A memory, maybe? He closed his eyes and tried to pull it forth. He even used the Synapse symbol to try and recover it.

Nope. Nothing. Just my mind wanting to make sense of things. He sighed.

"We should try to get some sleep," Hoyt said with a yawn. "We're going back into the Realm in just a few hours."

The three Balance Keepers exchanged wary glances.

"I'll keep looking while you guys are gone," Petra said. "I'll find it, if there's anything to find on this person. I'm good at stuff like that."

"Thanks, Your Highness," Albert said.

"Come *on*, man!" Petra tossed an old book at Albert, and he dodged it with ease, then turned to leave the Library. Petra waved good-bye as they all went to catch up on their sleep.

Another round of quakes came with the morning light.

The warning alarms were blaring by seven a.m., and Albert, Leroy, and Hoyt pulled themselves out of bed, looking like triplet zombies.

They ate a quick breakfast, then shuffled their way to the Main Chamber, ready to take on the Realm again.

The Main Chamber was empty, save for three people standing by the doorway to Belltroll.

Birdie waved hello, and beside her, Professor Flynn and Trey were waiting. To Albert's non-surprise, it looked like his dad still hadn't gotten any sleep. His hair seemed grayer than normal, and the skin beneath his eyes drooped like melted candle wax.

He's never looked so old, Albert thought.

"What's up?" Albert asked when they met in front of one of the winding tunnels. "Came to see us off?" He wanted to tell his dad about last night, how they'd listened in. He wanted to say thanks, to both Trey and his dad, for sticking up for him.

But he didn't want to get his team into trouble for sneaking out.

"You can't go just yet," Professor Flynn said, his voice low. "We have to make a stop somewhere first."

He motioned for Trey to lead the way. After exchanging wary looks with one another, Hydra and Farnsworth followed.

They walked on and on, past doors Albert had entered before, and some he still hadn't. A few doors were hanging on broken hinges, and some of the torches were scattered on the ground, having fallen from their brackets on the wall.

Farther down, a massive chunk of rock had fallen from the ceiling, taking up most of the tunnel. Hydra had to walk single file behind Professor Flynn and Trey, crawling up and over the mess.

They passed by Lake Hall.

The double doors had been chained and locked with double padlocks, and a yellow sign was placed out front.

"Caution, Hot Lava," Leroy read aloud. He groaned, and they moved along.

Everywhere they went, it seemed the Core was

damaged. Cracks had spread their way across the tunnel
floors and walls like spider webs. One was wide enough
that Albert scooped up Farnsworth as they passed by,
just in case the little dog got curious and tumbled in.

Every Core Cleaner was out, trying to repair the damage, but they looked dumbfounded.

"It's useless," one woman said as they passed by. "With
every quake, we take ten steps back."

"I'm totally sick of this traitor thing," Birdie said. "It's
putting everyone on edge."

"I just wish we could have everything go back to
normal," Albert said. What he wouldn't give for a term
without an Imbalance, where he and his friends could
just explore the Core and learn all of its secrets, like Petra
could.

Sadness and fear washed over him each time they saw
more of the Imbalance's effects, and by the time they
were nearly to the end of the tunnel, he felt as if a giant
fist was squeezing his rib cage, pressing in on his lungs,
making it harder and harder to breathe.

This had to end. They had to stop this, once and for
all.

"Where are we going?" Birdie asked.

Professor Flynn turned and put a finger to his lips,
and that was that.

They took a sharp right, heading down a tunnel that
had no torches at all. Farnsworth turned on his eye

beams, lighting the way. This tunnel got smaller and smaller, and goose bumps rose on Albert's arms.

Finally, after walking deeper and deeper, they stopped before an old, crumbling statue of a howling wolf.

"Were we followed?" Professor Flynn whispered.

Farnsworth circled the group, sniffing the ground. When he didn't bark or growl, Professor Flynn nodded and turned to Trey.

"This doesn't need to be said," Trey told the group. "But the secret of this place must be carried to your grave."

Despite the depressing journey here, Albert's body thrummed with nervous excitement. Trey turned, satisfied, and reached his hand into the wolf's open mouth. There must have been a hidden lever or button, because suddenly there was a click, and the statue began to move. Dust fell from the ceiling, and the ground trembled a little as the great wolf slid sideways to reveal a hidden elevator.

"Stand guard," Professor Flynn said, his hand landing on Trey's shoulder.

Trey nodded as the rest of them filed into the elevator. The statue slid back behind them.

Professor Flynn pressed a button, and as the elevator moved downward, Albert began to hear a strange noise. He recognized it, but couldn't place it. A few moments later, the elevator door opened.

They were standing in a cave of fire.

Not fire, Albert thought, and then Birdie finished the thought for him.

"Firefalls," she said, her voice nearly lost in the noise.

Albert stood there, his neck craned back, as he took it all in.

The cave was massive, by far the largest they'd entered since coming to the Core. It spread the length of two football fields, towering even taller, with rocky sides all around. There were holes every twenty feet or so, and liquid fire—that was the only way Albert could think to describe it—spilled out of them like water, cascading into a giant river that ran in a strange, jagged pattern all over the cave floor.

It was like standing in the belly of a live volcano. The falls crackled and popped like massive sparklers on the Fourth of July. Albert stared into the river, at all the shades of the fire. Buttercup yellow, to neon orange, to sunshine golden, to a bubbling, angry, blood red.

"It's incredible, Dad!" Albert said. He practically had to yell to be heard over the roar and crackle of the falls. "How did you find this place?"

"The real question," Leroy called out, after they finally got over the shock of standing in a room full of actual firefalls, "is why aren't we all burning to ashes right now? It's not hot, is it?" He stepped forward, toward the fire river, but Professor Flynn held out an arm.

"It's cool to the touch, but poisonous," Professor Flynn said. "Beautiful but deadly, I'm afraid."

Just like the Realms, Albert thought.

"This," Professor Flynn said as he stood back, with his arms spread wide like a painter showing off his latest work of art, "is the Cave of Fire."

There was a large rock island of sorts sitting in the center of the fire river. Professor Flynn led the group to it over a trail of smaller rock islands. They took their seats on the rock, careful not to get too close to the fire.

"Why are we here?" Albert asked. Again, he was nearly yelling to be heard, but his dad smiled.

"For privacy," Professor Flynn said, leaning in. "This is one of the only places I feel safe discussing the matter at hand."

Albert knew exactly what that matter was.

"The traitor," he said.

Professor Flynn nodded, a grave expression darkening his eyes. "Trey and I have been working around the clock, searching for clues. We've yet to come across anything. It's been quiet, since he or she split the door to Belltroll." He shook his head, like he was disappointed. "Way too quiet."

Albert shifted on the rock. "Do we know for *sure* the traitor has even been inside of Belltroll?"

Professor Flynn inclined his head. "If a Realm goes out of Balance by *natural* causes, it's always evident. We discover the Means, we go inside, and we solve it. Typically, the Core Watchers are able to get that information through their Readers."

Leroy spoke up. "We saw those thingies when we had detention in the Heart of the Core last term."

"Exactly," Professor Flynn said as a red, gold, and yellow bird soared just above his head, its long, flaming tail feathers nearly touching his shoulders.

"Firebird," Professor Flynn explained as he dodged the flaming feathers. "This time, the Core Watchers are baffled, which leads us to believe the traitor has gone inside. With the quakes, it would be hard to get a read on Belltroll's vitals anyway, but again, we think there's someone messing with the Readers. There's a sort of magical damper that's not allowing any of the Watchers' instruments to work right."

"That sounds like Master Tile stuff to me," Hoyt said.

Albert had almost forgotten Hoyt was there. It was still strange to have him on their team. Albert tossed a pebble into the fire river. "You've never been inside Belltroll, have you, Dad?"

Professor Flynn shook his head. "Only once, long ago. But I know enough to know it's a baffling Realm. And though we know about the strikers now, finding them may not be easy."

Birdie pulled her knees to her chest. "What if we're wrong about the replacement strikers? What if all that work was for nothing?"

Just then, the Cave of Fire filled with birdsong.

It was beautiful, but very different from birdsong on the surface, so melancholy it made Albert's very soul ache. He had never heard anything like it.

There were maybe twenty Firebirds, all in shades of red and orange and yellow, their massive wings slicing through the air like living, dancing flames. A single Firebird emerged from the group. It was older, that much Albert knew, and its colors were fading.

Before his eyes, the Firebird's feathers changed from red to a dull, sickly gray as it soared by overhead. It landed in a nest beside a Firefall, high above their heads. The other Firebirds continued their sad song, and Albert couldn't be sure, but he thought he saw Hoyt wipe a tear from his cheek.

Albert watched, and listened, as the old Firebird nestled down and closed its eyes.

Then, suddenly, the birdsong ended. The flock landed on rocks and crags in the cave, little specks of color amid the falls.

The old Firebird let out a single, solitary note. Low and sad and soft. A moment later, it crumbled into a pile of ashes and was gone.

"What the . . . ?!" Leroy said, as Birdie cried out.

Professor Flynn put a hand on Birdie's shoulder. "Watch," he said, pointing.

The Firebirds perched silently for a moment, the roar of the falls the only sound in the cave. Then one bird began to sing.

It was a high note. Hopeful, and happier than the last. Then another bird joined in, and another, until every Firebird was singing, chirping out a symphony of their own making.

They took flight, swarming in a circle, around and around the cave over Albert's head.

"Now," Professor Flynn said. "Pay attention."

Albert stared at the nest where the old Firebird's ashes were. There was a flash, a spark, and suddenly a brightly colored bird burst from the flames. It was small, only a baby, and its feathers were blue and purple and electric green. It shot upward, testing its wings, and its tail feathers unfurled like ribbons.

"Whoa!" Albert and Hoyt said together. The look on Birdie's face said the same thing.

It was Leroy who spoke up. "The Firebird," he said. "You mean, like a phoenix, right? They rise from their own ashes, born again."

"Close," Professor Flynn said. "In the Core, the Firebird takes on new color, and new life, and is stronger every time. It's a sign," he said as they watched the blue bird join in the song, finally soaring on its new wings. "There is always hope in the Core. Always a new beginning, and light after the darkness."

He placed his hand on Albert's shoulder, then looked pointedly at all of Team Hydra.

"You will do better today in Belltroll. You will find the other two strikers and you'll save the Core. I've never doubted your team, and I won't start doubting now."

"How can you be so sure?" Albert asked.

There was a traitor they couldn't find or catch. A Realm they'd already failed in. And the worst Imbalance they'd ever seen.

But his dad's face lit with a grin, and he looked into Albert's emerald eyes.

"The traitor might be strong," he said. "But you four have light, and goodness, in your hearts. That always overcomes the darkness in the end."

Albert held his dad's gaze. Any other time, that line would have sounded super cheesy, but right now, it was just what Albert needed to hear. He could feel his teammates relax a bit, too.

Professor Flynn reached into his jacket and produced a gleaming black short sword, as long as Albert's forearm. It was as black as the Master Tile, like solidified oil.

"The rest of the Core thinks this sword was lost to us, long ago. Not even the Apprentices know of its existence. It was made by the very same substance your Tiles were made from," Professor Flynn said. "It has magic in its very center, just like the Tiles. Like the Core. The Professors and I have decided you need to keep it with you, Albert. The CoreSword may be able to keep you safe when nothing else can."

He held the sword out, handle first.

It shimmered in the light of the firefalls. Albert reached out, his fingertips itching to touch it.

"This is for me?" he asked. He gripped the handle of the sword. It felt like it was made for him, a perfect fit, and strangely lightweight, seemingly made of the same material as his Master Tile. Energy buzzed through his fingertips, and suddenly Albert had a vision of himself holding the sword at the peak of Troll Mountain, facing the traitor. *Winning.*

Why me, though? Albert thought. The question was still tugging at him, though he wasn't sure he wanted to bring it up in front of his friends.

His dad seemed to sense Albert's question, but before he could speak, another quake shook the Core. Albert's instincts took over, and he grabbed his friends' arms. They all held tight, leaning on each other so they wouldn't topple into the fire.

It lasted two minutes, the longest quake they'd faced so far.

When it was over, embers floated down around them like falling stars.

The loudspeaker came on, even here, this deep in the Core.

"Balance Keepers on Team Hydra," Professor Bigglesby's

voice rang through the cave. "Please report to the Main Chamber immediately."

The speaker crackled off, and Albert turned to his friends. Leroy's new hat was on sideways, and Birdie had an ember fizzling out on her shoulder, burning a little hole in her T-shirt. Hoyt was shaken up but actually looking a little more confident than he had been lately.

They all stood and brushed themselves off, and Professor Flynn led them back across the rocks. When they were safely on dry land, Professor Flynn paused and turned to Team Hydra. "Be safe today. You know I'd give anything to be here when you get back, but . . . I have to go to the surface."

"Why?" Hoyt asked. "What's going on up there?"

Professor Flynn's face was grim. "Quakes, same as here. But this morning, part of the Brooklyn Bridge crumbled in New York. And in Dallas, Reunion Tower toppled sideways, destroying half of downtown."

"I live half an hour from there," Leroy said softly, disbelief in his eyes. Hoyt put a hand on his shoulder.

"What about Oregon?" Birdie asked.

"Nothing there," Professor Flynn said. "But the destruction is spreading." He looked at Albert, then back at the group. "Why don't you three start down the tunnel. I'd like a moment with Albert." Birdie, Leroy, and Hoyt nodded and headed back toward Trey.

"It's bad up there, Albert," Professor Flynn said when

they had gone. "I'm going to check on Pap, then go and make sure I get your mom somewhere safe."

"Tell Mom I love her," Albert said. "Tell her thanks. For letting me do this. Make sure she's okay."

His dad chuckled. "She's a tough lady, and Pap's as fierce as he ever was. They probably don't even need my help."

Albert knew his dad was just being positive for his sake.

Professor Flynn laid a large hand on Albert's cheek, the way he used to do when Albert was a little boy. "You're strong, Albert," he said "But even the strongest of us have weaknesses. Don't be afraid to ask for help, should you need it."

Professor Flynn tied an old leather sheath around Albert's waist. The CoreSword hung neatly at his side. Albert felt like a knight from centuries ago.

"If you find the traitor, use this to cut the Master Tiles from the chain around his or her neck."

Albert nodded and stood tall and proud, staring up at his dad.

"Go and find Mom and Pap," he said. "Make sure they stay safe."

"I will. Good luck today," Professor Flynn said. "I love you, kiddo."

"I love you, too, Dad."

Albert turned and ran to catch up with his friends, leaving his dad and the Cave of Fire behind.

The tunnels back to the Main Chamber were full of dust, with new cracks and fallen rocks from the latest quake. As they made it to the Main Chamber and passed by an impatiently waiting Professor Bigglesby, the dwarf looked up and met Albert's eyes.

"Be careful with the sword," Professor Bigglesby said. "Some things are more powerful than you know."

A wicked grin split across his features, spreading his wrinkles out like the cracks in Belltroll. His eyes looked incredibly dark. Darker, even, than the Master Tile.

It chilled Albert to his very core.

CHAPTER 20

The Strikers

The Pegasi were true to their word, and were waiting for the Balance Keepers in the Ring of Entry. Thankfully, Petra had an in with the kitchen staff and came armed with a giant bag of red-and-white peppermints just as Hydra left for Belltroll.

Spyro stamped his hooves as he devoured more peppermints than was healthy, and by the time the rest of the herd had had their fill, Hydra was mounted on their backs and ready to take flight.

"This is like flying first class," Albert said as he held on to Spyro's mane. Hoyt was in back today. The one real striker they had was in Albert's pack, wrapped safely inside.

The replacement strikers were with Birdie and Leroy,

one stuffed in each of their packs. Albert hoped with all his might that these would work. Today, they'd head to the center of the Realm and try to stop this Imbalance once and for all.

"What's first class?" Hoyt asked as he held on to Albert's pack.

Albert laughed. He'd forgotten Hoyt was born and raised in the Core, and wasn't up to speed on surface-world things. "Never mind. You good?"

Hoyt nodded, and Birdie and Leroy each agreed from their Pegasi.

"Spyro! Giddy up!" Albert shouted. He tapped the Pegasus's sides with his heels. "Hi-yah!"

Spyro turned his neck so that one big dark eye focused on Albert. He didn't have to use Creature Speak to know the Pegasus was totally confused.

"I don't think he speaks normal horse, bro," Leroy said from atop his white Pegasus. "And people don't really say 'giddy up.' At least, not real cowboys."

Birdie giggled and Hoyt muffled his laugh behind Albert's shoulder.

"Oh. Right. . . ." Albert nodded and simply pointed in the direction of Troll Mountain, far in the distance beyond a layer of fog.

Spyro's wings shot out of his sides, spreading wide over Albert's and Hoyt's heads.

His herd followed suit, and before they knew it, they

were rocketing into the sky like speeding bullets. Up and up they went, high over the Realm.

Albert looked down at the mess that was Belltroll. Since they were last here, it had taken a serious hit.

The ground was like a big puzzle. There were jagged cracks all over, some of them *way* deeper than they had been yesterday. The moors seemed to be full of more water and less land, like some pieces of land had simply broken off and sunk away.

Spyro banked right, soaring through the clouds, and Albert saw the Trundlespikes down below, scattered on a hillside. A big crack ran through the hill and the giant creatures rolled like bowling balls away from it.

And somehow, the grass looked less green, almost like Belltroll was sick. It was subtle, but the brilliant emerald color didn't hurt Albert's eyes like it had before. Now it was really just plain green, like the grass in Central Park back in New York.

I hope my family is okay up there, Albert thought. *The Brooklyn Bridge. What'll be next to fall?*

"I hope this works!" Hoyt shouted into Albert's ear. "Because that doesn't look good!"

He pointed past Albert's shoulder as Spyro broke through the fog and Troll Mountain came into view.

The cracks that spread out from the base of the mountain were far, far more in number. Albert marveled at how the mountain was still standing with that many cracks around it. They spread out from the mountain's base like fingertips, stretching into the Ring of Emerald.

Troll Mountain had been higher than the other two mountains yesterday. Now it was perfectly even with them, all three standing in a line. How much farther did it have to sink into the ground before it destroyed Belltroll for good?

Spyro whinnied loudly, and the other Pegasi cried back.

The sound was mournful, striking a crack in Albert's heart as wide as the ones scattered across the Realm. It was as if the Pegasus herd noticed the difference, too. Their home was in danger, and Albert could sense Spyro flying faster.

I can't let this break me, Albert told himself. *I have to save the Realm. For the Pegasi. For the Trolls. For the entire world.*

He made a promise in that moment.

He would not be broken like this Realm. He would not let the fear or the anger get to him any longer.

He would not let the traitor win.

Spyro soared around the peak of the leftmost mountain, his wings dancing in the wind and the rest of his herd following behind.

"We'll figure this out," Albert shouted so that everyone could hear. He looked at the Counter on his wrist and noted the time they had left.

Forty hours wasn't much, just under two days.

But it was enough. It had to be.

"So what's the plan?" Hoyt asked. His voice carried over the wind.

"I think we need to plug in the replacement strikers first, and then the real one. Something tells me the real one has to be the final one in place," Birdie suggested.

"She's right," Leroy said. "I mean, when you add up the odds, of course."

"Okay," Albert said. "Let's get moving then."

"Leroy and I will call out when we've hung our replacement strikers," Birdie said, tapping her backpack. "Then you guys plug the real striker in, and it's up to fate. And if that doesn't work, we'll cross our hearts and hope to die."

Leroy looked at Birdie. "You know that statement doesn't really work here, right?" he said. "It's only correctly used when someone's talking about keeping a secret. And can't we lay off the whole *dying* thing?"

"Geez," Birdie said. "It works good enough."

"No way. I have a dictionary, like, *for a brain*," Leroy said back. "Trust me on this one, bro."

Birdie threw a hand up in the air. Even her Pegasus tossed its head like it was bred for sass. "I am not your bro!"

"Bro or not, we should get moving," Albert suggested,

stepping in before they could get too far off track of the mission.

Albert could hear Birdie's and Leroy's bickering as they steered their Pegasi away, leaving Hoyt and him behind.

"Those two," Hoyt said, rubbing the spot between his eyes, "give me the worst headache ever."

"It's kind of nice," Albert said with a grin as he and Hoyt relaxed on Spyro's back. "Their arguing kind of made it less stressful when our teams were competing in the Pit the first two terms."

Hoyt nodded and stared out across the Realm. "We're one team now," he said. "And we'll solve this Imbalance in time."

"Sounds good to me," Albert said.

He hoped that Hoyt was right.

CHAPTER 21

The Great Awakening

The replacement strikers were in place, and Birdie and Leroy's Pegasi carried them back to Troll Mountain only ten minutes after they had left.

Things were moving quickly. *But not quickly enough*, Albert thought.

"You guys ready?" he asked when everyone was back together, their Pegasi hovering in the sky near Troll Mountain.

"Couldn't be any readier," Leroy said.

Birdie and Hoyt both agreed.

Together, Hydra turned toward the Bell. Was it Albert's tired eyes, or was it a little less shiny today, like the dull sheen of a coin kept in someone's pocket for too long?

Albert unzipped his backpack and pulled out the real striker.

"If this doesn't work . . . ," Hoyt said, but stopped when he saw the look on Birdie's face. The striker was beautiful, that was for certain. The Troll markings stood out, ancient and undecipherable on its golden surface. Albert wished, so badly, that he could read what they said. But there wasn't a Tile symbol for that—at least, not yet.

Everyone sat back on their horses to watch as Albert called forth the Float symbol again.

When he dropped sideways off Spyro, there was that same strange feeling of weightlessness, the same glorious feeling that he was doing the impossible.

He imagined himself floating forward, and his Tile responded, sending him slowly across the sky, into the gap of the forked mountaintop beneath the belly of the Bell. From here, he could look up at the underside. There sat the empty hook, just waiting for the striker to be hung back in place.

Albert's hands shook as he lifted the striker and fit it into the hook.

It was such a simple act. But it felt important. It felt like a step toward saving the Core, toward saving the world.

He floated backward, his breath a little lighter in his lungs. "Well, that's that," he said. He looked over his shoulder at his friends. Even the Pegasi were watching, all of them holding their breath in hopes that it had worked.

"Should we hear it?" Birdie asked. "Shouldn't it, like, magically start striking or something?"

Leroy shrugged. "Maybe it's not time for it to strike. Maybe we have to wait a little bit."

Albert nodded, but he felt his strength waning. He floated up to Spyro and settled into place behind Hoyt on the horse's warm back.

Seconds passed. It felt like there was a giant clock ticking in Albert's head. Every moment was one step closer to the Imbalance reaching its splitting point. Every tick was one more tick toward the traitor winning.

"That's it," Hoyt said a minute later. "I can't take this anymore." He urged Spyro forward and reached out and gave the Bell a little shove.

Albert squeezed his eyes shut, expecting a giant *RING!* to explode in his ears. But all they heard was the sound of the wind blowing across the mountaintop, and the faraway rumble of the Trolls' snores beneath their feet. Spyro flew back a few feet to give them some distance from the Bell.

"I keep feeling like we're missing something," Albert said.

"Try to use your Tile," Leroy suggested. "Supersonic Hearing?"

Albert focused, bringing the image of the hearing

symbol into the front of his mind. It picked up every single sound and frequency, even the supersoft ones, like a predator stalking the heartbeat of its prey.

There were a *lot* of sounds. Hoyt, scratching his head as loudly as someone scratching sandpaper. The Pegasi's powerful wings, flapping as they held the Balance Keepers in the sky. The Trolls, snoring as loud as motorcycles far beneath them. He even heard the anxious pounding of Birdie's heart.

But there was no ringing. No sound of the striker doing anything different to the Bell.

Albert shook his head, clearing the symbol from his mind. "Maybe we didn't hang it right. . . ."

He leaned out to get a closer look, and as he did, something fell out of his pocket. Hoyt caught it just before it tumbled into the open sky.

It was the red gem that they'd found on the first day in the Realm, in the moors.

"You still have that?" Birdie asked. "Why'd you bring it with you?"

Albert nodded. "It felt weird not bringing it here. But I still don't know what it's for."

"Weird Troll mojo, probably," Hoyt said, holding the gem up so that it shone in the daylight.

Leroy suddenly snapped his fingers. "Let me see the gem," he said.

Hoyt tossed it to him, and Leroy turned it round and

round in his palm. His eyes lit up.

"I can't believe I'm asking this, but . . . Albert, can you take me to the Bell?"

Albert nodded slowly. "If I concentrate. . . ."

"Let's go, then," Leroy said. "Before I change my mind."

It was double the concentration, and double the nerves, now that Leroy's life was on the line. But Albert mustered up the strength of the Float Tile and the Weightlessness Tile and merged them together.

"If you let go of my hand, you'll fall and die," Albert said as he helped Leroy down from his Pegasus.

"Oh, that's encouraging," Leroy said.

But he put on a brave face and grasped Albert's hand hard.

Together, they floated into the small gap between the Bell and the mountain's two sides. Albert's mind throbbed from the effort.

"We're literally flying, dude!" Leroy said, his voice trembling.

"Albert Flynn, if you drop our best friend I will pummel you!" Birdie shouted from her Pegasus.

They reached the underside of the Bell. Before Albert could stop him, Leroy reached up and removed the striker from its hook.

"What are you doing?" Hoyt shouted. "You could have messed with the system!"

"Just hang on," Leroy said, his voice echoing in the giant bell. Albert floated them backward a few feet.

"I can't believe I didn't think about this before," Leroy said as he held out the striker with his free hand. "Look at this!" The striker had an empty octagon-shaped hole on the end that hit the bell. Albert had assumed that was just the way it was shaped, like maybe the hole helped the ringing hit the right vibration and pitch. He wasn't an expert on bell strikers.

Leroy went on, voice rising with excitement. "It's just like in the Pit, how we had to match Tiles with their correct pillars? Only this," he said, holding up the striker, "is matching the *gem* to its striker! Here, hold this."

Leroy passed Albert the striker and then pulled the gem out of his pocket. All the while he kept on iron grip on Albert's hand.

Albert's eyes widened as Leroy held up the gem. Slowly, Leroy pressed it to the end of the striker.

It fit perfectly, like the two were made for each other.

It was magic. In an instant, the gem lit up as if set on fire from within. More Troll symbols appeared all over its facets, ones that definitely hadn't been there before.

"That's *it*," Birdie gasped from her Pegasus. "Memory Boy, you're a genius!"

Leroy grinned. "Plug it back in," he said to Albert.

"No way," Albert said. "You do the honors. You figured it out!"

He floated them back to the underside of the Bell.

Leroy beamed.

They all held their breath as Leroy hung the striker back up. Albert crossed his fingers and begged it to work. When the striker was safely in place, he floated them quickly away, out of range of the Bell and back to their Pegasi.

It was almost too perfect, how quickly the striker began to move! Back and forth, it struck against the sides of the Bell. There was no sound.

"Use your Tile and listen." Hoyt nudged Albert when he landed beside him again on Spyro. "See if it worked!"

Albert's whole body buzzed with anticipation as he conjured the image of Supersonic Hearing.

And his head almost exploded from the sound.

He yelped, clapping his hands to his ears. It was horrible, the effort it took to force the Tile symbol away.

But when the ringing faded, and Albert looked up, there was a massive grin on his face.

"It's ringing," he said. "It's time for the Trolls to wake up."

CHAPTER 22

The Trolls of Belltroll

Theywaited, their hearts pounding in time with the Bells of Belltroll.

But the Trolls didn't wake.

Hydra had been sitting for five minutes already. The horses' wings were getting tired and Albert's mind was doing that strange warning thing again, repeating the same two thoughts over and over.

It didn't work. You let the traitor win.

The one golden Bell, with the one real striker and gem, was ringing on a constant loop that only Albert, with his Tile, could hear.

The others were ringing, too. But something was still missing.

There was no *Realm-ish* magic to it.

Leroy sighed and turned to his friends. "My suspicions are correct, I believe," he said.

Everyone turned to look at him. His Pegasus tilted its ears back, like it was listening, too.

He went on. "We've missed the golden ticket, dudes. *The Realm always provides the Means to Restore Balance.*" When nobody seemed to catch on, he held his arms out. "The *Realm!* Not us. The only Bell that Albert can hear is the one with the gem and the striker the traitor gave us! Our replacement ones aren't doing anything."

"He's right," Albert said.

Leroy spit over his Pegasus's side, into the abyss below.

"If he's right," Hoyt said, his arms crossed over his chest, "then why have the Trolls stopped snoring?"

The rest of Hydra whirled around to stare at him just as the mountain trembled.

This wasn't a quake, though. There was a strange, heavy *boom . . . boom . . . boom*, like in a movie Albert had once seen about giant dinosaurs attacking a city. From far away, each footstep rumbled the ground like an explosion.

"It's the Trolls," Albert said. "It has to be."

"They're up!" Hoyt shouted.

"Oh, man," Leroy said. "Oh man oh man oh man. This isn't good."

"Why not?" Birdie cried out. "They're waking up! This is what we wanted to happen."

"Not like this," Leroy groaned, pointing at the base of the mountain just as a giant, wart-covered Troll stepped out into the light. "There was only one color Professor Bigglesby said wasn't okay."

"And remind us what that was?" Hoyt said.

Albert, Birdie, and Hoyt all turned to look at Leroy right as a second Troll, and then a third, came stomping out of the middle mountain.

All of them were the same color.

"Green," Leroy said, unable to tear his eyes away from the massive beasts below. "The bad color was green."

He barely got the words out before the three green Trolls raised their heads and let loose angry roars that could have knocked a Guildacker from the sky.

The Realm was a punching bag, and the Trolls were furious enough to use it.

Their fists were the size of boulders, their feet twice the size of that. They were even worse than Bigglesby had described them to be.

The Trolls probably could have kept a T. rex for a pet and made them look as small as toy poodles when they stood side by side.

"What have we done?" Hoyt was saying over and over. He had his hands pressed over his eyes. "We did something wrong!"

Troll Mountain spun on its axis, deeper and deeper

into the ground. With every furious stomp the Trolls made, their fists took out trees like they were little toothpicks. The mountain seemed to spin faster.

And the cracks in the Realm got deeper.

"We woke them up," Birdie growled. "That's the best anyone's done so far!"

"We're gonna die!" Leroy howled like Farnsworth.

"Be quiet!" Albert said.

He angled Spyro into the shadow of the mountain, and the other Pegasi followed just in time. One of the Trolls turned his ugly head and looked up at the spot Hydra had just been flying in.

He was darker than the other two, and at least ten feet taller.

And something told Albert that a darker green meant an angrier Troll.

The Troll bashed his fist into the ground, creating a fissure that lightning-bolted across the meadow and into the trees, knocking a cluster of them down.

He lifted his head and roared, and the other Trolls beat their chests with their fists.

"Tarzan Trolls!" Leroy whimpered. "It's even worse than I suspected."

"Oh man oh man oh man." Hoyt shook like a Chihuahua.

"Chill out, you two!" Birdie said.

Albert's mind was racing. "One Bell worked enough to wake them up. But if they're up, what made them this way?"

"Who knows! It's not like we've got a handbook on Trolls," Hoyt said, poking his head out of the shadows to watch as the Trolls stomped away, heading for the Ring of Emerald.

"The traitor planned this," Leroy said, his hands balling into fists.

"Duh." Albert glanced sideways at him. Leroy was pumped up.

"This guy or girl is obviously smart," Leroy explained. Albert could see trees flying in the distance as the Trolls bashed them out of their path. "Why else do you think the traitor just *gave* us a perfectly good striker? Not two or three, but one?"

Albert, Birdie, and Hoyt stood there silently, clearly not understanding where Leroy was going with this.

He spread his hands through his hair, and it was sticking upward like he was a crazy professor as he shouted, "Because he knew what would happen if we only used *one* striker, meaning only *one* Bell would be ringing at the right frequency!"

"But the replacements are ringing too," Hoyt added.

"Not in the same way," Albert said, finally starting to understand.

Leroy nodded furiously. "What if all three Bells have to ring together, at the same frequency? What if that magical red stone thing—"

"Gem," Birdie corrected him.

"Gem," Leroy said, nodding her way. "We know the Realm provides the Means, and the Realm provided those strikers and those gems hundreds of years ago! We just came in here, thinking we could replicate magic that powerful!"

"Which isn't possible," Birdie said. She slapped herself across the forehead. "How could we be so stupid?"

Albert shook his head. "Not stupid," he said. "Desperate."

"Uh, guys?" Hoyt tapped Albert on the shoulder.

Albert turned to look at him and saw how pale Hoyt's face had become.

"We should probably stop them before they get too far. Because . . . well, there's only one way out of here," Hoyt said. "And they're heading straight for the exit."

The Core. Albert's head was pounding with fear and adrenaline, and his stomach was flipping and turning itself into one big knot. The mountain was still spinning and spinning, sinking deeper toward the tectonic plates that could rumble this Realm to nothing but flecks of mountain dust.

If something as old and well-constructed as the Brooklyn Bridge had collapsed because of the quakes, what would happen to the rest of New York City if the Imbalance wasn't stopped?

What would happen to every city, in every state, in every *country*?

The chaos would be unstoppable.

Leroy let out a little crazy laugh, bringing Albert's imagination back to reality. "How are four kids supposed to stop three furious Trolls?"

"Four *Balance Keepers*," Birdie said.

"And one of them has the Master Tile," Hoyt added.

They all turned to Albert, eyes wide, but for once, he had completely drawn a blank.

They weren't heroes, and they certainly weren't Troll wranglers. Heck, Albert could barely hang on to a Pegasus, and that wasn't exactly impressive. . . .

"A Pegasus," Albert said suddenly as an idea came to life in his mind. "A horse. With *wings*. For *flying*."

"Oh, poop on a pecan pie," Leroy said. "He's lost his mind. He's gone mad! Quick, Birdie, knock him over the head before he turns on us."

"He isn't a zombie, you dodo!" Birdie yelped. "He's just . . . oh, goodness, I'm with you. He really has lost it!"

But Albert could barely hear them. He hadn't lost his mind.

Well, maybe a little bit, with the plan he was forming. But there was a method to his madness. And there was a tiny vial, packed safely away in his backpack, and two more, packed away with his friends.

"We're going to take them down," Albert said, swinging his backpack around to the front. He unzipped it and pulled out the strange vial of lavender liquid that Petra had brewed up for them. He held it above his head and smiled as he thought of how crazy this was. *Thanks for this, Petra.* When he saw the looks on his teammates' faces, he knew they were catching on. "We're going to need some help from our flying friends, and we're going to have to move quick."

"What are you planning?" Hoyt asked. "Fill us in."

Hydra and their Pegasi huddled together over the mountaintop, beside the Bell that had caused this new, angry problem.

When they were done, and everyone was on board, they pulled out their purple vials and tucked them into their front vest pockets. Birdie and Leroy each had one. Albert and Hoyt kept the third.

"We get one shot," Albert said. "We can't screw it up."

"Wouldn't dream of it," Birdie said, tightening her ponytail. Now she was ready. Determined.

Leroy sat a little taller atop his horse, and Hoyt puffed up his chest.

"Team Hydra," Albert said. "Like the old days. But stronger."

Hoyt smiled and stacked his hand on top of Albert's.

Birdie leaned out and placed her hand on top, and then Leroy did right after.

"Team Hydra!" they all shouted, together, like one voice.

One team.

Then Albert turned, harnessed the power of his Master Tile, and told the Pegasi his plan.

CHAPTER 23

For Petra

Albert didn't have to work hard to convince the Pegasi to help. The horses had seen the Trolls of Belltroll. Now their dark eyes were open wide, and their neighs echoed across the sky like a battle cry.

It was decided without speaking.

Together, Hydra and the Pegasus herd would become an army, their sole mission to save the Realm.

Albert was too distracted to notice that the Counter on his wrist had suddenly, strangely, dropped from thirty-nine hours . . . to just one.

The Pegasi were like black and white rockets, their giant feathery wings tucked in close to their bodies as they careened down toward the ground.

Albert felt like a pilot riding a fighter jet. He pressed low to Spyro's neck, clutching on to the thick, silky mane. Behind him, Hoyt shouted in Albert's ear to slow down.

But neither Spyro nor Albert were going to listen to that. Today, they were on a mission.

Faster and faster Spyro and his herd flew. Albert was sure they were going at a speed that only magic could produce. He wasn't sure he'd ever get over his awe at the things the Realms could do.

The mountains faded away, and the Ring of Emerald sped by beneath Albert's feet in flashes of green. Albert's Master Tile flapped in the wind, the only thing darker than Spyro's coat.

"What happens if we miss?" Hoyt shouted into Albert's ear.

Albert shook his head. "We die."

"That's encouraging!" Hoyt shouted back.

They were silent until Spyro's wings rose high, bringing them to a sudden halt in midair. Albert's face smacked against Spyro's neck, and the wind was knocked out of him. But Spyro was hovering just on the edge of the Ring of Emerald, high in the clouds so the Trolls wouldn't see.

The other two Pegasi followed, gently flapping their wings as they stopped beside Spyro. Birdie and Leroy both looked like they'd been spat out of a wind tunnel.

"You guys good?" Albert asked. "You ready?"

Leroy patted his horse's pearly neck. "Definitely not ready how the dictionary defines it, but something like that, yeah."

Birdie looked like she was going to say something to him, but thought better of it. "We'll stop them, you guys. We've *totally* got this."

Albert turned to look at Hoyt. Hoyt patted his vest pocket gently, where the very top of the purple vial from Petra was just poking out.

For one moment, Albert closed his eyes and let the wind dance across his skin. The beat of Spyro's wings was constant and steady.

Down below, Albert could just barely make out the Trolls, three ugly bald heads bobbing as they stomped about.

"Remember. We need to lure them back toward the mountain," Albert said. "Do whatever you have to do to get them to follow you. Then we'll make them angry enough to roar, and once their mouths are wide open, we'll throw the potions in, putting them all back to sleep. We'll find the strikers, wake up the Trolls the *right* way, and solve this Imbalance for good."

We've got almost two days left, Albert thought.

They could do this. They would do this. There was no other choice.

"I call dibs on *not* tucking them in," Leroy said.

Albert let out one booming laugh. Leave it to Leroy

to make a joke in the final moments before what felt like the biggest battle of Albert's life. The warmth of the laugh gave him renewed energy. He dug his heels into Spyro's sides, and the Pegasus rocketed toward the earth.

Albert and Hoyt held tight. It was like the wildest roller-coaster drop of Albert's life. The wind was screaming in his ears, but he could still make out Leroy's shouts from across the sky.

"WE'RE NOT GONNA MAKE IT!"

He pushed all thoughts from his mind and focused.

Three Trolls, three Pegasi, and three bottles of Petra's potion left.

"Here we go!" Albert shouted, and he felt Hoyt's body tense behind him as Spyro rocketed past the first Troll's giant head.

The smell alone was nauseating. It was like that time his little half brother left an egg sandwich in the back of his mom's hot car for three days.

Focus, Albert told himself. It was what his dad would say.

Spyro's wings flapped, pulling them right in front of the Troll's face. The Troll roared as he noticed the Pegasus and lifted a giant, boulder-sized fist to smash them.

"Dive!" Albert shouted, but Spyro didn't need any orders.

The horse tucked his wings tight to his sides, and suddenly they were speeding down, soaring in between the

Troll's legs, and then back out behind him.

The Troll roared furiously, the sound vibrating through Albert's chest. Then he turned around, his steps like two massive drumbeats, and followed the Pegasus like a cat chasing a mouse.

"It's working!" Hoyt shouted.

Albert threw his hands in the air and cheered.

But then the Troll picked up speed.

"Uh-oh," Hoyt said, wrapping his arms tighter around Albert's middle as Spyro flapped his wings faster. "It's *really* working! Too well!"

Leroy's Pegasus soared past. "IT HAD TO BE TROLLS, DIDN'T IT?!"

Birdie swooped by, too, whooping and hollering at the top of her lungs.

Spyro flew at top speed, his hooves only feet above the grass. The Troll roared from behind them as it swiped with its fists, blasting Albert's and Hoyt's heads with rotten air.

"FASTER!" Hoyt yelped. "He's gaining on us!"

"I don't think we can go any faster!" Albert yelled. He looked backward, and his eyes nearly fell from their sockets. A giant fist was inches away from Spyro's tail. He tried to reach down for his CoreSword, but Spyro suddenly banked left, and Albert nearly flew off. He gripped Spyro's mane, and he and Hoyt screamed as the Pegasus zigzagged like a rat in a maze.

But they were already halfway across the Ring of Emerald, leading their Troll back away from the Core, back to where he belonged.

He saw flashes of Birdie and Leroy on their separate Pegasi, dipping and diving. Troll fists swung about, trying desperately to grab them as they all avoided capture.

It was a furious dance.

One Pegasus soaring left, a Troll chasing after it.

Another Pegasus flying to the right, and a second Troll beating his fists against his chest in a show of outrage.

They were angry, all right. But they were following, and that was all Team Hydra wanted.

"The Hulk has nothing on these guys!" Albert shouted.

"The *who*?" Hoyt shouted back.

They both ducked their heads as a Troll's green fingertips just barely flitted past them, inches from plucking the Balance Keepers off Spyro's back.

"Look out!" Hoyt shouted.

Spyro pulled up, just as a second Troll lunged for his tail. His hooves kicked off the Troll's warty hand, propelling them out of the way just in time. They flew over his shoulder, heading back up into the sky, just out of the Troll's reach.

"We need to do this now!" Hoyt shouted. He pointed at the ground.

They were just at the edge of the Ring of Emerald, reaching the forest. The mountain range was ahead.

As Albert looked down and back at where they'd come from, despair struck him. The Ring of Emerald was destroyed.

Massive Troll footprints, like crash sites for meteorites, left scars on the ground. With every step, there was another crack jutting out in the grass, and Albert could see from here that the entire Realm was shaking angrily. Even the Trolls looked like they were uneasy on their feet from all the quaking.

In the distance, there was an earsplitting grinding noise. Troll Mountain was getting closer and closer to sinking so deep that any kind of recovery would be out of the question.

Below, a blur of green caught Albert's eye. He turned just in time to see one of the Trolls clip Birdie's Pegasus with its ugly fingernail.

"No!" Albert shouted. "Birdie!" The Pegasus's screech pierced Albert's ears. He saw a slash of red on its white side as it soared past, carrying itself and Birdie to safety.

Spyro reared, his hooves pawing the air. He let out a bellowing neigh, that of a leader pressing his team onward.

The Trolls arrived, angry and ugly and ready to destroy the world.

But Hydra wouldn't let them.

Albert reached backward, and Hoyt placed the purple vial into his palm.

"It's go time," Albert said. *Thanks, Petra. You're a life-saver.*

He tapped his heels. Spyro turned to face the Trolls, and Albert pulled forth the Tile symbol that seemed like it was invented for this moment.

Aimtrue.

CHAPTER 24

The End, End

Last term, in Ponderay, Albert had used his sense of aim to help save the day on top of the Ten Pillars.

This term, it wouldn't be quite so easy. Because while the Pillars moved, they stayed on a relatively predictable path. Circles could only rotate in one direction or the other.

Trolls were a different story, capable of thinking for themselves.

Hydra flew together like an army, a solid line of Balance Keepers and Pegasi. The winged horses had their ears flat back on their heads, ready to move like the wind.

"Ready?" Albert called out, using Amplify to make his voice seem as if it were coming through the Mega-Horn.

"READY!" his teammates called back in unison. The Trolls were bounding toward the mountain range.

"Let's go!" The Pegasi shot forward in formation. They were eighty yards from the mountain.

Seventy.

Sixty.

Fifty. They closed in with every flap of the Pegasi's wings.

The Trolls' eyes widened, their massive tree-trunk-sized fingertips stretching to grab ahold of the team.

"Albert, now!" Hoyt shouted in his ear.

Albert squeezed Spyro's sides, two fast pumps, and the Pegasus shot ahead, using the strength and speed that only a leader could have. But it wasn't fast enough.

They had to be a rocket, or they'd get caught in the Troll's fist.

They had to be a blur of black in the sky.

Albert closed his eyes, pulling on the strength of his Master Tile. He'd done this before, in Calderon, and today, with Leroy. But Spyro was massive.

I can do this, Albert thought. *I have to be able to do this.*

He pictured the Merge symbol, imagined Hoyt's Speed Tile alongside it, and as Albert's hands gripped Spyro's mane so hard his fingers went white, he felt the power surge from him into the Pegasus. It was like Albert and Spyro were one.

A blast of wind, a beat of the Pegasus's wings, and

they rocketed ahead, leaving Birdie and Leroy behind with their vials clutched in their fists.

One shot, Albert thought. *We get one shot.*

They were so close now.

Albert was about to tell Spyro what to do, but the Pegasus seemed to sense it. His entire body tensed, and suddenly he was flying straight toward the first Troll's feet. Then, using the speed from Albert's Tile, Spyro *ran* up the Troll's body, over his pudgy stomach, up toward his face.

His hooves went *pound pound pound*, and the Troll opened his mouth, fury and pain raging out.

Then came the roar.

It was explosive. Albert wanted to close his ears and hide away, but he looked back, past Hoyt's shoulder, and shouted "NOW!"

Birdie came in like a Guildacker, all fire and fury. Her Pegasus swept upward, using a fresh draft of wind to lay on the speed.

"FOR BELLTROLL!" Birdie shouted.

It was a beautiful sight, Birdie uncorking the vial with her teeth and spitting the cork into the wind. Her Pegasus soared right over the open mouth of the roaring Troll, and she launched the vial right into the Troll's screaming mouth.

It was a perfect shot.

Down it went, disappearing in a flash. Birdie's Pegasus

sped into the clouds, soaring to safety.

The effect was nearly instantaneous. The Troll swallowed, let out a massive, stinking belch, and then dropped like a swatted fly and landed on the ground facedown. The grass swayed around it, and then, for a moment, time seemed to freeze.

It worked, Albert thought. *It actually worked!*

Then Leroy was shouting, "Go, go, go!" and everything suddenly sped up again.

"One down!" Hoyt shouted. "Two to go! Let's move, boys!"

Spyro responded to the sound of victory, and again, Albert lent his Pegasus the Speed of his Master Tile.

Spyro sprint-flew up the side of the second Troll, and as soon as it was angry enough to release an air-bending roar, Leroy arrived.

He was like a cowboy out of the old West, his dark hair waving in the wind. He uncorked the vial, and as his Pegasus soared close, Leroy shouted, "SAYONARA, DUDE!" and let the vial fly.

"SCORE!" Hoyt pumped both fists in the air.

Leroy soared away, and then they were faced with the final Troll.

The biggest Troll.

And by the looks of his dark leaf-green skin, he was the angriest.

Albert's head was pounding, his body exhausted from

all the Tile symbols he was using. He thanked the adrenaline coursing through his body—it was the only thing keeping him alert right now.

Still, everything was going according to plan. The Trolls were going down. They would find the other two strikers and get this Imbalance fixed before it was too late. They'd been this close to the splitting point before, in both Calderon and Ponderay. They could do it in Belltroll, too, and come out on top, traitor or not.

"Let's ride!" Albert shouted. Hoyt let out an exuberant cry.

Albert engaged the Speed Tile and Spyro began sprint-flying up the front of the Troll. The giant beast's roar came out even louder than the other two. They'd sprint-fly up and over the Troll's head in just a few moments. They had agreed to toss the vial when they were at the very top of the Troll's head and it was almost time.

"You ready?" Hoyt shouted. He leaned past Albert and placed the vial into his hands. "You do it! I'm not going to screw this up like last term!"

"You sure?" Albert shouted back.

Hoyt nodded.

Albert's mind pulsed, buzzed, and he was starting to see spots in his vision. Spyro was still moving incredibly fast; he wasn't sure he'd be able to toss the vial correctly at this speed. But he had to do this, use one last Tile to bring down this Troll.

Two at once took practice.

But Albert wasn't sure if three at once could be done.

He pulled forth the symbol for Aimtrue, like a perfect crosshair target.

He focused on seeing the Speed symbol, Aimtrue, and Merge as *one* image, all of them mixing together. His mind screamed with the effort, but Albert held on. He had to be stronger than this. He had to *win.*

Spyro carried them up and over, but as Albert got ready to throw, Hoyt suddenly cried out.

The Troll wasn't as stupid as it looked, because suddenly it lifted a fist. And *swung.*

There was a horrible screech from Spyro, and Albert saw a flash of long black feathers float past his eyes. The Troll had clipped Spyro's wing!

They were going down, spiraling toward the ground too fast.

"THROW IT!" Hoyt shouted to Albert. But Aimtrue slipped away as another Tile symbol took its place.

Float.

Albert latched onto it with every ounce of strength he had, crying out as his head pulsed like a dagger was ripping through his skull. Spyro floated, keeping them in the air thanks to Albert's Master Tile.

"NOW!" Hoyt shouted.

Albert lifted one arm while the other held on to Spyro for dear life. The Pegasus flapped with one good wing, dipping them sideways over the Troll's open mouth.

Albert launched the vial and it tumbled down, down, down.

It slipped between the Troll's teeth . . . and landed on its outstretched tongue.

Hoyt screamed "YES!" as the Troll fell to the ground.

Albert's vision dimmed. He felt Spyro spiraling toward the ground and then a hard thump as they landed in a heap. His vision came back into focus as the Tile symbols faded from his mind.

Birdie and Leroy landed beside them, cheering.

But something was wrong. Albert's Counter was blinking bright red.

THIRTY SECONDS.

"No," Albert whispered. "No, it . . . WHAT?!"

"What is it, Albert?" Birdie asked.

Leroy started dismounting, but Albert said, "Stay on your Pegasus!"

"What's wrong?" Hoyt asked, behind Albert.

He lifted his wrist. The seconds on the Counter ticked down.

"That's not right," Birdie said. Her voice rose in pitch. "We had . . . we had over a day! I saw it! Right, Leroy?"

Leroy was staring at Troll Mountain. It was spinning faster than before, just a blur. The ground began to shake so badly that the Pegasi screeched and leaped into the sky.

Spyro fought to stay afloat and Albert wished so desperately that he could concentrate to help Spyro out, but he was confused. The Counter had to be wrong, didn't it?

Albert's heart stopped cold in his chest as Troll Mountain itself roared in fury. Then, in one swift motion, over half of it sunk into the ground. A giant *CRACK!* rang out.

The Counter hit zero.

A fault line crept out from the base of the mountain. Trees cracked in half as the Realm literally opened up and split in *two*. A giant dark gap was spreading toward Hydra.

"Fly!" Hoyt shouted. "Everyone, FLY!"

The sky seemed to split and Albert could hardly believe what he saw—a funnel of darkness was spiraling up into the surface world. Maybe his eyes were still playing tricks on him.

Albert barely had enough strength to hold on as Spyro carried him back toward the Core. There was one thought in Albert's mind as the Realm of Belltroll sunk into chaos.

They had failed.

The world was going to die.

CHAPTER 25

The Fight for the Core

The tunnel was as dark as the traitor's soul.

Hydra stood just inside, watching the Realm tear itself apart. The Pegasus herd stood with them, stamping their hooves in the tunnel, crying out as their home slowly fell to pieces. Albert knew they should be on their way back to the Core—they had done all they could here—but he couldn't look away from the destruction in front of them.

"We tried," Birdie whispered as she grabbed Albert's hand.

He held on like it was an anchor.

"We tried, yes," Albert said. "But we failed." He stared at the Counter on his wrist. "You all saw it, right? You all saw we had time."

Was he going crazy?

Everyone looked at Leroy. He rubbed his forehead. "We had thirty-nine hours, bro," Leroy said. "I know we did. My Tile doesn't lie."

"But someone does," Hoyt said, finally speaking up. He was just a shadow in the darkness, leaning back against Spyro's muscular side. "Lucinda. She gave you the Counter. She did something to it, to make us think we had enough time, and probably to the countdown clock in the Main Chamber, too."

Birdie gasped. "He's right!" Her hand squeezed Albert's so hard he almost cried out. "Last term in Ponderay, the Counter was perfect, down to the last second of time. Same with the countdown clock in the Main Chamber."

Leroy nodded. "What if Lucinda bewitched it, or something like that, using her Book of Bad Tiles? If she's the traitor, there's no telling how much power she has with both Master Tiles and that book!"

"But what about Bigglesby?" Hoyt said. "He's the one who gave us the map. He probably hoped it would confuse us and make us think we were still safe. He's the one who knew we'd be out in the middle of the Realm trying to find the strikers. We almost *died*! Maybe Lucinda and Bigglesby are working together. With his fake injury, it gives him plenty of time to be in the Core with her, plotting our deaths, without people suspecting him."

"And your dad doesn't trust the dwarf, so why should we?" Leroy said.

"He's always staring at my Tile," Albert added. "It's like he's hungry for it, and I can't explain it, guys, but I just have this awful feeling that it's him. Yesterday, after my dad gave me the CoreSword, Bigglesby said something really weird to me. Every time he's around, it just feels like . . . we can't trust him."

"He helped us with the fake strikers, though," Birdie said. "Maybe we're wrong."

Leroy wasn't buying it. "He helped us with those so he could lead us in the direction he wanted us to go. He knew putting in those fake strikers would cause the Trolls to wake up and go all psycho on us."

Albert covered his face, unable to look at the Realm anymore. Unwilling to accept the failure before them. The Counter felt heavy on his wrist. He wanted to rip it off and throw it back into Belltroll. But he couldn't, he realized. It was evidence.

He turned and stared into the darkness of the tunnel. There was no telling what would be happening in the Core when they arrived.

"It's time to go back," Albert said. "We're going to find Professor Bigglesby and Lucinda and stop them. They won't get away with this."

"Which one's the traitor?" Birdie asked.

"It doesn't matter," Albert said. "They both have to be stopped."

Nobody said a word. The Pegasus herd stood there, staring out at their Realm with sadness in their big, dark eyes.

"I'm sorry," Albert heard Birdie tell them.

He turned away, a horrible sadness ripping through him as he left the crumbling Realm behind.

His hands lingered on the top of the CoreSword at his hip. It reminded him that this Imbalance wasn't the only issue. Soon, he would use it to cut the two Master Tiles from the traitor's cord.

And when it comes to that, Albert thought, *I'll do what I didn't do here.*

I'll win.

By the time they reached the halfway point in the tunnel, Albert's boots were soaked through. The stream was tiny, but it did not belong.

"This isn't good," Leroy said as he waded through the water behind Albert.

The closer they got to the Core, the deeper the water became. It rose past the soles of their boots, soaking through their socks. Up past their knees, heading toward their waists.

And suddenly, it was an effort to keep moving forward.

It was a river, flowing in the darkness.

"What's it from?" Birdie asked.

Albert was about to answer when a light shone from up ahead, cutting through the darkness like a sword.

And with the light, there were shouts.

Screams.

"It's coming from the Core!" Hoyt shouted from behind.

They waded through the water as fast as they could, their thighs burning from the effort. Albert stopped cold the second he saw the entrance to the Core. Birdie, Leroy, and Hoyt all slammed up against his back, pressed together like an accordion.

The door to Belltroll was blown from its hinges, and the stream of water that normally stopped at Belltroll's door poured through like a waterfall, heavy and angry.

But that was nothing compared to the scene on the other side.

The Main Chamber was full of Core creatures, and *not* the companion kind.

Hexabons swung from the giant copper chandelier, screeching and pounding their six arms against their hairy chests. Core workers were dodging flying poison spit by Hissengores slithering across the floor. Albert could see flashes of Lightning Rays' electric skin glowing beneath the water, too. Poison Toads burped and flicked their tongues as other Balance Keepers sprinted past.

He hoped his fellow Balance Keepers knew enough to stay out of the creatures' way. From the looks of it, nobody in the Core knew quite what to do.

Leroy came up beside Albert. "Dude," he said. "We screwed up bad."

As they watched their Professors and Apprentices, Balance Keepers and Core workers fight against an army of angry creatures from *every* Realm, Albert knew Leroy was right.

There was nothing to do but press on into the fight.

CHAPTER 26

Petra's Secret

It was a massacre. Albert should have rushed in, but his feet seemed frozen in place.

"How did this happen?" Birdie screamed. There was so much noise her voice hardly broke through it all.

"The Imbalance!" Leroy shouted, water dripping from his face, as he'd just dodged an angry Lightning Ray that should *not* have been in the Core.

Suddenly there was a flash of dark blue in the water, and Hoyt shouted, "HAMMERFIN!"

It was enough to get Albert moving. They all scrambled to the dry edge of the river as a Hammerfin swam past, its tail thrashing and its hammer-shaped nose ready to bash anything in its path. Suddenly the CoreFish came out of nowhere and slammed into the Hammerfin.

A huge wave erupted, soaking Hydra.

Albert turned in circles, dread forming a tight knot in his throat. The door to Calderon wasn't just open. It had been *blasted* apart, by fire.

By a creature he'd faced before.

"King Firefly!" Birdie shouted.

Sure enough, two of them came buzzing through the smoldering doorway, shooting fire like giant spitwads as Balance Keepers dashed about trying to avoid the flames. Slink and Mo were in the group, shouting commands to others, trying to help them gain some sort of upper hand. But everything was happening too quickly.

Albert whirled around and saw that the door that led to Ponderay was blasted apart, too, just barely hanging on its hinges.

A Jackalope hopped past, leaping over the stream, its strong back legs using the door to get a higher bounce. What was left of the poor hinges snapped, and the door was swept away into the current, disappearing into the darkness of the tunnel.

"It's *all of them*," Albert said, horrified. "All the doorways are open!"

He looked for Professor Bigglesby or Lucinda in the crowd, but didn't find them. They were probably hiding somewhere, laughing as the Core tore itself apart.

"What do we do?" Birdie yelped.

Albert turned to look at his friends. "We fight through

it," he said. "And we find Professor Bigglesby and Lucinda and stop them once and for all."

"We'll help you!" Leroy shouted.

Hoyt nodded and dodged a fireball from a King Firefly.

Albert whirled around. Where was Farnsworth? Was he safe?

He heard a familiar howl, then an angry bark, and turned to see Farnsworth on the top of the last remaining bridge. He was guarding a dark-haired boy from an angry Jackalope attack.

"Petra!" Albert shouted to his teammates. "Come on! We have to help him!"

"I'll catch up to you guys!" Hoyt shouted. "I've got to go help Slink and Mo!"

It was a mad dash to get to Petra. Farnsworth's eyes kept flashing as if they'd just been plugged into a light socket. He was blinding the Jackalope to keep Petra safe.

"Over here!" Petra shouted. He had a big fat book in his hands and was brandishing it like a blade, swinging it back and forth to try to keep the Jackalope back. But it tumbled from his hands as the beast's antlers knocked it away. "HURRY!"

Just then, someone burst through one of the tunnels, shouting at the top of his little lungs.

It was Professor Bigglesby! And he was holding a shield twice the size of himself.

"Not my intern!" Bigglesby shouted. He leaped, doing a flip in midair, and landed in front of Petra.

He slammed the shield against the Jackalope, sending the giant beast tumbling over the bridge and into the water below.

"If he's here, fighting," Birdie said, "then . . ."

"I knew he was faking his injury!" Leroy shouted. "He's the traitor!"

"I'm going to pummel him!" Birdie growled as a Hexabon swooped in and stole Leroy's glasses right off his face. The two of them ran after it, shouting.

"Guys! Wait!" Albert yelped.

At the sound of Albert's voice, Professor Bigglesby whirled around. His eyes locked on Albert. He started marching toward him and Albert took a step back.

Then two steps, and three, his heart threatening to burst in his chest.

This was it. This was the moment he would face the traitor. He turned to look for Birdie and Leroy, but they were lost in the fight.

"Please," Albert said, hands out. "Don't do this."

"Albert." Professor Bigglesby was stumbling toward him. "I have to tell . . ."

A giant tentacle reached out of the waters, wrapping itself around Professor Bigglesby. The dwarf's eyes widened, and then he was lifted into the air.

"The Hendeca," Albert heard himself say. It was the

great beast from the waters inside Calderon Peak. Shock coursed through his veins.

Like a giant thrashing snake, the Hendeca lifted Professor Bigglesby higher and higher. The old dwarf was shouting, his little voice like a cat's screech, but suddenly he brandished a short black dagger. Albert recognized it as the one he'd used in Calderon to paralyze the Hissengores.

"We can't help him!" Petra said as he reached Albert's side.

"FIND . . . HIM!" Bigglesby was shouting. "FIND . . . TOO . . . LATE!"

He was looking at Albert as the Hendeca thrashed him around high above their heads.

"Albert, we have to go!" Petra said. "We have to go *right now!*"

Albert wouldn't budge, because something in him was shouting that he'd had it all wrong. If Bigglesby was the traitor, he wouldn't be here right now, fighting against the chaos he'd caused. Would he?

He watched as the dwarf shouted one final word before the Hendeca pulled him under into the waters. The name rang out, clear and true.

Festus.

CHAPTER 27

The Battle

They were in the tunnel, running toward the Library.

"Petra! Stop!" Albert shouted, but his friend wouldn't release his grip on Albert's arm. Had he always been this strong?

"There's no time," Petra said.

With each step, they were getting farther and farther away from the Main Chamber. Albert had to turn back. He had to help his friends protect the Core. He'd lost Birdie and Leroy, and without him, would they be safe? What about Trey, and Tussy? And Hoyt and Slink and Mo?

"We have to go back," Albert said. "What's gotten into you?"

Finally, Petra stopped and whirled around. "I figured it out, Albert. I know everything, and there's no time!"

"Know *what*?" Albert asked as he ripped his arm away from Petra's iron grasp.

"The traitor," Petra said, gasping for breath. "I know who it is."

Albert's eyes widened, and his chest throbbed. "Who is it? Is it Lucinda?"

"*Not here*," Petra whispered.

Why was *everyone* saying that this term? Albert looked back over his shoulder. He could still hear the shouts. Was Professor Bigglesby okay? Did his dad make it out to the surface before it was too late? Had the chaos spread all the way up there?

"Tell me who it is, now," Albert commanded, whirling around to look at his friend. "Please, Petra."

"It will take five minutes," Petra said. "You have to see it to believe it, Albert. Right now, this is your duty. If you want to save the Core, you have to come with me."

Albert's friends were back there.

But ahead, with Petra . . . it was the answer he'd been waiting for.

"Show me," Albert said, nodding. *Please, be safe out there*, he thought in a silent message to his friends.

He let Petra lead him along.

*   *   *

It was horribly quiet inside the Tower. The door swung open with an awful sound, creaking like the dead branches of the Troll Tree waving in the wind.

"I wasn't thinking straight yesterday, but Lucinda kept showing me books, promising she'd help me find it," Petra said as he shut the door behind them and locked it. "This has the oldest documents in the Core. This has all the answers."

This was the very room where Albert and Petra had once come together for detention, the very room where they discovered what the Master Tile was, and what it did.

Really, this was where everything began.

Bookshelves lined the walls, and there was an old, comfortable hammock swinging in the corner. Half of Albert begged him to run back to the Main Chamber to rejoin the fight, but the other half desperately wanted to fall into that hammock. Now that he was away from the chaos, the exhaustion had set in.

"Over here," Petra said. "They've had me covering some shifts since the disappearances, so I came up here after the Library to help clean. I was dusting this shelf when I discovered *this*."

Petra shuffled over to the farthest bookshelf in the room. It was full of old leather-bound books and smelled of rich mahogany.

He lifted a hand and tapped a dark-red book. *Low-Carb Eating—Fuel for the High-Energy Balance Keeper.*

"It looks like a book nobody would want to read," Albert said.

Petra nodded. "Exactly. But check this out."

He pulled the book off the shelf and Albert realized it wasn't a book at all. The pages were cut out, like one of those awesome book safes for people to hide things in.

And behind it was an old copper lever.

Albert's eyes almost popped out of his head.

"Go ahead," Petra said. "Try it."

Albert pulled the lever. There was a click and a hiss, and a section of the bookshelf swung backward like a door.

"Whoa," Albert said. This was super-spy stuff.

"Whoa is right," Petra said. "Who knew this was here all this time, huh?" He reached past Albert, into the open doorway, and flicked a switch on the wall.

A single light bulb flickered on, dangling from a cord in the center of the hidden room. The space was no larger than Albert's bedroom back at his mom's apartment in New York. There were a few bookshelves along the walls and an old oak table in the very center.

An ancient scroll was sprawled out across the top. Old candles, burned to nubs, sat around the scroll, guarding it like little army men.

Petra stepped inside, and Albert followed.

"Look at this," Petra said. He gently unfurled the curls at the edge of the scroll. It spilled out, like a long tongue stretching to the old stone floor. When the cloud of dust cleared, Albert's eyes widened.

It was a replica of the Core Family Document in the Library.

But this one looked much older. Its edges were tattered and the rest of it was worn through with holes in some places.

"Why are there two of these?" Albert asked.

Petra ran his fingertip along the document, searching down the long list of names. "I wondered the same thing. But I studied this for a while before the big explosion happened, and I think this one might be the original."

"Which means the one in the Library is a replica?"

"Exactly," Petra said. "Look."

He pointed to the bottom of the document, to the *F* section.

The Flynn family line was there, just like in the Library.

There were Flynns from the past on there, ones Albert had never heard of. There was Philo Flynn, Tegen Flynn, and "Big" Nell Flynn. Albert saw Pap, his dad, and his very own name.

But that wasn't all.

There was another name on there. Albert's dad was right below Pap, but there was a second name beside

Bob Flynn, directly to the left.

"Your dad has a sibling," Petra said, and pointed at the extra name. It looked as if someone had tried to scratch the name out. Beside it, written in red ink, was the word *BANISHED*. Albert looked more closely at the scratched-out name. He could see the *F* for *Flynn*, but there was a second *F* too, just visible beneath the scratch lines, about one inch before his last name.

And suddenly everything made horrible, terrible sense.

Albert's dad had a brother, which meant Albert had a secret uncle, someone he'd never met, and never even heard of. And not just a secret uncle, but an uncle who had been *banished* from the Core.

He looked at the scratched-out spot, and his mind whispered *traitor*.

"Festus Flynn," he said. "Festus Flynn is my uncle."

For a second, the room felt like it was spinning, and Albert had to grip the table to stand up straight.

"But I can't have an uncle," Albert said. "I mean, my dad doesn't have a brother. He's never, in my entire life, talked about a brother!"

"I don't think the document is lying," Petra said. Then he looked Albert right in the eye and said, "What kind of person is so bad, every trace of them is completely wiped from the Core?"

And so bad he's been hidden from me my entire life? Albert added to himself.

Albert ran his thumb across the name. Impossible. But there it was, written in nonerasable ink, still visible even beneath the scratch marks.

"He's the traitor," Albert said. "It has to be him. This whole time, I thought it was Professor Bigglesby or Lucinda, but Bigglesby kept bringing up this name, and everyone kept shutting it down."

Petra sat down on a little stool beside the table. "But if he was banished, how would he have found his way back to the Core? The Memory Wipers are supposed to protect that from happening by stealing all memories of the Core from people who leave."

"But even if it was possible, and Festus did make it back somehow . . . who is he?" Albert stared at the old document, begging his mind to come up with *some* sort of memory, anything that would tell him who Festus was.

"I know this is the answer, Albert," Petra said, but then he shook his head. "I've been in the Core my entire life, and I've never known anyone by that name. We don't have time to sit here and research. We don't have time to figure out his past, or where he might be. . . ."

"What if he's been here this entire time, using a different name?" Albert asked. But then he thought better of it. If Festus was here, nobody would have allowed it.

Judging by how freaked out Professor Bigglesby was by the very mention of his name . . . "Who *is* he?" Albert asked.

"I can help you with that," a voice said.

There was a creak and a hiss, and suddenly a dark shadow loomed in the doorway to the secret room.

Albert whirled around and froze.

Lucinda stood in the entryway, staring down at them.

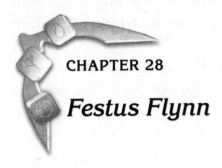

CHAPTER 28

Festus Flynn

Had Albert been wrong?

Was Festus not a brother, but a sister? Was it *Lucinda*?

"Please," Albert said, backing up until he knocked into the table. "If it's you . . ."

Lucinda took another step forward, closer to the light. And at the sight of her, Albert knew she was the traitor.

The strange woman was crying, tears streaming down her cheeks.

And she was looking at Albert as if she was experiencing the sort of pain that broke a person from the inside out.

Kimber slithered down her neck, over her shoulders, and onto her arm.

"What's going on?" Petra's voice was just a squeak.

He shuffled away as Lucinda came closer. She practically collapsed onto the stool where Petra had just been sitting and let the tears fall faster.

"The truth," she said through sobs. "It's time you know the truth."

Albert and Petra just stood there staring in disbelief.

"He was just a boy when we met," Lucinda said, sniffing back her tears. "I remember the day the Flynn twins came into the Core. I was working beside my mother at her shop, the very same place where I first met you, Albert." She looked up, and Kimber hissed. "You look so much like they did at that time. So much like Festus. But it was always his eyes that drew me to him. So strange, and so beautiful."

Albert didn't have the strength to argue with the craziness of her story. His dad didn't just have a brother . . . he had a *twin*.

He swallowed, hard, and listened as Lucinda went on.

"We were in classes together, and we sat at lunch together, but he never paid much notice to me. Bobby was always the kind one, Festus the one to get into trouble. But everyone loved him. He was whip smart, and funny." She smiled. "So, so funny. Everyone wanted to be his friend." Her eyes took on the glaze of a person lost in her memories. "There was lots of talk when Festus plucked a Master Tile from the Waterfall of Fate.

You wouldn't believe it, the whispers. He and your dad were on a unit together, with one other boy. The dream team, really. Excellent speed in the Pit, with how fast they overcame the obstacles. I was there watching every Competition, just like you, Petra."

She looked up and smiled at Petra, but he just stared back with his mouth hanging open.

Lucinda went on. "Everything was fine until Festus started pulling ahead, learning how much his Tile could really do. He . . . he started doing things nobody should have done. Their teammate, Curt, was nearly killed during Competition, and it was Festus's fault. He had used a symbol from the Book of Bad Tiles." Lucinda shivered. "And he didn't care. He apologized, but I remember the look in his eyes when they hauled Curt away. Festus didn't *care*."

She reached up to pet Kimber, and a fresh round of tears began to fall. Albert leaned on the table. This was so much to process at once.

"Things got bad when Festus entered a Realm of his own accord. Without anyone else. Your dad, Albert, tried to stop him, but Festus went in anyway. He caused so much destruction. The Imbalance nearly shook this earth off its axis and created a tsunami so large that over two hundred thousand people lost their lives."

Albert was only a boy then, but he remembered doing a project in World History about the tsunami in Haiti.

He'd studied the horrific news stories; thousands of families had lost loved ones to the disaster. Homes were destroyed, and lives forever changed.

His uncle had caused that? Albert felt sick.

"Professor Bigglesby's mother was . . ." Lucinda sniffed, and a huge sob came after it. "Professor Bigglesby's mother went in after him, she was a Professor at the time, and she caught him, and she got his Tile, but after, she was never the same. Whatever she saw in that Realm, it changed her."

She kept crying, unable to finish her story. But Albert wanted her to push on, because the tears weren't right. They didn't seem like sad tears for the loss of a friend or from remembering something tragic. They seemed like guilty tears, like how his little half sister cried after she was caught stealing candy from the pantry before bed.

"And then what?" Albert asked. "What else happened?"

Lucinda looked up, her eyes wide and full of fear.

"There was a trial, in the Pit. Festus was stripped of his Tile for what he did, banished forever from the Core. But your dad believed there was still good in his brother's heart. He believed that anyone could still come back from the darkness, and so he offered up an alternate punishment for Festus."

Kimber's hiss was the only sound in the room, and

that strange, methodical rhythm of his forked tongue flicking in and out of his mouth.

"Festus was given a choice. Leave the Core and never come back, or remain as a servant to it for the rest of his existence. He chose the latter," Lucinda said. "He chose to remain here, protecting the very place he worked so hard to destroy."

"So he's here?" Petra asked. "I mean, he's been here the whole time?"

Lucinda nodded, but wouldn't speak.

"Who is he?" Albert asked. "Where is he?"

Kimber slithered away from Lucinda. This time, she didn't try to hold on to him as he reached the ground and disappeared into the stacks.

"The Path Hider," she whispered. "He's . . . the Path Hider."

The room suddenly felt impossibly small. Albert's hands went to the Master Tile around his neck, and in his mind, he saw two eyes.

One, a crystal blue as bright as a summer sky.

The other, dark and dangerous.

There was a voice in Albert's head. That strange, shaky Pegasus voice, from the winged horse Albert had tried to ride that first day. *Its eyes*, it had said. *Its eyes were so horrible.*

Everything clicked into place. The way the Pegasus

had screamed about Albert's blood, how it smelled like *the one who came before.* The spidery fingerprint on the Bell, too large for a child, larger than an average adult's, but smaller than Professor Asante's.

He thought of the scribbled note on the striker, the handwriting that reminded him a little too much of his dad's. The black smudge they'd found on the door to Belltroll that had looked like oil. And then, of course . . .

"He was the only one not in the Pit when the door to Belltroll was cracked," Albert whispered.

"A recording," Lucinda whispered, finding her voice again. "He wanted to ensure that people *thought* he was present, while he entered the Realm." She shook her head. "I never meant for anyone to get hurt. Please, forgive me."

"What do you mean, forgive you?" Albert asked. He took a step back, knocking up against the bookshelf. "What did you do?"

Lucinda wiped her tears with the back of her ring-covered hand. "He was always so smart, so cunning. He discovered a way around the punishment. And I . . ."

"And you *what*?" Albert asked. "Lucinda, what did you do?"

She sobbed so hard her entire body shook.

"I loved him," Lucinda said. "I always have, and he knew it, and he used me to help him, and I fell for it."

Albert was tired of her sobs. He just wanted to get away from her.

"I helped him, all this time." Her head snapped up, and her sobs stopped. "He wants you, Albert. He wants your Tile, and he's waiting for you. He intends to take it himself."

"Where is he waiting?" Albert asked. A flash of courage surged through him. "Tell me."

"I never meant to hurt anyone," Lucinda said.

"I trusted you," Petra cut in. There were tears in his own eyes, and his voice cracked. "And last night, in the Library, you were keeping me there so I wouldn't come here and find out his name! You lied to me. How long have you been lying to me?"

"Forgive me." Lucinda cried and cried and cried. "If Festus doesn't get Albert's Tile, he will destroy the world. But you can't go to him, Albert—he's too strong and powerful. And he doesn't care what he has to do to you to get that Tile. I won't allow you to go."

Albert saw the begging in Lucinda's eyes before she buried her face in her hands and resumed her sobbing all over again. Her concern for him surprised him. He put out a hand to touch her shoulder, but suddenly, Lucinda stopped crying.

"You can't go to him. But . . . if someone brought the Tile to him . . . if I . . ."

Her eyes widened. She stood up and lunged at Albert.

It happened so fast. There was a flash of black from the direction of the bookshelves. Albert and Petra both screamed and jumped back. Lucinda cried out and fell to the ground.

It was *Kimber*. He'd wrapped his body around Lucinda, holding her captive like he was a coil of thick black rope. She tried to fight, but Kimber held strong.

His dark eyes looked up at Albert's and the snake nodded once, a message. *Run.*

"You can't go!" Lucinda yelped.

"Tell me where he is!" Albert yelled. His face felt hot.

"No," she whispered.

"We have to go," Petra said. "We'll find him, Albert. We'll look together."

They shuffled past her to the freedom of the door.

They were almost out when Lucinda called Albert's name. He turned around.

"Just give him the Tile, and don't fight him," Lucinda whispered. She gave up fighting against Kimber, all the hope sucked from her voice. "He . . . he has your friends."

"Where?" Albert asked. "Please."

But Lucinda's eyes shone with love. Not for Albert, but for Festus. She wouldn't betray him, not even now.

"Albert," Petra said. "Come on."

Birdie. Leroy. Farnsworth. Not safe.

Albert gave Lucinda one final glare.

"He won't win," Albert said. "Because I'm going to stop him, tonight."

Then he turned and sprinted from the room, the faces of his friends the only thing in his mind.

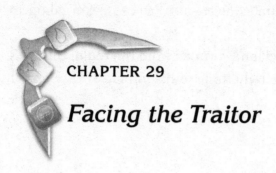

CHAPTER 29

Facing the Traitor

They made it to the Main Chamber in record time, using the system of hidden tunnels and back routes Hoyt had shown them. Albert and Petra burst out into the light.

Professor Asante had organized the Balance Keepers and they were fighting in their individual units.

Terra, fighting against the Hexabons.

Slink and Hoyt and Mo on Team Argon, battling the Hendeca. They slashed at its arms as a little man with a sword and shield shouted out commands.

"Professor Bigglesby!" Petra shouted. "He's alive!"

The dwarf caught Petra's eye and winked, then did a flip and roll beneath the Hendeca's slashing arms. When he stood back up, he looked at Albert and nodded once.

A truce.

Albert nodded back, but quickly returned to scanning the room for his friends. They were nowhere to be found.

A cold sweat broke out on Albert's brow. If Lucinda was right, and Festus had them, they wouldn't be here. They'd be somewhere hidden. Away from all of this.

But where?

The Cave of Fire? The Cave of Souls? Maybe in Lake Hall, or one of the Professors' classrooms? Could they be in the Path Hider's domain, where Festus had been this entire time? There were too many possibilities and not enough time.

"LOOK OUT!" Petra screamed.

A King Firefly buzzed toward them from one of the tunnels. It shot a fireball and Albert and Petra dove. But there was a raging roar, and Jadar the Guildacker zoomed down from the rafters, swallowing the fireball in his giant, open jaws.

He took off, chasing the Fireflies, helping the Balance Keepers below round them up. Trey ran past, shouting as he tried to get some of the older Core workers to safety.

"Have you seen Leroy and Birdie?" Albert shouted.

"Not in a while!" Trey shouted back as he herded the workers away.

Albert kept looking, but every second that ticked by

was another second Birdie and Leroy could be in danger.

His body was numb.

"I don't see them!" Petra yelled.

Thoughts raced through Albert's mind like a round of bullets.

They aren't here. Festus is the traitor. The Path Hider is Festus. Festus is my crazy secret uncle. My crazy secret uncle has my friends.

"I have to go," Albert said to Petra. "I have to find them."

"What about your Tile?" Petra said. "There has to be a symbol you can use to find them."

"I can't think right now." Albert pressed his fingers to his temples. "I can't . . ."

"You can," Petra said. "You have to."

There was too much noise. Too much chaos all around.

Albert took a deep breath and forced himself to focus the way he used to do in the Pit when things got tough.

Please, he thought. *Help me find my friends.*

It must have worked, because an image appeared in his mind. It looked like a giant magnet with two squiggly lines on either side. He didn't know what the symbol meant, but he didn't have another plan.

Albert thought of the Master Tile and focused on the first day he'd met Leroy and Birdie, standing in the Path Hider's domain. Birdie had her hands on her hips, and

Leroy's hat was on sideways. He remembered the yo-yo in Leroy's hands, too.

Suddenly, an overwhelming need to go *left* filled Albert's body.

He looked left, and there it was. The tunnel that led to the Pit.

It was as if there was a magnet in his very soul, tugging and pulling at him to go down that tunnel.

Albert turned to Petra. "Get somewhere safe," he said.

But Petra shook his head. "I've waited on the sidelines for too long." He reached out and shook Albert's hand. "Go find them." Then he turned and sprinted into the fight.

Albert could only be in one place at one time. A part of him shattered as he turned away from the battle.

Be safe, he thought. *Fight well.*

Then he unsheathed his sword and sprinted into the tunnel that led to the Pit.

The Magnet symbol kept pulling and tugging, and Albert obeyed. His hands trembled as he held the CoreSword, and suddenly it felt way too small. Festus was so much bigger than him, a beast.

Though the fight raged on behind him, every step brought on a horrible, eerie silence. Soon the only sounds Albert could hear were his own breathing and his footsteps echoing off the stone walls. The green torches flickered.

"I'm going to the Pit," Albert whispered to himself. "I'm just going to the Pit, and I'm going to do a Competition, and I'm going to win."

It got darker and darker as Albert moved down the tunnel; torches were flickering out. Albert wondered if the Path Hider might pop out of the shadows right now.

Would he still look the same? Or would he be in some sort of evil, magical armor that would make it impossible for Albert to cut the Master Tiles from their chain?

"Just keep walking," Albert said to himself. He came to the end of the tunnel, where the door to the Pit Path stood slightly ajar.

Albert lifted a trembling hand. If he went inside, would he ever come back out?

"Birdie and Leroy," he said to himself, and their names gave him just enough bravery to swing open the door.

It was dark inside, except for two blue flashes at the very tip-top of the path.

Farnsworth!

The little dog was barking his head off, standing on the orange platform right before the entrance to the Pit.

"Farnsworth!" Albert yelled. "I'm coming, buddy!"

Suddenly Albert was sprinting, all the fear in his body having given way to adrenaline that fueled him forth.

Was Farnsworth okay? Was he hurt?

Nobody touched his dog and got away with it.

It was a strange sensation, sprinting up the Pit path alone. Albert had never done this without his friends, and suddenly his stomach became a pit, too. Dread was filling it faster and faster, so much that Albert was afraid it would overflow.

He reached the top.

"I'm here," Albert said. "It's okay now."

Farnsworth whimpered and scratched at the door. His fur was standing up on the back of his neck, and he wouldn't budge when Albert tried to coax him away from the door.

"Are they inside? Is it Birdie and Leroy?"

At the mention of their names, Farnsworth's barking started anew. They had to be inside the Pit. This was it.

Albert dropped to one knee and allowed himself a second to pet his dog. "Good boy," he said. Farnsworth's eyes dimmed a little as Albert's fingers ran through his fur. "I'm going to go and get them. Now you need to get away from here, buddy. Or go and get help. Find Trey or Professor Asante or Bigglesby and bring them here."

Farnsworth whimpered, but licked Albert's chin like he understood.

"Go," Albert said.

The little dog didn't budge.

Albert gave him a nudge, and Farnsworth howled just once. Then he turned and sprinted down the path, and Albert was alone.

He turned to the door, a sick feeling running through him.

He had to do this, now. Before it was too late.

For Birdie and Leroy, Albert thought to himself.

For my dad.

For Petra, and all the Professors.

For the Core, and the surface world.

He turned the handle. The door swung open, and before he could stop himself, Albert went inside.

Silence.

Pure, uncomfortable silence inside. Albert was afraid to take a step.

But something told him Festus already knew he was here.

You're strong, Albert's dad's voice rang in his head. *Just . . . remember who you are. Remember that the Flynns are the good guys.*

But Festus was a Flynn, too. And he was anything but good.

Albert tightened his grip on his sword and walked a little farther inside. The room was dark, but not so much that Albert couldn't see.

And then, suddenly, torches blazed all along the rocky

walls of the giant room. This fire wasn't cool blue or sickly green, but a deep, angry red-orange.

And it illuminated the figure sitting on the bleachers, calmly waiting.

He looked the same as always, save for the miner's cap that was missing. But there he was, with that strange coppery hair. They must have been fraternal twins, because other than their height and build, Festus and Bob Flynn didn't look very much alike.

The tall, slim figure sat with one leg crossed over the other casually, as if he were waiting for a friend. He wore a coat similar to Professor Flynn's, but instead of emerald green, this one was jet black.

Albert glared at Festus from across the Pit. "You," he said. "Where are my friends?"

Festus chuckled, a sound that carried across the gap to Albert's ears. "Is that any way to greet your uncle?" He spread his arms out.

"You're no uncle of mine," Albert said, making sure to speak up so that Festus heard him loud and clear.

Festus burst into laughter and slapped his knee. Albert didn't think he'd said anything funny.

"Always so clever, so quick. But of course, all the Flynns are. It's in our blood." Festus was staring at him now. "I'll admit, I was beginning to wonder if you'd show."

"I'm here now," Albert said. He didn't want to get any closer to Festus, but it felt stupid to be shouting across the

Pit. He took a deep breath and moved forward, halving the distance between them. "Give me back my friends."

"Slow down, nephew. Let's enjoy this family reunion." Festus rested his chin on his hand, his strange eyes bright as if he were truly delighted to see Albert. But there was a darkness beyond it all. Albert could see it even from here. "You didn't need anyone to tell you where I was, did you? No, you figured that out all on your own. Of course, that insufferable dog wouldn't stop barking."

It was good Farnsworth wasn't here now—he would have ripped Festus's throat out for that comment.

"I trusted you," Albert said. "You were the first person I met in the Core. I thought you were my friend."

His uncle sat a little taller, his back straight. Even though the Pit loomed between them, Albert felt like Festus was staring into his soul.

"You and I aren't friends, Albert. We're so much more than that. We're so much more than *everyone else*." He raised his hands, and twin flames flickered to life in his outstretched palms. Albert's eyes widened as the flames turned from fire to floating orbs of water.

He'd never seen magic like that in the Core.

Festus raised a brow and stood. The orbs of water twirled above his palms. "You see what makes us different, nephew? We can do things that no one else can. We're strong. We're powerful." His strange eyes flitted toward Albert's Master Tile. "If you join me, I can teach you things beyond your wildest dreams. We can share the power. Imagine the world bowing at our feet. I know you feel it. I know you hunger for more."

Albert shook his head, and inside, his body felt like it was crawling with ants. "You're wrong."

"Wrong?" Festus raised a brow. He clenched his fists, and the orbs of water exploded.

"I'm nothing like you," Albert said. "I will *never* join you."

Festus glared back. He didn't move his mouth to speak, but suddenly his voice was *inside* of Albert's head, tickling his brain. *I was afraid you'd say that,* Festus said. *Which is why I've set up a challenge.*

"What challenge?" Albert said. He gripped the sword harder; his uncle inside his head made him feel incredibly vulnerable. His whole body burned with anger. "My friends. Lucinda said you had them, and I want them back. *Now.*"

Festus curled his lip in disgust. "Lucinda," he hissed. "What a useless Apprentice." Then he laughed and looked back into Albert's eyes. "Your friends are in this very room." He waved a long, spidery hand toward the Pit. "See for yourself."

Albert's whole body turned to ice. He edged forward, afraid to look into the Pit, but knowing that he had to. What would he see at the bottom?

Horrible images flickered through his mind. *Birdie and*

Leroy injured and broken. Birdie and Leroy just barely holding on to life. He shoved the images away and focused on the truth.

The Pit was nothing like it used to be. It was as if Festus had plucked the blueprints for it right out of Albert's nightmares and brought them to life.

In the center of the Pit, a giant, razor-sharp pillar emerged, spiraling up from the ground. Albert had no idea what the pillar would do when the Pit actually sprang to life . . . but he knew it wouldn't be good.

It wasn't the pillar, though, that gave Albert a fresh layer of dread in his chest.

It was the creatures that stalked back and forth across the Pit's floor, waiting for their prey.

The first was a massive lizard-like beast covered in serrated spikes, with a cluster of them on the tip of its tail. As if it sensed Albert's eyes on its back, it looked up and hissed, revealing two rows of jagged teeth, and a black, forked tongue that probably held a lethal amount of poison.

"What have you done?" Albert asked.

Festus took a few steps down, off the bleachers. "Hybrids," he said. "Aren't they beautiful, nephew?"

The second creature had a giant wolf's body, large enough to fit its bear head, and claws so long they click-clacked across the floor as the creature paced. If the animal's claws made that sound, then the floor of the Pit probably wasn't the usual soft, squishy floor that it was in Competitions.

The third creature was a colossal black bird with talons like a hawk, its black beak long and ragged like the edge of a steak knife. It soared from the Pit and landed on Festus's outstretched arm.

"My friends," Albert said, forcing himself to look at Festus. "Where are they?"

Festus laughed. "Not as observant as I hoped you'd be." He lifted his arm, and the bird soared from it, flying down to the Pit to land on the wolf-creature's back.

It was then that Albert noticed the cave in the Pit's wall.

The three awful hybrids were guarding its entrance. A firefall suddenly sparked to life too, liquid fire cascading over the entrance to the cave.

"A little adjustment," Festus said, waving his arm. The firefall split like a curtain, revealing the inside of the cave. "And there you are. Your pathetic little friends."

Birdie and Leroy were lying against the cave wall—or at least that's what he thought he saw from the distance he was at. There were others in the cave, too, crumpled figures. Albert's panicked mind screamed, *They're dead!* But the calmer, braver side of him begged him to look a little closer.

Albert called forth the BinocuVision symbol and let his Tile do the work from there. His eyesight zoomed in until he was looking at his friends up close. They were both unconscious, their eyes closed as if they could be sleeping. They looked fine, not a single bump or bruise on them, not a single thread out of place on their clothing. He looked at the other people trapped inside. There were the two Core Cleaners who had disappeared, and the old Core Historian. But Albert couldn't see if anyone's chest was rising and falling with each breath because the firefall shut, covering them from view.

Were they alive?

Albert couldn't bear to think of the alternative.

His mind was racing. How did Festus get to Birdie and Leroy? How had they been caught?

And then he thought, *How could I have let this happen?* It was stupid to leave Birdie and Leroy behind in the Main Chamber. Stupid to run away with Petra while his very best friends fought for the Core without him.

It was his fault they were trapped behind that fire.

"Only I hold the key," Festus said, snapping Albert from his thoughts. He pointed to the right of the firefall, where a simple keyhole sat in the wall of the Pit. Festus reached up to his collar and pulled out a chain. It was black and thicker than the cord around Albert's neck. Festus had the two Master Tiles, glittering black, and next to them dangled a golden key. "Get the key to turn off the fire, and voilà! Your friends are free."

"Let them go," Albert growled. His hands clenched

into fists. He didn't know when he'd moved closer to Festus, who was now less than a car's length away, with a smug smile on his face. "Let them all go *now.*"

Festus simply nodded. "Oh, I will," he said. "But first, you'll have to prove you're as powerful as me. Let's see what you're really made of, nephew."

Albert took a deep breath. He would fight to save his friends, he had no doubt about that. But he could see the hurt in the Path Hider's eyes. This wasn't really about Albert.

"Don't do this," Albert said. "Please. You can still turn back. We can start over and be a family. You and me and my dad, and Pap."

Apparently, it was the wrong thing to say.

Festus's eyes practically glowed with fury. "We were *never* a family," he said. "Never."

Then he lifted his arms and the Pit sprang to life.

CHAPTER 30

The Fight to the End

*T*his is just like any other Competition, Albert told himself. *Only if I win, I get my friends back instead of a Medallion.*

Two floating orange platforms appeared, and Albert felt like he was in a dream as he stepped onto one. Festus took the other, their eyes locked on each other the entire time.

"It's all fun and games, nephew!" Festus said. "All fun and games, *especially* when someone gets hurt."

He burst into laughter, and Albert's body seized with fear. He could tell himself this was just like any other Competition in the Pit, but Albert knew, in the bottom of his soul, that this would be a fight to the death.

The CoreSword in his hand felt so small and pathetic.

How could it possibly cut through the thick chain around Festus's throat?

Albert looked over his shoulder at the exit door to the Pit. If he used Speed, he could probably be out the door in less than three seconds. But then his dad's voice rang in his head. *It's incredibly powerful, made from the very same substance that created your Master Tile.*

If Professor Flynn believed in the CoreSword, then Albert had no choice but to believe in it, too. Besides, it was all that he had left. His Master Tile was powerful, but not as powerful as the Path Hider's two.

The platform sank down, down, down to the bottom of the Pit, seemingly deeper than it had ever gone before, as if Festus had tripled the size of the Pit.

Now Albert couldn't escape if he wanted to.

Festus's platform carried him *up* and over to the center of the Pit. He stared down at Albert, arms crossed over his chest.

"What is it they used to say, in Competitions?" Festus called down. His two Master Tiles twinkled even from such a distance. "Oh, yes. Balance Keepers . . . begin!"

Albert took off running across the Pit toward the firefall. Festus's laughter boomed from overhead, making Albert's knees tremble. Key or no key, he was going to get his friends out of here.

The bear-wolf lunged for him first, its awful jaws snapping.

Albert dove, rolled to his feet, and tried to go left.

But the lizard-beast came next. Its forked tongue shot out of its mouth, impossibly long. It was like the Poison Toads in Belltroll!

Albert leaped, narrowly avoiding a hit to his ankle. Now the bird swooped in, its beak clicking and clacking as it aimed for Albert's head.

He ducked and dodged it, but landed a little too close to the firefall. There was a piercing slice of pain in his arm. Albert cried out and stumbled back.

A fresh burn bubbled up along his wrist.

"What's the matter, Albert?" Festus laughed from above. "Too slow to defeat my hybrids?" He clicked his teeth and shook his head. "You're the great Albert Flynn, bearer of the third Master Tile. Use it, you foolish boy!"

Albert's head spun. He stumbled backward to the side of the Pit farthest from the creatures. Spots appeared in his vision.

"Poison," he said to himself, remembering the river in the Cave of Fire. The Firefall must have been laced with it.

He had to think.

Festus was taunting him, and he wanted Albert to fail. But he also seemed like he wanted a true battle. The Master Tile . . .

I need to heal, he thought. He called forth Leroy's Synapse symbol, and could nearly feel his brain pulsing with the need to see and calculate everything around him. *I need a symbol for healing. . . .*

The Black Book popped into Albert's mind, like he was staring at a TV screen. There was the Black Book, the thousands of Tile symbols spread out across all the pages. His mind mentally flipped through it until Albert was staring at a symbol he'd never even *known* he'd seen.

It was like the red medical cross from history books.

Albert harnessed it, ordered the symbol to work for him.

He felt the dizziness fade, as if a cool bucket of water had been poured over his head. His limbs felt stronger, and though his burn didn't disappear as he'd hoped it would, the pain faded to a dull throb.

Albert looked up at his uncle, floating safely above the chaos.

So much evil. So much hate in one man's body.

"That's all you've got?" Albert yelled. "Come down and fight me yourself! That's what you want, isn't it? To take my Master Tile from me? Come and get it!"

Festus's voice boomed like he was speaking into the MegaHorn, but Albert knew it was the magic of his two Tiles. "We'll fight," he said, "but only if you make it up to me. Prove you're a worthy opponent!"

Albert looked back at the firefall.

He could try to keep going, try to find a way around the hybrids and rescue his friends. Maybe with Hoyt's

Speed Tile? Or maybe he could use Creature Speak, to try and control them?

But the creatures saw him staring. The bear-wolf growled, and the lizard hissed, and Albert knew that he was wasting precious time. Even if he got through the creatures, he wouldn't be able to get through that fire-fall. He could use a Tile to help protect him from the heat and the poison . . . but Birdie and Leroy and everyone else stuck behind it wouldn't come out of there safely.

No, Albert couldn't save them now. He had to get through Festus first.

He turned to look at the pillar.

Before his eyes, the outside layer of the pillar morphed into a massive staircase, spiraling its way around the rocky pillar. There wasn't a guardrail or anything to hold on to, and the higher it went . . .

The harder the fall would be.

You have to do this, Albert. It's the only way.

"I guess I'm coming to you, then," Albert said with a growl.

He took one last look at the firefall, then shook his head and sprinted for the staircase.

He was almost to the first step when the bear-wolf lunged for him. Albert dove to the right, narrowly avoiding the creature's swiping claws. He was barely back on his feet when the beast lunged again, snarling and spitting black liquid that oozed from its poisonous teeth.

Albert lashed out with his sword and the bear-wolf took a half step back.

But it wouldn't be good enough.

Albert hadn't trained in sword-fighting. How would he defeat a massive beast with a weapon he hardly knew how to use?

The creature snapped its jaws, and Albert twirled the sword in front of him to ward it off. Festus laughed from overhead.

That laugh is getting old, Albert thought. But he took his annoyance and funneled it into his fight. He swung at the beast once again.

The sword was too short. The bear-wolf swiped a claw, and Albert barely held on to the sword as beast and blade clashed.

It didn't even cut through the hybrid's fur!

"I protect my investments," Festus said. "You think a simple sword can defeat my creations?"

Albert glared up at Festus. "This isn't a simple sword," he said, wiping sweat from his brow.

But it sure seemed like it now.

The blade wasn't sharp at all. Where was the magical, mystical feeling Albert had felt when his dad first handed him the CoreSword?

Albert would have to use his Tile instead.

He tucked the sword into its sheath and called forth the Strength symbol.

Don't be afraid, Albert thought.

He pictured Birdie, how she always tightened her ponytail and got ready for battle. Albert would channel her strength.

The bear-wolf advanced, and Albert clenched his fists and sprinted for it.

They both leaped at the same time, the bear-wolf with its jaws open and claws outstretched, Albert with his Master Tile's power coursing through his veins.

For Birdie, Albert thought.

He swung his fist in midair.

There was a crack, and Albert felt the hybrid's coarse fur against the back of his hand, felt the beast's roar as the punch hit true.

The bear-wolf was no match for the Strength symbol. The great beast soared backward, ten feet, twenty feet, before slamming into the Pit's rocky wall.

Then it lay still.

Albert gulped. The power scared him, but it also felt good.

He'd done it.

Then he looked up at his uncle. For once, Festus was silent, his jaw clenched tight.

Albert stepped calmly onto the staircase and began the climb.

Albert had barely made it ten steps when there was a single click, to his left.

His body reacted on instinct, calling forth the SlowMo symbol. The Master Tile responded, and Albert saw everything in slow motion.

A giant black spike jutted out from the pillar, moving at the speed of a snail.

In reality, Albert knew, it was moving like a strike of lightning, faster than should be possible.

Albert sucked in his stomach, and the spike pierced the air, inches from where he'd just been.

It didn't stop there.

A second click, and a second spike jutted out, this one so sharp that its tip shined like a diamond.

"Oh, brilliant!" Festus clapped his hands in slow motion from above, and Albert gritted his teeth and forced his uncle's voice into the background.

Spikes came like an army. So many Albert could hardly keep up, even with the SlowMo. He needed to get creative.

He conjured up Merge and harnessed the SlowMo and Speed symbols at once.

Every time one spike jutted from the wall in SlowMo, Albert had less than a second to duck or leap or flatten himself before he was skewered. But the Speed symbol rang true, helping Albert move like the wind.

He was halfway up the staircase now. The pillar seemed to have run out of spikes, and Albert shook the symbols from his mind.

"Oh, this won't do," Festus said. Albert was closer to him now and could make out the strange multicolored eyes that the Pegasus in Belltroll had feared so much. "I think, perhaps, we should turn the heat up."

"Whatever you throw at me, you won't win," Albert said.

"You have the confidence of my brother," Festus said back. "It's time we crush that."

Albert rolled his shoulders and got ready for the next attack.

At first, nothing happened.

He took another step up the spiral staircase, wondering what would come.

More spikes? Another hybrid creature?

Another step, and nothing.

He took one more, feeling a little braver, and suddenly it came.

A fireball blazed from the side of the Pit, soaring toward Albert like a rocket.

Albert was ready. Two circles, one half the size of the other, appeared in his mind.

Size Shift! His entire body grew smaller until he was half the size that he had been seconds before.

The fireball blazed right past him, where the other, taller Albert's head had just been, and exploded into the side of the staircase.

Heat. So much heat. This wasn't cool Core fire. No,

this was real fire, the kind that could burn him to ash.

Albert thought of Leroy, how good his friend was at avoiding the most dangerous things, how he'd scurried up the side of a spiral pillar once in this very Pit, moving fast in the face of fear.

This one's for you, Leroy, Albert thought, and as the fire-balls raged, Albert raged, too.

Every explosion, Albert was ready.

A fireball shot from his left, and Albert's tiny body flattened against the wall of the pillar. The fireball blazed past, but then another was coming from his right.

He squashed himself to the stairs, letting it soar past his head and explode against the Pit wall far away.

Sweat was dripping down Albert's neck and back, the entire Pit's temperature suddenly hotter than Calderon.

But he wouldn't let that slow him down.

More fireballs, this time from all sides.

Albert called forth Double Vision, one he'd used before in this Pit, too, but this time, conjuring up the image was as easy as breathing.

It was like he had a *second* pair of eyes. When a fireball shot from behind him, Albert saw it from the back of his head. He twirled, stooped to his knees, and let the fire-ball explode just over his shoulder.

Another came, and another.

One singed his shoulder, and Albert cried out as a burn bubbled on his skin, melting through his shirt. The pain made him lose control of the Size Shift symbol, and he popped back up into his normal size.

"Not so fast, are you?" Festus shouted.

But his voice was angrier than it had been. He knew Albert was getting closer, and he wasn't happy.

At least Albert seemed to have reached a height on the pillar that was out of the fireball zone. What could be worse than fire?

Spinning. So much spinning.

The pillar was rotating and it made even the speed of the Pillars of Ponderay look like child's play. The staircase spun so fast Albert felt like his face was going to fly right off.

He stooped to one knee to lower his center of gravity and grabbed the staircase-pillar's rocky wall with his fingertips. But the handholds were so tiny. Even if Albert used the Shrink symbol again, he'd probably slip.

He needed something. . . .

The stairs disappeared beneath him.

Suddenly, impossibly, the staircase had turned into a slide coated in slippery black oil. Albert began to slide. Too fast, way too fast, and he knew he was slipping back into fireball territory.

Oil, he thought. *Oil is flammable!*

Think! Albert told himself. *THINK, ALBERT!*

His arms flailed.

He scrambled to grab hold of something, but Festus

was laughing so loud, and his mind couldn't focus. He felt so weak, falling, falling . . .

Just like in Belltroll, when Spyro was falling from the sky.

"Float!" Albert yelled through gritted teeth. Somehow saying the symbol's name made it all the more real.

Suddenly he was floating. He imagined himself floating up, just above the surface of the slide, so the oil couldn't touch him any longer. He flipped onto his stomach, like Superman.

Then he reached out and used his hands to push himself along the side of the pillar, as if he were an astronaut hauling himself through a spaceship in zero gravity. Up and up he went, following the spiral pillar's shape.

Albert didn't look at Festus. He just looked straight ahead, pulling himself higher, until the slide suddenly faded and the stairs reappeared in its place.

Albert released the symbol's power and sunk to his stomach, gasping for breath. His brain was going to explode.

His heart might explode too, and his lungs with it. He was so tired.

Good will always win in the end, Albert's dad's voice rang in his head.

There was still a chance for Festus. There was still a chance for his uncle to change this, turn it all around for good.

"You can stop this!" Albert said through gasps. He knelt on the staircase, his head leaning against the rough rocky wall to the left, and looked up at his uncle. "You can stop this right now and we can turn in our Tiles together! We can fix this, Festus. It's not too late!"

Festus stared down at him, his face frozen in a mask of pure, unrelenting hatred. He bared his teeth like the hybrid wolf, and Albert heard his uncle's voice in his brain, hissing, sizzling with hatred.

"You will die today, Albert Flynn. You will die, and I will use your Tile to take over the world."

Festus raised his arms to the sky and a wall of fire erupted around his platform, covering himself from Albert's view. The bird cried, and Albert hauled himself to his feet and turned around.

The great bird soared toward him, its talons aimed for the kill.

Albert unsheathed his sword.

CHAPTER 31

The Master Tiles

S parks flew as Albert's sword clashed with the bird's talons, but with every flap of the beast's wings and swipe of his sword, Albert's arms grew heavier and heavier.

He tried to harness the Strength symbol, but his mind was flickering like a candle flame in the wind. He swung the sword, and more sparks flew as the bird's talons clipped it. The beast let out a piercing cry and lunged with its knife-beak.

Albert dodged.

He tried to pull forth the Speed symbol, but it didn't work.

"You're exhausted," Festus's voice whispered into Albert's mind. *"Give up, Albert. You won't make it."*

"No," Albert said. He closed his eyes as the bird backed away, its great wings flapping and cooling the sweat on Albert's face.

Please, don't let me fail, Albert thought. It struck him that this was the first time he'd fought in the Pit without his friends beside him. *I don't know if I can do this on my own.*

Heat singed his hand, and for a second Albert thought he'd been burned by a fireball. When he opened his eyes, though, the sword's blade had turned red at the edges, as if it were an ember fighting to stay aflame.

As the bird came in for a final attack, Albert lifted the sword and swung.

The bird's talons struck, and there was a blast that shook Albert's body.

The bird was rocketed backward, screeching. It fell to the ground of the Pit, its wings crumpled over its body.

Albert gasped and sheathed his sword. His hand was hot, but not burned, where he'd held it.

What just happened?

He didn't have time to think. He had to climb higher before something else attacked him. He ran as fast as he could without using Speed, making it to the top of the pillar.

But he wasn't done yet.

Festus was waiting inside his wall of flames, atop his platform.

It floated high over Albert's head, higher than Albert could jump. He could use the Jackalope symbol to get up there, but the pounding in his head had intensified, and all the focus he'd had while fighting the bird seemed to have evaporated. How could he keep using his Tile with the pounding in his head? Festus was whispering, *You will lose, Albert. You will not win.*

Albert was bleeding, and burned, and his clothing was ripped and covered in oil. Sweat covered his whole body, and he couldn't remember the last time he'd eaten or had a drink of water. His throat was like cotton. If he could just close his eyes . . .

He looked over the edge of the pillar, down to the firefall below. It glittered bright and fierce like a deceiving smile.

If it was him in that cave, and Birdie and Leroy up here . . .

"They wouldn't quit," Albert whispered. "Not ever."

He was so close. He'd made it this far.

He stood tall, shoulders back, the way his dad always did.

Then he wrapped his fingers around his Master Tile. The Tile that would be used for good instead of evil. The Tile that was impossibly dark, but would be used for light at the end of all of this.

If he could just survive.

Albert pictured the Jackalope symbol, and for one

second, he chuckled to himself as he imagined Leroy riding Jemima like a true cowboy from the Wild West.

"Let's do this, Tile," he said.

He felt the buzzing in his legs, the eagerness to jump that he hadn't felt only moments before. He opened his eyes and stared at the wall of fire, and he knew Festus would be ready just beyond.

Albert would be ready, too.

He bent his knees.

And leaped.

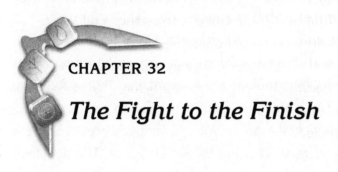

CHAPTER 32

The Fight to the Finish

High and wide he leaped, and as he came to the wall of fire, Albert pictured the AntiHeat symbol. His body felt like a chunk of ice, soaring through the air.

He slid straight through the flames and landed in a crouch, fists clenched and teeth bared like a warrior.

Then he looked up into the eyes of Festus Flynn.

"Marvelous," Festus said. He did a slow clap, but didn't make a move for Albert. Not yet. "Great form, nephew. I must say, I do see a lot of myself in you."

Albert practically growled. "I am nothing like you."

"Oh?" Festus spread his arms wide. "But here we both are, high in the air above the Pit. The very place we have always excelled. It's you and me, the Flynn boys. Masters of the Great Black Tile." His eyes fell onto Albert's chest. "I'll give you a final chance to join me."

"Join you how?" Albert said. He'd made it this far, and now all Festus wanted to do was talk? Enough was enough. Albert took a step forward, but Festus followed suit, stepping back.

Festus sighed dramatically. "Join me in greatness, dear boy. Imagine, the Realms as our kingdom. The people of the Core and the creatures of the Realms bowing before us, bending to our every will."

"But *why*?" Albert said, his rage fueling him another step forward. "What good does that do? What's the *point*?"

Festus was circling him now. Albert moved opposite him. They were like two sharks waiting for the kill.

Who would strike first?

"It doesn't do any good at all," Festus said. "That's the point."

"That doesn't even make sense," Albert said. He put a hand on his sword.

Festus laughed and took a step toward Albert. "That's exactly what my useless brother said. And after I destroy you, I'm going straight to your father, to show him what true power really is."

At the mention of his dad, Albert let out a battle cry and swung his sword.

Festus danced out of the way with ease, chuckling. "A

sore spot, it seems," he said. "Perhaps instead of ending your father, I'll keep him as my personal slave."

Albert lunged again, swinging his sword for the chain around Festus's neck.

"He tried to help you!" Albert shouted.

"I didn't need his help," Festus said. "I needed him out of the way."

Albert swung yet again, but Festus was on the other side of the platform before the swing was done. Albert couldn't think of a single symbol that did that. Which one was Festus using?

Round and round they went, Albert swinging the sword, Festus somehow gliding out of the way so fast that Albert could hardly see him.

"You have to stop this," Albert said. "Let my friends go. I'll leave the Core, and I'll never come back."

"That would defeat the purpose of defeating *you*," Festus growled.

Albert screamed and swung the sword again. Festus shoved him on the shoulder, and Albert face-planted on the platform.

"Get up," Festus chided. "Get up and face me like a real Balance Keeper would. It's time to fight, Albert Flynn, and I'm tired of your childish games."

That was when it hit Albert.

Festus was *playing* with him. His uncle wasn't even sweating or breathing hard.

Albert would have to try a little harder if he was going to make this a real fight.

That meant using his Master Tile. The one, tiny, *single* Master Tile against double the power.

Festus raised his arms into the sky. "You want to be a brave little hero and save the day?" He clicked his tongue and shook his head. "Then you'll have to do better than this."

From the darkness above the Pit, two shining sticks of gold buzzed through the air, soaring toward Festus's outstretched arms.

Albert's eyes grew wide as he realized what they were. "The other two strikers," he said.

They landed in Festus's hands. "Took you long enough to realize what the cause of the Imbalance was. Imagine my pleasure when the little note I left you sent the entire Core into a blessed uproar!"

Festus gripped the strikers. Had they been here this entire time, hiding in the shadows around the Pit?

If they could somehow get these strikers back to Belltroll . . . then maybe they could reverse the Imbalance, wake up the Trolls, and solve at least that problem. There would still be Festus to deal with, but the people of the Core and the surface world wouldn't be in so much danger.

Festus twirled both strikers in his hands and then held them out like twin swords.

"If it's a sword fight you want, then it's a sword fight you'll get. Only the best for family," Festus said, with a wink that made Albert's toes curl in his boots.

Then Festus attacked.

Albert threw up his CoreSword, blocking the striker from view. Golden sparks erupted between them, and Albert stumbled back, gasping.

Festus swung the left striker, and Albert blocked it. But then Festus jabbed with the right, and Albert had to spin to escape the hit.

He has two Tiles and two weapons, Albert thought. Festus now literally had double the chance of winning over Albert . . . and Albert had double the chance of losing and letting the whole world die.

Festus laughed, and swung again.

Albert dropped to one knee and felt the *whoosh* of wind as the striker nearly shattered his skull.

"Two Master Tiles, two weapons," Festus said. "What would your friend Leroy say? Ah, yes. Looks like the odds are *not* leaning in your favor."

Albert was sick of this.

He focused on his Master Tile, calling forth what was left of his Strength and Speed, and struck.

It was like a lightning storm. Festus's two strikers were twin bolts, erupting against Albert's sword. Thunder boomed as they hit again.

They circled, and Albert laid on the Speed.

Come on, Tile, he thought. *I need more than this to win.*

Festus leaped into the air, soaring high above Albert's head. He landed, and the platform shook like a Belltroll quake, rocking sideways in the air. Albert had to drop the Speed and Strength symbols and focus on Balance to avoid falling off.

But Festus was advancing again, with the platform still tilted unevenly.

Albert swung with a Strength that could shatter the world, a Speed that rivaled the gods. He swung with all his might, but he knew he wasn't going to win. Not like this.

He tried the Invisibility symbol and felt his body fade. But the CoreSword was still visible, and Festus laughed at Albert's weak attempt to disappear.

"Think smarter," Festus said as he swung a leg out at Albert.

Albert used the Jackalope symbol to jump over Festus's leg and landed on the other side of the platform.

Festus charged again, and Albert whirled around to deflect the twin strikers.

The power of Festus's swings increased until Albert's hand went numb. He dropped his sword.

"Not good enough," Festus said. "Pick it up, and give me a real challenge."

I won't win, Albert thought again. *Not like this.*

"Use the Tile as it was meant to be used, boy," Festus

growled. "I'm getting bored."

Suddenly, an image appeared before Albert. It wasn't from the Black Book.

It was a horrible symbol from the Book of Bad Tiles, one that could block out someone's vision so they saw only darkness.

Albert knew what it meant to use that symbol, to cross that line from good to bad.

But he had to save his friends, the Core, the entire world.

He focused on Darkness and his entire body trembled with the weight of evil. It was an awful feeling, but he pushed through. He pictured the symbol, like an eye with an X where the pupil should be.

With a violent tremble, Albert felt the power of Darkness surge out of his body and into Festus.

His uncle stumbled for a moment and blinked twice.

Albert swung his sword and it was a perfect hit. Festus dropped one of the strikers. He held on to the Darkness symbol in his mind.

"Do you feel it?" Festus asked, unfazed even as he couldn't see. "The power that comes from using *my* kind of symbols?"

Albert gritted his teeth and called forth the Darkness symbol in his mind even clearer than before. He didn't like the way it made him feel, but he was out of other ideas. Maybe he could maintain this one and layer another on top of it? What else had he seen in the Book of Bad Tiles?

Fear.

He knew it was wrong, even as he called forth the symbol. He thought of Festus and imagined sinking his hands into his uncle's soul, plucking out his very worst fears.

The power of the symbol slipped over Albert's body like a second skin.

"What are you afraid of, uncle?" Albert heard himself say, the words slipping from his lips.

An image of a spider popped into Albert's brain, and he harnessed it, picturing hundreds of tiny black spiders crawling all over Festus's skin. *Merge*, he thought, and together, Darkness and Fear struck Festus.

His uncle let out a gasp. "You're learning," Festus said, his hands shaking as Albert kept his focus on the Fear symbol. Festus writhed with the feeling of thousands of invisible spider legs all over his arms and legs and face. He clearly wasn't enjoying Fear, but it hadn't had the effect Albert was hoping for. He let Fear go.

Albert tried to think of another symbol to combine with Darkness, but his body was growing heavier. His head began to throb, and his vision was peppered with spots of black. He thought he might throw up.

I can't let go, he thought. *I'll lose without it. And there's something about seeing Festus suffer . . .*

Suddenly, he felt the Darkness power leave his body. Festus was using his own two Master Tiles to push back against Albert's. The symbol faded from his mind.

"Very good," Festus said, shaking his head as his vision returned. "You're joining me, little by little. Now try again."

The words were like icy water, shocking Albert back to the truth. He wouldn't try again. He wouldn't join Festus, not ever.

And yet, the power . . .

Albert stumbled. No, that little taste of bad magic was enough. It wasn't just the physical strain of it. He felt as if his very soul had lost some strength. But if he didn't use the Bad Tiles, what could he do? His arms felt like dumb-bells. It was like every symbol he'd memorized from the Black Book had turned to mush in his mind.

Festus swung the striker, and Albert held up the sword, his arms trembling. He would lean over the edge of the platform and empty his stomach any minute now.

"You won't win," Festus said as he pushed back against Albert. "You're too pathetic to use my magic, nephew." Then Festus raised a hand, and without even touching Albert, shoved him to the ground.

Albert tried to get up, but it was like two hands were pressing on his shoulders. The pressure forced him down until he was lying flat on his back.

Festus approached, walking as lazily as a cat.

The CoreSword was barely in Albert's grip. *This is it,* Albert thought. *This is the end.*

Festus stopped over him, arms crossed. "I guess I was optimistic, to hope for a fair fight." He frowned, and Albert felt those invisible hands again, pushing against him. Against his chest, his rib cage, his heart.

He couldn't breathe.

He couldn't think.

Please, he mouthed, but no sound came out.

"Begging," Festus said. "Begging like the pathetic little child you are."

The invisible hands pushed Albert closer to the edge of the platform. His head was dangling over the edge. Now his neck, and his shoulders.

Blackness took over Albert's vision as his breath left his lungs. There was no hope, no chance, no . . .

A sound rang out, in the distance.

It started low, far enough away that Albert could just barely, barely hear it. Albert turned his head so that he could see the Pit's door, off to the left, far below.

"It's time to say good-bye," Festus said.

The door to the Pit burst open, and a blur of black shot through the opening. And then came the howl. *No,* Albert thought, *the roar.*

The fire around the platform flickered away and back again, and in those moments Albert could see two brilliant, blazing blue lights.

Farnsworth!

A stream of people flowed in behind him. Balance Keepers, Professors and Apprentices and Core workers, everyone rushed into the Pit, their faces looking up at Albert arranged precariously on the edge of the platform.

"An audience," Festus said. Albert couldn't tell if he was glad they were there or not, if their presence would provoke Festus or distract him. Albert hoped it was the latter, but had a feeling that wasn't the case.

Professor Bigglesby shot an arrow from the CoreBow at Festus, but Festus simply waved an arm and the arrow was knocked off course, soaring into the shadows.

Still, that momentary distraction took a little weight off Albert's chest and he had a chance to breathe.

"Albert!" Professor Flynn burst through the crowd.

Dad.

"Not him again," Festus growled. He swung an arm, and a wall of fire blazed around the Pit's edges, stopping the crowd from entering. Albert heard them change direction and rush into the bleachers. The wall of fire crackled, but Albert could hear them chanting his name. Louder, then louder still.

Festus was standing over Albert, clearly trying to gather his thoughts. The crowd had distracted him after all.

"ALBERT!" He heard his dad screaming below, then

the whole crowd joined in. Farnsworth's howls chimed
in, too.

AL-BERT, AL-BERT, AL-BERT!

Albert lifted his head to look at Festus. He needed to
give this one more shot, for all those people out there.

AL-BERT, AL-BERT, AL-BERT!

For the Core that had become his family.

AL-BERT, AL-BERT, AL-BERT!

For Leroy and Birdie below. For his mom and all the
people on the surface above.

AL-BERT, AL-BERT, AL-BERT!

Albert studied Festus—he'd have to time it just right.
If the crowd got just a bit louder he might be so distracted . . .

"ENOUGH OF THIS!" Festus shouted. He released the
invisible force from Albert and lunged at him.

Albert held the CoreSword out and in an instant it
turned red around the edges, just as it had done earlier.
His chest and hands burned, but Albert could handle
this. This was the right kind of hurt, and Albert trusted
this power. Something deep inside him recognized the
good in it. It grew stronger with every chant of his name.

Albert dodged the striker and snapped to his feet.

"You will never hurt anyone, ever again," Albert said,
feet wide, ready for whatever Festus had coming next.
"You will never enter another Realm and destroy it."

Festus's eyes widened, and his hands were shaking.

Tired as Albert was, he could tell Festus was getting ready to use some too-horrible-to-even-imagine bad magic.

But it was no match for whatever was happening with Albert.

Every Tile symbol he'd ever so much as glanced at in the Black Book was now laid out in his mind, like a giant touch-screen tablet just waiting for Albert to tap.

Albert latched onto the Creature Speak Tile. *The hybrids . . .* Albert's mind and Tile were one, and suddenly the bird soared up to Albert, now bowing to his command.

Call your friends away from the firefall. The hawk cried out and a moment later, the bear-wolf and lizard dispersed. He looked back to Festus, who seemed to be concentrating hard. "You will never touch my friends, or my dog, ever again."

Hardly thinking it, Albert harnessed the TieDown symbol, and invisible ropes wrapped themselves around Festus, squeezing his legs together. That symbol was from the Black Book—Albert assumed it was meant for tying down sails on boats or something like that—but no one said Albert couldn't be creative.

"No," Festus said, looking as surprised as Albert at how fast he was conjuring up symbols and acting on them. "This isn't how . . ."

The Merge symbol appeared in Albert's mind, and then Speed and Strength together, and a third one he'd never used before—it looked like the medals soldiers got after doing something brave in battle.

Albert lifted the CoreSword, which was now flaming red.

A fourth symbol appeared. He effortlessly called up Leroy's Synapse Tile—had he seen this image before? No, definitely not. It wasn't in the Black Book, he was sure of it.

But the symbol of three figures linked together gave him what he needed.

Albert flicked his sword toward Festus, just barely hitting the golden striker in his hand.

BOOM!

The striker flew from Festus's hand. It fell from the platform and landed on the Pit floor with a loud *CLANG*.

Festus tried to hide his surprise. "You are finished!" he shouted, and started trembling with bad magic again.

"No," Albert said. "Nobody will die today." He swung the sword toward Festus's neck.

A spark flew off the thick black chain that held Festus's Master Tiles as Albert's sword connected. He screamed and held on to the blazing CoreSword as an explosion burst between him and his uncle.

Then a flash of black as the chain broke. The two Master Tiles tumbled from Festus's neck.

With the TieDown symbol wiped from Albert's mind

during the explosion, Festus scrambled to the ground and grabbed the Tiles, howling like a wounded beast.

But Albert was quick. He shoved his uncle with the butt end of his sword and Festus flew back with the power of the CoreSword. Albert hadn't used SlowMo, but it seemed like he had as his uncle fell from the platform, his face a mixture of hatred and horror, the Tiles held close to his chest.

He hadn't used Creature Speak again either, but Jadar swooped to the falling Festus and grabbed the Tiles with his outstretched talons, then flew back to the platform.

Albert reached out a hand.

Clink.

The two Master Tiles landed in his palm, and with them, the glittering firefall key.

Albert fell to his knees, gasping. He dropped the Core-Sword, and this time, his hand was scalded. An angry red burn covered his palm.

The crowd had gone silent.

Leroy and Birdie.

Albert didn't even have to think of a symbol to harness the power of the three Master Tiles together. They might as well have been a key to the universe, with the amount of power Albert felt inside.

Albert willed the platform to sink, and it did. Just like that.

When he reached the ground, he stood slowly, carefully. Then he walked across the Pit floor, stopping in front of the firefall.

The creatures whimpered and bowed before him. Albert waved his hand and the animals turned to ash, which was swept away a moment later in an invisible breeze Albert wasn't sure he had created.

So much power.

Albert walked to the firefall keyhole, standing taller than he'd ever stood before.

He stuck the key in the hole. It turned easily, and the firefall sizzled to a stop. Albert knew it would. Everything would go his way starting now. He just had to think it.

He ran to Birdie and Leroy and knelt down in front of them.

"Wake up," Albert said and reached a hand out to shake Birdie.

But his voice felt different, like it was too big for his throat.

"Leroy," Albert said, shaking his friend. Yes, his voice was different, too. Brave, confident, persuasive. He could do a lot with a voice like that—be an Apprentice, or a Professor, or even something . . . more.

He looked down at himself. The Balance Keeper suit he wore suddenly felt pathetic.

He was better than a mere Balance Keeper. He was Albert Flynn, who had saved the Core from an evil traitor. He deserved to be ruling the entire Core. The Professors would report to him and everyone would have to do what he said. He would lock the doors to the Realms, bar them off for good, or perhaps he alone would have access to the magic of those worlds.

But why stop with the Core? He would rule the surface world, too. He would make decisions and the world would fall in line. Nothing and no one would be able to stop him from whatever he wanted to do, anytime he wanted to do it.

He reached up to place the Master Tiles around his neck, where they belonged.

But then a voice rang out.

"Give them to me." It was the sound of a broken man.

Albert looked up and saw the Professors hauling Festus away from the edge of the Pit.

"I NEED THEM!" Festus howled, and sobbed. "GIVE THEM TO ME!"

Albert gasped. This was what the Tiles had done to his uncle. Would it be what the Tiles would do to him?

Had he not been thinking just a moment ago that he could rule the Core, rule the world? Yes, he could use his power for good, but even that suddenly seemed ridiculous. No one person should have that much power. It would be too dangerous, too unfair to everyone else.

It was an effort to lift his arm, to open his palm and free the Tiles.

He threw them as hard as he could, across the Pit, then dropped to his knees.

He saw Birdie and Leroy waking, then rushing to him, shouting his name. Albert closed his eyes. *So tired.*

Suddenly the ground shook, a familiar feeling by now, only even more intense. Albert was disappointed, though not surprised, when a split worked its way through the floor of the Pit and rocks rained down from the ceiling.

"The strikers," Albert said as his body wobbled and weakness sunk his body to the floor. "Get them . . . to Belltroll."

The quaking worsened, and Albert's head spun and hit the floor of the Pit.

And then everyone, and everything, went black.

CHAPTER 33

Waking Up

I t was so bright, and so soft.

Albert groaned and opened his eyes. He was lying in a hospital bed in the Core.

Balloons and flowers and a strange copper statue of some sort sat by Albert's bed. His right hand was bound up with cotton and wrapping.

Albert sat up suddenly. *Festus. The fight. Birdie and Leroy. Belltroll!*

He swung himself out of bed and swept the curtain aside. He took a tentative step, unsure if he'd be steady on his feet. He felt a little out of it—like maybe he was in a dream—but other than that, he felt fine.

All the other beds were occupied, and Albert

recognized lots of the sleeping figures. Harold, the Core Cleaner who had disappeared at the beginning of the term. Betsy, a red-haired woman who was always sweeping the halls at night.

There were voices coming from the waiting room of the hospital wing, so Albert hastened his pace, a smile forming on his lips.

Birdie and Leroy were sitting on the floor in front of an old, barely working TV.

"I could win, you know," Birdie was saying. "If you would just stop using your Tile!"

"That's like asking me not to breathe!" Leroy whined. A game of Tiles was laid out between them, and Farnsworth was chewing on a blue bone, his eyes flashing.

Albert's dad was sitting on a couch nearby, snoring. Hoyt, Slink, and Mo were there, too.

Everyone he cared about was here, in one place.

"This looks like fun and all," Albert said. "But I'm starving."

Everyone whirled around. "ALBERT!"

Farnsworth reached him before anyone else did, and then it was a flurry of hugs and slobbery dog kisses and Birdie slapping Albert's arm, telling him she'd pummel him if he ever scared her like that again, and Albert was laughing.

"Is Mom safe?" he asked his dad. "What about Pap?

What about the surface world?"

Professor Flynn nodded. "Mom and Pap are perfectly fine. The surface world will take a while to recover." He looked down at his hands for a moment. "Lives were lost, and many homes were destroyed, but . . . it's all over now. You did it, Albert. You stopped Festus."

"Lives were lost," Albert said slowly, nodding. He sank to the couch, beside his dad. "If we'd stopped the Imbalance in time . . ."

Birdie and Leroy scooted closer.

"Bad things happened," Birdie said carefully. "But it's not anyone's fault but Festus's. He did this."

"And you stopped him," Leroy said.

Albert let out a deep sigh. He allowed himself one moment to think about the chaos that was caused because of Festus. He allowed himself to feel the pain of the loss on the surface world, the fear that those people must have felt.

Then he swallowed it down and looked around at his family and friends.

They were safe. They were all here with him, and after everything that had happened, he couldn't have asked for much more.

Birdie leaned in and hugged him again. "Thank you for saving us," she said. "Me and Leroy. I don't remember much about when he took us, but . . . thank you."

"I couldn't have done it without you," Albert said.

Birdie pulled back. "What do you mean?"

Albert smiled and shook his head.

Then he remembered the strikers. "The Imbalance! What happened?"

Hoyt nodded, and Albert noticed the fresh cuts on his lip, the bruises all over Slink's and Mo's faces. "We took care of it."

His dad patted Hoyt on the shoulder and smiled. "They're more than a backup unit, Albert. Got the strikers hung back up and working in record time."

Hoyt's face reddened. "We wouldn't have made it without you, Albert," he said. "It's thanks to you for helping us get those Trolls back to sleep before we got there. And for helping Spyro agree to give us a ride."

"We do still have to go back and give them peppermints," Slink said. Mo shrugged beside him.

"And in case you're wondering, Lake Hall construction is under way. We should be eating real food again in no time," Leroy added.

Once Albert started laughing, he couldn't seem to stop.

The hugs resumed, and he was so relieved he could have slept for days.

But he'd slept enough.

He had some business to take care of.

"We need to call a meeting," Albert said. "The entire Core. And we need to do it now."

His dad nodded. "We were waiting for you to wake up."

"Festus?" Albert said. "And Lucinda?" The names made a shiver go through him, but his dad put a hand on his shoulder.

"Their trial is happening in a few minutes. They'll both be there, but I promise, the security is under control. And the Tiles are safe for now. If you don't want to go . . ."

Albert held up a hand. "I have to see the traitors one more time, and make sure everyone knows the truth."

As for seeing the Master Tiles again . . . that would be a battle Albert would have to face on his own.

A few minutes later, after the cyclops nurse had officially declared Albert well enough to be released, everyone left the hospital wing together, Albert's dad behind him, and his best friends at his sides, as they headed for the trial.

It was over. It was *almost* over, as soon as Festus and Lucinda were banished.

"I'm glad you're awake," Birdie said. She slung an arm across Albert's waist.

"Thanks again for saving us," Leroy added. "That jerk-butt caught us off guard."

"Jerkbutt?" Birdie asked. "Is that even a word?"

"He's smart enough he can make up his own words," Hoyt said, catching up.

Albert smiled as they walked along, Farnsworth leading the way.

CHAPTER 34

The Core Trial

They avoided the Main Chamber, heading instead down the tunnel that led to the Library.

When they got there and Professor Flynn opened up the two heavy wooden doors, Albert's eyes widened.

The Library had been transformed.

Bookshelves were moved aside, and the giant zip line and rock-climbing wall were gone for the day. In their place was a set of bleachers, pulled right out of the Pit. The Library was already packed with everyone from the Core. Whispers spread throughout the crowd as Albert arrived.

"If this is too much too soon . . . ," Professor Flynn whispered, but Albert shook his head.

"It's okay, Dad. I'm fine."

He was better than fine, because here was proof that the Core was alive and safe. Only a few faces were missing from the stands, and some of them were the ones he'd already seen recovering in the hospital wing.

"Some people left for good," Leroy explained as they walked along. As they approached the bleachers, a few people cleared a spot in the front row for Albert and his friends.

"They were too scared of a repeat traitor event happening," Birdie added.

"It'll never happen again," Albert said.

And just as he said it, he saw Festus and Lucinda.

A small stage had been set up in the center of the Library, and a podium with the MegaHorn on top. Professor Asante and Professor Bigglesby were sitting on the stage, waiting. Festus and Lucinda sat side by side in metal chairs on the other side of the stage, their wrists and ankles bound in copper handcuffs.

Festus had looked so giant yesterday, so looming and terrifying.

Today, he looked incredibly small. His hair was greasy and stuck to his scalp.

Lucinda didn't look much better. Her fingers were completely bare, no giant rings. And no Kimber slithering from her neck.

Instead, the snake was coiled up on the stage nearby,

watching. Guarding them.

Festus's head whipped up toward Albert. His multi-colored eyes were sapped of all emotion, but he didn't look away as Albert took his seat in the stands. He was squeezed between Leroy and Birdie, with Hoyt, Slink, and Mo on the sides. His friends, guarding him like an army.

But there's nothing to be afraid of, Albert told himself. *Not anymore.*

Professor Asante stood and moved to the podium.

"We are gathered here today to decide the punishment seen fit for Festus Flynn and his accomplice, Lucinda Lore."

Murmurs spread throughout the stands, but nobody seemed all that shocked to hear that Festus was related to Albert. Apparently, news had traveled fast while Albert slept.

Professor Asante pulled out a scroll, which unraveled to the floor. "We will begin with the reading of the crimes."

Festus was charged for entering every Realm, for trying to sabotage the peaceful nature that kept them each in Balance, and for tampering with the instruments of the Core. He was charged with theft for stealing both Master Tiles, and with attempt to harm not one Balance Keeper, but many. His final crime was breaking the laws of his previous punishment, which had banished him from the main Core to the Path Hider's realm many years ago, without the freedom to leave that space for any reason whatsoever.

That last part surprised Albert. He had never seen the Path Hider anywhere other than the Path Hider's realm, but he had just assumed the Path Hider was a solitary person. How many years had he been confined there? Albert thought of being cramped up in his tiny Manhattan apartment during that big hurricane a few years ago. He was batty by the time it was safe to go out. But what would have happened to him had he *never* been able to come out?

Professor Asante cleared her throat and stepped closer to the MegaHorn. "Festus Flynn, how do you plead? Guilty, or not guilty?"

Festus lifted his head, slowly, his eyes focused only on Albert.

"The Tiles," he said, his once-powerful voice cracking. "Give them back to me." He shook against the handcuffs, and Albert felt himself flinching, afraid for a second that Festus could break away.

But his power was gone, along with the three Master Tiles that were hidden somewhere safely away.

The absence of Albert's own Master Tile around his neck was strange, but also, he realized, freeing. It was fine with him if he never saw those black Tiles again. Still . . .

I wonder if I'll get another Tile, Albert thought. *I wonder if I'll ever be a Balance Keeper again.*

Leroy nudged Albert. "You good, man?"

Albert nodded. He'd figure it out. After fighting Festus, he was sure they'd at least allow him to pick another Tile from the Waterfall of Fate.

Right?

Next, Professor Bigglesby came up and read off Lucinda's crimes.

She was charged with fraternizing with the enemy Festus, tampering with crucial Core devices such as Albert's Counter and the countdown clock in the Main Chamber, and attacking a Balance Keeper without just cause.

"Forgive me," Lucinda said, weeping. "I was under the spell of love."

"I'm going to puke," Hoyt said beside Albert.

The crowd glared at Lucinda, and some called out their disappointment.

"We trusted you!"

"I let my children play in your Library!"

"I want back all the Medallions I've spent in your Canteen!"

Albert knew at least a little how they felt. The Path Hider had always been there behind the scenes, but Lucinda had walked among them. She'd attended meals with them and cheered them on in the Pit. He had thought of her as a friend, just like Petra and so many other people in the Core had.

Lucinda was crying harder now, begging the Core to forgive her. Festus wouldn't stop staring at Albert with his strange, hungry expression, which was making that fuzzy feeling from the hospital wing come back. Albert did his best to shake it off as the Professors calmed the crowd. He needed to pay attention.

"The prisoner Festus has declined speaking at today's trial," Professor Asante said. "But his accomplice Lucinda has agreed to enlighten us as to how everything happened."

"What a coward," Birdie hissed under her breath. "He can't even speak for himself?"

"I'll pummel him," Hoyt said.

It struck Albert suddenly how alike the two of them were. Maybe that was why they'd always been at odds.

"Lucinda," Professor Asante said, "you may proceed." Albert leaned his elbows on his knees.

"Years ago," Lucinda began, "Festus and I started meeting in secret. He was so alone, stuck in that prison of pipes and steam."

Festus just stared at his hands as she spoke.

"At first, we simply meant for Festus to leave the Core for good and get to the surface world. But when Albert Flynn arrived in the Core and plucked a Master Tile from the Waterfall of Fate . . ." She looked toward Albert but turned away before meeting his eyes. If he wasn't mistaken, Lucinda was afraid of him.

"When Albert got the Master Tile, our plans changed. Festus didn't want to simply be free." Lucinda looked sideways at Festus, her eyes lighting up. She lowered her voice. "He wanted to *rule*."

"Oh, I'll show you who rules," Birdie growled, and Hoyt leaned past Albert and bumped her fist in agreement. Festus continued to just sit there, head hanging. Was he even listening?

"How did you do it?" Professor Asante asked. "Honesty, Lucinda, is most advised."

Lucinda sniffled and continued. "We knew that Festus's father on the surface had one Master Tile, and we knew that Bob Flynn had the one that had been taken from Festus."

Whispers broke out around Albert. Apparently, most of the Core didn't know that Professor Flynn had watched over Festus's Master Tile after Festus had been banished. That made sense—Albert himself hadn't known until a few days ago.

"Hey," Birdie said. "What's Trey doing?"

Trey was approaching the stage carrying a chair, which he placed next to Lucinda and Festus.

"Who's that for?" Albert whispered. Was there another accomplice? He heard similar questions from the crowd buzzing around him.

Albert looked to his dad, who had stood up from his

place next to Professor Bigglesby. Professor Flynn glanced at Albert.

Then he walked across the stage . . . and sat down in the third chair.

Trey fastened handcuffs on Professor Flynn's wrists. Professor Flynn didn't even flinch.

Albert leaped to his feet. "NO!" Birdie and Leroy held him back from rushing onto the stage. "No! What are you doing? He didn't do anything wrong!"

He felt sick.

How could this be happening?

Albert tried to pull away from Birdie and Leroy, but another hand pressed down onto his shoulder. And then another, and another, until Slink, Mo, and Hoyt were all holding him back, too.

"Let me go," Albert said. He yelled at the other Professors. "WHAT DID HE DO? HE HASN'T DONE ANYTHING WRONG!"

A couple people around Albert shouted their agreement. Others were crying.

But Professor Flynn just sat calmly in his chair, his hands folded in his lap, his emerald jacket sparkling.

"Dad!" Albert shouted. "What's happening? Tell them you didn't do anything wrong!"

Professor Flynn smiled sadly.

The crowd hushed.

"It's okay, Albert," Professor Flynn said. His voice

was calm and steady. He looked away from Albert and addressed the crowd. "It's time that I 'fess up to the entire Core about my mistakes." He took a deep breath. "It is true that I had a Master Tile."

The crowd was silent.

"After Festus was sent to become the Path Hider, the Tile was thrown back into the Waterfall of Fate. It was our hope that the waterfall would keep it safe. But I didn't trust that, and so I went in myself that night and plucked the Tile back out."

No, Albert thought. *Stop talking! You're going to make it worse!*

His dad kept going. "I kept that Tile safe until just recently. I went to visit my brother in the Path Hider's domain, and . . ."

Festus started to laugh, slow at first, then rising to a cackle. "And he told me he'd kept the Tile safe! What a fool you are, brother!" His laughing made every hair on Albert's neck stand on end. "I know my brother. And when he told me he would keep the Tile safe, I knew it meant that he'd removed it from the waterfall himself. Predictable, as always. Pathetic." People booed and shouted at Festus, but he continued laughing until he started to cough.

Professor Flynn's face had gone white.

Lucinda continued for them. "After Festus learned of this, he told me of a book that existed, one he'd kept hidden in the Library that would help lead me to the Master Tile that Professor Flynn had hidden."

The Book of Bad Tiles, Albert thought.

"I used the book to find the Master Tile. I plucked it straight from Professor Flynn's hiding place."

Professor Asante looked at the three prisoners. "Where was the Tile hidden?"

Albert's dad sighed deeply. "In my office."

"It was too easy," Lucinda said. The tears were gone, now that she was telling her story, caught up in the excitement of it. "Once I delivered the Master Tile to Festus, he was free to move about his domain. There are tunnels hidden all throughout it. Tunnels that lead inside the Core. All it took was a little prodding from the Master Tile, and we were able to access the tunnels."

Everyone gasped.

Even the Professors.

Festus laughed again, delighted. "So mindless, so weak. All of you. You don't even know the depth of this place. The mysteries that it holds."

"Enough!" Professor Asante yelled. She stood taller, like a proud soldier. "If you don't silence yourself, Festus, we will do it for you."

He grimaced and nodded at Lucinda to continue on.

"After some studying, Festus used his Master Tile to convince Professor Flynn to steal the *second* one from his dad, on the surface," Lucinda said.

Professor Flynn cut in. "I felt the need to go and get it, to keep it safe," he explained. "It was like I couldn't ignore it. I had to have it."

Albert shivered. Festus had controlled his dad's mind, with only one Tile, and a very dark, dark symbol.

"On the night of the Float Parade last term, Festus mixed up a sleeping potion that I could use," Lucinda said. "All I had to do was slip it into Professor Flynn's drink. He fell asleep in his office, and it was too easy to sneak in, while everyone was in the Main Chamber partying, and take that second Tile, too.

"Once I delivered that one to Festus, and he had two Master Tiles, his strength grew. We planned some more, to lure Albert into the Realms. We'd heard that when a Balance Keeper dies in a Realm, their Tile is given back to the Waterfall of Fate. If Albert died in a Realm, it would be the easiest way for us to get the third Master Tile."

Albert glared at Festus and Lucinda. They were two horrible, evil people, who didn't think twice about killing Albert, all in the name of power.

Lucinda went on. "So Festus went inside the Realms at night, created Imbalances, and Albert and his team blazed forth in the Pit, just like we expected. He had the third Master Tile, after all, and we know what happens when a Balance Keeper holds so much power. They will always succeed, eventually."

Albert had walked right into their plan.

And his friends had been in danger the entire time, just for being near him.

"I'm sorry," Albert whispered.

But Birdie and Leroy sat tall beside him. "It's not your fault, Albert," Leroy said.

"When Albert kept solving the Imbalances, despite all of Festus's efforts," Lucinda said, an air of annoyance finally reaching her voice, "Festus had no choice but to enter Belltroll and create the greatest Imbalance ever known."

"And the note?" Professor Bigglesby spoke up. "Why give Albert the single striker, and the note, if you wanted him to fail in the Realm?"

Festus chuckled. "Fun and games," he said. "All fun and games. You locked me in that maze of pipes for thirty years. Thirty *years*, without seeing the sun or another human being save for the annoying children arriving as new Balance Keepers a few times a year. And it was always the same. I had to watch while the Balance Keepers came through, calling themselves the defenders of this world." He swallowed and looked at the crowd. "You are not worthy. You will never be worthy of the titles you have been given."

"That is enough!" Professor Asante said. "You will only answer the questions we ask of you, understand?"

Festus looked at her with a sly smile.

Lucinda told the rest of the story quickly. She described

how easy it was for Festus to enter the Realms, for him to tamper with the creatures. She described how annoying it was when Birdie and Leroy proved to be stronger than she and Festus had originally hoped.

The crowd pressed closer together, as if that would help keep the chill of Festus's words away.

When Lucinda was done, Professor Asante cleared her throat again. "Festus, Lucinda, do you have anything else to add?"

"No, Professor," Festus said with a smirk. Lucinda just shook her head.

"Very well," Professor Asante said. "Professor Bigglesby?" She sat down and Bigglesby took her place at the podium. The MegaHorn squealed as it always did.

Farnsworth didn't howl this time. Instead, he glared at Festus, a growl ripping through him.

Bigglesby pulled out a third scroll. He cleared his throat and spoke slowly, as if he didn't want to say the words. "I will now read the crimes of Professor Bob Flynn."

Albert wanted to scream and shout. Professor Flynn had made a mistake, taking the two Master Tiles and losing both of them. But that was all it was.

A mistake.

And Lucinda herself had admitted that Festus had used the first Master Tile's power to trick Professor Flynn into taking the second Master Tile from Pap.

Please, Albert thought. *Let them go easy on my dad.*

"Professor Bob Flynn," Bigglesby read. His beady eyes flitted to Albert's, but instead of menace, they held pity. "You are charged with the crime of harboring two hidden Master Tiles and losing track of them, therefore placing the entire Core and the entire surface world in danger. There is an amount of leniency, for Lucinda's admittance to Festus controlling you for the second Tile. But the first was your own choice, and you endangered the Core by choosing to remove your brother's Tile from the Waterfall of Fate yourself." He sighed and shook his head. "Bob Flynn, how do you plead?"

Professor Flynn looked up. His eyes scanned the room and fell on Albert. He swallowed, hard.

"Guilty," he said. "I plead . . . guilty to the crimes."

CHAPTER 35

The Punishments Given

Everyone was quiet.

Albert's heartbeat pulsed in his ears, and he held his breath as he waited for the punishments to be dealt.

"Lucinda Lore," Professor Asante said. She held a small copper hammer, much like the kind that judges always had in shows Albert's mom watched.

Lucinda looked up, fresh tears in her eyes.

"You are hereby banished from the Core," Professor Asante said. "You are never to return, and your memory will be taken care of by the Memory Wipers. From here on out, you are a member of the surface world."

She banged the hammer, and Lucinda flinched.

Then she began to sob silently while Professor Asante turned to Festus.

"Festus Flynn," she said, her voice full of authority. "We made a mistake, keeping you here the last time around. If it weren't for Albert Flynn and his extreme show of bravery . . ."

Professor Asante looked to Albert and gave him an approving nod.

"Festus, you are hereby banished from the Core, never to return. Never to harm these Realms or their Balance again."

Festus kept silent, but he raised his head to Albert.

There was so much hatred in him. So much disgust.

"You can't keep the Tiles locked up forever," Festus said. "I will spend the rest of my days trying to get back here to them."

"Not if the Memory Wipers can help it," Professor Asante said.

Albert felt Festus staring at him, even as he looked away.

"Professor Bob Flynn," Professor Asante began.

Albert closed his eyes.

Please, he thought. *Please don't banish my dad. He belongs here.*

"You have been a dear friend to the Core for many, many years," Professor Asante said. Her voice was stern, but not harsh. "You and I used to work alongside each other, training to become Apprentices, and finally, Professors. I consider you a dear friend."

"And I you," Professor Flynn said. His face was grim.

"We have had our differences," Professor Bigglesby spoke up in his squeaky voice. "But I have seen a good heart in you, Bob."

It seemed that the entire Core was holding their breath, not just Albert.

Birdie grabbed his hand and held on. Even Trey, who hardly showed emotion, looked as if he was going to faint.

"Due to your admittance to your mistake," Professor Asante said, "and your complete willingness to cooperate during this trial, we have come to a unanimous decision on your punishment."

Albert could hardly bear this. He squeezed Birdie's hand tighter. Farnsworth hid behind Albert's legs.

"Bob Flynn," Professor Asante said. "It is our belief that, in any other case, you would be banished."

Birdie's nails dug into Albert's skin.

"But . . ."

But? Albert thought. That was a good word. That had *hope* mixed in with it.

"Because you were tricked, and because you have come forth of your own accord, Professor Bigglesby and the Core Watchers and I have decided that you will remain in the Core. You will take your brother's place, as the new Path Hider, where you will remain for the next two years, one for each Tile lost. During that time, you will protect the Core, hiding the paths at all cost. Meals will be delivered to you, and you are allotted one companion creature by your side. Twice a year, until your punishment ends, you will be given a six-hour leave to return to the surface world. After your two years are up, you are free to do as you please." She stopped and gave a quick wink to Professor Flynn. "Perhaps maybe even take on a job as our new Pit Supervisor, a position we could possibly create for you, given your obvious talents in the Core. For the time being . . . may you guard and protect the Core with all your worth, Path Hider."

She banged the hammer. Professor Bigglesby motioned for Trey to stand, and Trey helped remove Professor Flynn's emerald coat.

The Library fell silent.

Professor Flynn's face was wet with soundless tears. "Thank you," he said. His voice carried gently across the room. "Thank you for showing me mercy."

Albert's face was wet, too.

His dad, his hero, was no longer a Professor. At least, not for the next two years. It was a brutal blow, stealing the one thing from Professor Flynn that he'd worked his entire life to get. Albert was furious for a moment.

But really, two years was nothing. And his dad would get to stay in the Core, and after that? He was *free to do as he pleased.* It was the best possible outcome when all was said and done.

Albert's dad had done something wrong. He was facing that now, his head held high like a true Balance Keeper. Bravery wasn't always about doing the best thing. It was about doing the *right* thing, even if it meant it would cost you something.

And in that way, Albert knew his dad was the bravest man in this room.

CHAPTER 36

The Heart of the Core

Albert didn't go to see Festus and Lucinda off, but he heard their shouts coming from the Main Chamber as the Professors hauled them away, using Jadar as backup should they try to escape.

"I WILL FIND THEM!" Festus shouted. "I WILL FIND MY TILES!"

Jadar's roar blocked out the sound, but Festus's words remained in Albert's mind, even as he made his way back to Cedarfell.

But when he crawled into his bed, and Farnsworth curled up beside him, Albert closed his eyes and slept the words away.

*   *   *

It took two days for the Balance Keepers to haul all the Core creatures back into their individual Realms, and another three days for the Core workers to repair the broken doors to the Realms and put the arched bridges back up over the streams. Albert helped with every step, and with each creature he ushered back into a Realm and every board he helped nail back in place, he felt a little lighter, a little less broken.

They were making the Core feel like home again.

Albert's dad was sent to the Path Hider's domain immediately to begin guarding the paths, and though Albert had promised to visit him, he hadn't been able to bring himself to do it just yet. Albert didn't know if he could bear to see Bob Flynn in there, wearing the same old miner's cap that Festus had worn.

And he didn't know if he could bear to think of Pap all alone in Herman, waiting for a son who wouldn't come home for quite some time.

There was only one thing left for Albert to do, before everything was really safe. One thing, before the nightmares would go away and Albert could sleep without worry once again.

It was after dark when Albert and Farnsworth made their way through the halls of the Core alone.

A few days ago, the darkness would have creeped

him out, making his hair stand on end. He would have looked over his shoulder every few seconds, wondering who was watching.

Now, the darkness was like a warm hug, the crackling of the new blue torches on the walls a peaceful melody in Albert's ears.

They passed by Professor Asante's office, and Albert smiled as he thought of her. Rumor was she'd been visiting Albert's dad in the Path Hider's domain every single day this week, delivering him home-baked goods that nobody would have guessed she was talented at making.

Professor Asante was a strange woman, and certainly not Albert's number-one choice for his dad to date, but she was loyal. She was fierce, and she had been on Albert's side all through the chaos the traitor has caused.

And if she made Albert's dad happy, well . . .

That was okay with him.

Farnsworth's high beams came on as they stopped before an old elevator at the end of the tunnel.

"You ready for this, buddy?" Albert asked.

Farnsworth wagged his tail. Albert took out the key that hung from his neck, the key that had been delivered to him by Professor Bigglesby earlier this week.

When you're ready, Flynn, the old dwarf had said. *Make it count. And don't lose the key, or you'll have to write an essay explaining your mistake.*

"He's not the warmest old man on the planet," Albert

said to Farnsworth as he turned the key in the lock beside the elevator. "But he and the other Professors have trusted me with this."

He pressed the button on the door. The elevator opened with a hiss, and they stepped inside. It took them deep, deep down. The doors slid back open, and Albert and Farnsworth stepped into the Watchers' Cavern.

The Watchers were gone for the day, as the Professors had promised.

But someone else was waiting in their place.

Farnsworth yipped and scurried off to greet the surprise guest.

"Dad?" Albert asked. He couldn't believe his eyes. "What are you doing here?"

Bob Flynn stood beside the Heart of the Core, holding a black box in his arms. Even though he was wearing a grease-covered jumpsuit and looked like he hadn't showered in days, he looked *alive*. He looked happy, and younger, than he had in three terms.

Albert raced across the cavern and threw his arms around his dad.

"Hey, kiddo," Bob said.

"How did you get in here?" Albert asked. His voice was muffled into his dad's chest.

"I'll tell you when you let me breathe," Bob said, laughing.

Albert pulled away and looked up at his dad.

"I might be the Path Hider, but I'm not the same kind your uncle was. I still have friends here."

"But you're supposed to be hiding the paths!" Albert said, his voice squeaking like Petra's.

His dad smiled. "Trey's covering for me today," he said, waving a hand. Then he shrugged. "The other Professors *may* have looked the other direction as I walked past. They know what it means to me, to be able to be here for you."

Albert was so happy he could have cried.

He had wanted to be alone for this, but seeing his dad here now, one of the only people who truly understood how horrible the Master Tiles were . . .

"I'm so glad you're here," Albert said.

His dad smiled and held out the black box.

"Whenever you're ready. You can take your time if you need to."

Albert gently took the box, surprised at how heavy it actually was. It looked to be made out of the same stuff as the CoreSword.

"I've waited long enough," Albert said. "I'm ready right now."

He took a deep breath before opening the box.

Just one peek, to be sure they were inside.

The box was lined with black velvet. The three Master Tiles were nestled in the center, side by side.

Just seeing them, Albert felt the longing, the need, to

reach out and touch them, to wear them around his neck and feel the power surging through his veins. . . .

He snapped the box shut.

"Never again," Albert said.

Then he turned, and before he could blink, he tossed the box into the Heart of the Core.

The fire took them immediately, engulfing the box in flames. It was as if the Core had been waiting for centuries to swallow the Master Tiles whole.

In seconds, there was nothing left but a few strands of black, swirling inside the Heart. Then the lava bubbled up and the darkness disappeared.

"We did it," Albert said with a gasp.

His dad wrapped an arm over his shoulders and pulled him close.

"You did it, Albert," Bob Flynn said.

They stood there for a while, watching the Heart of the Core.

"I'll miss you," Albert said finally.

"I waited for eleven years to be able to share the Core with you." His dad chuckled, the slight breeze dancing across the top of Albert's hair. "Two years is nothing, kiddo. And besides, you're not planning on leaving the Core for good, are you?"

Albert was silent.

He'd given lots of thought to that, yes. Leaving the Core on the gondola, letting the Memory Wipers erase his memory of this place. *Festus, his evil stare and blistering laugh. Lucinda, with her lies and deception. The feeling of the ground trembling as the Core nearly ripped itself apart.*

But they wouldn't just erase the bad memories.

They'd erase the good ones, too.

Birdie and Leroy laughing with Albert as they held their secret sessions in the Pit. Lunch at Lake Hall, with Leroy shoveling cake into his mouth faster than was humanly possible. The Float Parade, with Petra's glittering Guildacker.

"I'm not going anywhere, Dad," Albert said.

He looked up at Bob Flynn, the older version of himself. They'd both made mistakes, but at least for now, Albert felt just like the Heart of the Core—warm and bright.

Albert's dad smiled down at him and pulled him closer. "You're the best Balance Keeper I've ever known, kiddo," he said. "And Tile or no Tile, that's not going to change."

Farnsworth yipped, and his eye lights came on.

"Now," Albert's dad said. "I've got about five hours left before I have to return to my post. What do you say we go and try our hand against Leroy in a game of Tiles?"

Albert laughed.

"We can try," he said. "But we won't win."

"It's not always about winning," his dad said.

They left the cavern together with Farnsworth leading the way.

CHAPTER 37

The Cave of Souls

The rest of his stay in the Core went by in a flash. There were endless games of Tiles in the Library, most of which Leroy won, but when Professor Bigglesby showed up, the match was pretty even. There were late lunches in the brand-new and improved Lake Hall, where Albert was pretty sure the Whimzies were dropping more desserts than usual.

The Pit was deemed safe, and friendly competitions were held. Albert and his friends sat in the stands, watching. They weren't quite ready to compete again just yet.

At night, they played games of hide-and-seek around the Core, and Albert was pleased to see that Hoyt now had his own companion creature. Spyro gave everyone rides on his back, as long as they paid him with a peppermint or two.

The rest of Spyro's herd was back in Belltroll, soaring over the mountains where once a day, the Trolls rose and cranked the mountain back into place.

On the final day in the Core before they had to return home, Albert, Birdie, and Leroy headed to the Core Canteen. It had been boarded up all week with a sign out front that said "renovations in progress," but rumor had spread this morning that it had reopened. Albert wanted to call his mom, and Leroy was eager to spend his earnings on a fresh bag of candy.

It was only when they arrived and found the spot behind the counter empty that they realized that with Lucinda gone, they had no idea who was running the Canteen.

"Oh look," Birdie said, gesturing to a sign on the desk. "It says to ring the bell if you need help."

"I'll do it!" Leroy said, sliding over to the bell. He banged it with a little too much energy and it slid off the desk and clattered to the floor. "Whoops," Leroy said. "My bad." Birdie rolled her eyes as Albert stooped down to grab the bell.

"Yes? How can I help—"

"Petra!" Birdie and Leroy's voices rang out together.

Albert popped up from the floor to see Petra behind the counter, grinning like Spyro with a peppermint.

"Welcome to the Core Canteen," Petra said with a

wink. "It's been hard to keep it a surprise from you guys, but the Professors gave it to me as a reward for helping you discover who the traitor was, Albert."

In mere minutes, Petra Prince became one of the most popular guys in the Core.

"I offer free phone calls to home!" Petra shouted out as a crowd gathered. "And if I can get it up and running, I'm going to install a TV, so you can keep up to date on the latest surface-world news!"

Which, Albert had learned from his dad, was also well on its way to recovering from the disaster. Plans were made for buildings going back up, teams had gathered to help rebuild homes. The surface world had a camaraderie of its own in times like these.

Hoyt and his teammates saved the day just in time, Albert thought.

"Well, I'd like to be your first customer," Leroy said to Petra.

He hefted a heaping bag full of golden Medallions onto the counter.

Petra whistled. "You're the best at Tiles, man. No doubt."

Leroy laughed and started a list of all the Core Candies he wanted as his prize. He even bought a fresh new blue bone for Farnsworth, and the little dog yipped happily as Petra tossed it to him.

"This is really something, Petra," Albert said, pulling

up a stool to the counter. The Core Canteen was bright and happy with new life. Candies were now half off, and colorful Tiles were going two for the price of one. Kimber slept happily on the topmost shelf.

Albert guessed he'd taken a liking to Petra, and though Petra wasn't a big fan of snakes, he was happy to let Kimber doze in the rafters of the Canteen. Albert figured the extra security of a big, scaly snake probably helped ward off any customer's thoughts of stealing an extra Tile or two.

"What do you think of the new addition?" Petra asked. "It came together pretty quickly, I think." He motioned to the right of the Core Canteen.

Lucinda's old ramshackle booth, which normally sat in the entrance to the Core, had been pulled inside. Now, Petra's mom stood behind the booth beneath a brightly painted sign that said *The Soda Fountain*.

Students and adults made up a long line of customers shouting out orders. Medallions were practically pouring in, and Petra grinned like a cat as he watched his mom mix up milkshakes and snow cones and all sorts of goodies.

"I just adore what you've done to the place," Birdie said. "And your mom looks so happy."

"She'll never have to sweep the Core floors again," Petra said. "So, obviously, it's going great!" He sat on Lucinda's old stool, with a fresh copper name tag on his chest. "I'm expecting tons of orders to come in for my new line of trick potions, and Professor Bigglesby offered to let me teach a class once a week on making them!"

Albert smiled. "You earned it, man."

"You were born for this, Petra," Birdie added.

"Thanks," Petra said. "Free candies for Hydra, anytime!"

"Now that's what I call a good deal," Leroy said, through mouthfuls of taffy. When Leroy was done collecting all his new loot, Hydra waved good-bye and set off back through the halls toward the Main Chamber.

"What now?" Birdie asked as she waved to a group of passing girls. They stopped to pat Farnsworth on the head, but quickly raced away after he slobbered blue all over them.

Albert laughed and slung his arms over his friends' shoulders.

"I was thinking maybe we'd make a stop somewhere special."

Leroy raised a brow. "Lake Hall for lunch? The new docks are freaking sweet."

"Later, Memory Boy." Birdie rolled her eyes, and Albert chuckled under his breath.

"Follow me," he said.

They headed down a tunnel, deeper and deeper into the Core, and stopped before a door that they'd entered once before.

*   *   *

The three friends lay on their backs, watching the blinking orbs of light float far over their heads in the Cave of Souls.

These were the souls of every Balance Keeper, new and old.

They were as countless as the stars.

"I wonder what it'll be like to leave this time," Birdie said.

Albert rolled onto his side and looked at her. "What do you mean?"

Birdie shrugged. "Well, I just think . . . this time, it's been more than it ever has."

"I'm not catching on, Guildacker Girl," Leroy added.

Birdie laughed and punched him. "Just think about it. Every time we've come, it's been the same. A horrifying Imbalance that mystifies even the Professors, and then us trying to figure out what in the heck we were going to do to solve it. But now that's over, right? I mean, the traitor causing these crazy Imbalances is gone."

"And the Tiles are destroyed," Albert said.

He still wore the leather cord around his neck. It was empty and light as a feather, but it was a good reminder. Nobody should have as much power as the Master Tile allowed.

"When we leave, we'll know that next time we come back, it'll be easier," Leroy said. "Less danger. I like the sound of that, dudes."

Albert smiled and pointed up at the flickering orbs of light.

"We're up there," he said. "I wonder which ones are us."

"Well, it's obvious, isn't it?" Birdie asked. "We're that little trio over there."

She pointed up and to the left. Sure enough, there was a trio of little soul lights, floating together through the others in the darkness. They stayed in a solid line, like they were tethered together.

"That could be any team," Leroy said. "And really, the odds of that being us are—"

Birdie let out a soft growl. "Way to ruin the moment, Leroy."

"But this is nice," Albert said. "We're back where it all started."

"Safe," Leroy said.

"And together," Birdie added.

They stayed there for a while, until their thoughts were interrupted by an announcement.

Trey's voice rung out over the loudspeaker. "Team Hydra, please report to Professor Flynn's . . ." He cleared his throat. "Please report to my office."

"I guess Trey hasn't settled in to his new position yet," Albert said. Trey as Professor was a rightful fit.

Albert wondered what his dad would do next, when his punishment as Path Hider was up. He didn't think his dad would take the position back, not now that Trey was enjoying it so much.

Maybe he'd take Professor Asante's advice and become the Pit Supervisor. That would be pretty cool, too.

"Let's go see what he wants," Albert said.

Birdie and Leroy exchanged sheepish grins.

The three of them got up and left the Cave of Souls, Albert taking one last look over his shoulder at the three blinking lights, still together.

CHAPTER 38

A New Beginning

Trey was waiting for them at the door to Professor Flynn's old office. He wore his own emerald jacket, perfectly fitted to his long, lean figure.

"What's up?" Albert asked.

"There's something we have to do before you leave," Trey said. There was a sparkle to his words.

He motioned for Albert to go inside.

Albert turned the handle. The roar of the Waterfall of Fate sounded from within, and with it, the rest of the Core was waiting.

They were all inside the room, standing patiently around the waterfall's pool.

"What's this?" Albert asked as Trey and his friends ushered him forward.

Birdie smiled. "We wanted to surprise you."

Leroy nodded and gave Albert a little nudge. "You're getting a new Tile, dude."

Albert didn't quite know what to think. He made the walk to the Waterfall of Fate, passing by all the people near and dear to him. They were silent, respecting the mighty presence of the waterfall. But that couldn't keep the smiles off their faces.

Petra was there, holding up his old *Team Hydra!* foam finger. Professor Asante and Professor Bigglesby, and Team Argon, and all the other teams of Balance Keepers, too. Jadar was nestled in the corner next to Leroy's Jackalope, Jemima. There was Spyro, his wings outspread in a display of pride. He bowed his head to Albert as he passed.

Tussy stood closest to the pool, next to . . .

"Dad!" Albert ran to hug him.

He was starting to think that maybe being the Path Hider wasn't so bad. If the Professors had already let Albert's dad out twice in one week, then maybe they weren't taking this whole punishment thing as seriously as Albert thought.

He pulled away from the hug and looked up.

Albert's dad beamed with pride. "This is all for you, Albert."

Birdie and Leroy took their places beside Bob Flynn, grinning as they watched Albert's look of awe.

"I'm getting a new Tile?" Albert asked.

"You can't be a Balance Keeper without one," Trey said when Albert stopped before the pool. "You earned it, Albert. Now get in there and pick the very best one."

Albert reached down to untie his boots. His fingers shook a little as he loosened the knots.

What if the Tile he chose was something he wouldn't be good at? What if he got something useless, like a Tile that gave him great dancing abilities, or made his hair grow long?

What if . . . he couldn't find one at all?

"Albert," Birdie spoke up. "It's going to be great."

"We know you'll get a good one," Leroy said, with two thumbs up.

Hoyt nodded from the crowd.

The water was cool today, a breath of fresh air. Albert stepped in and took one look back over his shoulder.

Everyone's eyes were wide, watching and waiting.

"Here goes nothing," Albert said.

He dove in.

The waterfall pounded over his head, and Albert swam deep and wide, his eyes closed the entire time.

Let it be a good one, Albert thought. Then he changed his mind. *Let it be the right one for me.*

He didn't want to look. He wanted to let the Core decide for him. So he swam and swam, his arms spread out before him, and just when Albert began to wonder if he was going to find a Tile at all, his fingers scraped the bottom of the pool.

A single Tile closed in his grip, and Albert swam up.

The crowd was silent as he emerged, dripping wet.

He kept the Tile tucked in his fist until he was completely out of the water, a towel thrown over his shoulders.

"Well?" Birdie asked. "What is it?"

"Come on, dude!" Leroy chimed in.

Albert opened his fist and looked down at his new Tile.

A smile broke onto his face, and he let out a single laugh.

It was perfect, the Master Tile power that had given them the most help in the Realms, and the one Tile his dad used to wear.

"Creature Speak," Albert said.

He held the Tile high, and everyone cheered. It was a roar of victory, a roar of thanks.

The sound stayed with him the rest of the day and into the next.

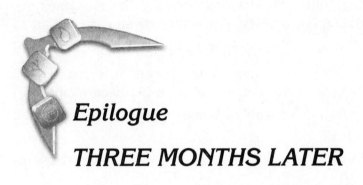

Epilogue

THREE MONTHS LATER

Albert Flynn stood at the edge of the woods in Herman, Wyoming. The wind blew gently, but it was full of summer heat.

An old truck whizzed down the street, stopping beside Albert. The window rolled down, and Pap leaned his head out.

"You forgot this," Pap said. He tossed Albert a duffel bag, which was full of Bob Flynn's favorite surface-world snacks and a fresh pair of boots. There was also a giant, extra-large-sized bag of catnip for Professor Asante's giant six-legged Guardian cat, which had long since moved in with Albert's dad in the Path Hider's domain. "And be sure to show him this," Pap said.

He held up a newspaper. On the front page was an ad for a traveling circus. Albert's eyes nearly popped out of his head.

There was a picture of Lucinda, her head wrapped in a big bundle of scarves, beaded necklaces and rings all over her.

"A fortune-teller," Albert said. "Well, I guess that's fitting. No news of Festus yet?"

It was still strange, talking about Pap's other son. But Pap shook his head.

"I'm keeping an eye out. You'll know as soon as I find anything."

Albert hoped that Festus was leading a normal life, somewhere in a small, sleepy town. Harmless. He hoped the Memory Wipers had done a good job of removing all traces of the Core.

Pap started to roll the window up. "Give your dad a hug for me. And tell him if he wasn't so good at hiding those paths, I would have come to see him by now."

Albert laughed. "He misses you, Pap. I hope you know that. He's counting down the days until he can come back up."

"Just twenty-one months left," Pap said with a nod, and revved the engine. "Go on, then. You're twelve years old now. No time to dilly-dally."

Albert waved good-bye.

Farnsworth yipped and circled around his boots.

"You ready, buddy?" Albert asked. "Just one more second."

Albert looked over his shoulder once at the town of Herman. There was the old, square post office where Pap pulled up his truck and sat with his porch buddies, playing a game of Tiles.

Beyond it, along the winding street, was the small house that Albert's dad would return to soon enough. Pap still lived there, and Albert had slowly started moving some of his stuff from New York.

He'd spend every break here now, thanks to his mom allowing it, to give Pap some company, and to make it easier for Albert to sneak down to the Core and spend a little time with the new Path Hider.

And someday, when Albert was old enough and graduated from high school, he had hopes of becoming a Professor in the Core.

"See you soon, Herman," Albert said. Farnsworth's tail thumped across the tops of Albert's boots. It wasn't the same without his dad here, but Herman was still the entrance to the most magical place in Albert's world.

Birdie and Leroy would be waiting for him at the Troll Tree. Leroy probably had a new hat, and Birdie had probably added new colors to her hair.

Albert smiled. "Lead the way, Farnsworth."

The little dog let out a howl that reached the heavens.

Then he raced off into the trees, a blur of black.

"Wait for me!" Albert shouted. He sprinted after Farnsworth, his white Tile bouncing on its chain.

He didn't know what adventure awaited him this time.

But he knew it would be good.

Acknowledgments

I don't quite know how to begin with this part.

Maybe it's because this is the fifth book I've written, not to mention the final book in the Balance Keepers trilogy. Maybe it's because I'm so attached to these characters that writing this means I'm really, truly letting go.

Maybe it's because this was the hardest book I've ever had to write, and now I am so incredibly attached to it.

What I do know is this:

Everyone below means the world to me.

Everyone below has helped shape a part of me, because you helped shape my writing, and writing is my heart.

Katie Bignell, my fearless editor, who might love Harry Potter just as much as I do: Please know that this is NOT a cheesy, meaningless thanks. Katie, you have taken my writing to new levels. You took a chance on a much younger Lindsay, offering your patience and incredibly thorough edit letters, and now, years later, I am so, SO much better for working with you. Thank you for your time. Your positivity. Your excitement for this series. You have been a complete and total joy to work with (I'm tearing up already, writing these freaking acknowledgments!).

Patrick Carman, my Wise Panda, my Yoda, my Sometimes-Intimidating-But-Only-Because-He-Means-Well Friend: thank you for giving me this gift.

Katherine Tegen: for having an imprint that feels like home.

Louise Fury: your encouragement, and excitement, and pure "fire and fury" agenting skills brought me here. Thank you.

The entire team at HarperCollins, from the cover designers to the copy editors, the marketing team, the people I'm inevitably forgetting: thank you all. SO MUCH.

My family—Mom, Sis, Dad, Grumpy Husband (I love you), extended family, new brothers, and of course, my legion of fur babies: thanks for putting up with my crazy.

Jackson Redmon: thanks for being the biggest Balance Keepers fan in Celina!

My amazing readers (#booknerdigans): thanks for buying my books. Thanks for loving them as much as I do. Thanks for being generally awesome.

And finally, to God: it may seem strange that I'm thanking you last, but the truth is, I simply wanted to close this series with your name. It started with you, after all . . . I am so, so blessed.

Thank you.

Thank you.

Thank you.

(It's not over. Stories never truly are.)